The Third Generation Series

Book 13

Prisoner 

by

Margaret Gregory

Cover designed by msgdragon
Cover images:
Pixabay

Also by Margaret Gregory

TYMOREAN TRUST SERIES:
Book 1 - Power Rising
Book 2 - Great Ones
Book 3 - The Return to Earth
Book 4 – Earth Mission
Book 5 – Alien Contact
Book 6 - Invasion

ATAPI SORCERESS SERIES:
Prequel – Korvu: The Beginning
Book 1- The Wild One
Book 2 – Atapi Sorceress

Maeven - Dragon Thief

THE THIRD GENERATION SERIES:
Book 1 - Wanda: From Bad to Worse
Book 2 - Wanda: Choosing Crime
Wanda – Early Days (anthology) Book 1 and 2
Book 3 – Wanda: Risking Life to Live
Book 4 – Erin: The Forcing of Wisdom
Book 5 – Wanda: A New Life Part 1 – Hidden Secrets
Book 6 – Wanda: A New Life Part 2 – First Mission
Book 7 – Wanda: Full Circle
Book 8 and 9 – Erin: The Call
Book 10 - Royal Favour
Book 11 - The Serpent's Shadow

For permission requests, address the request to the author c/o
Permissions,
TAT Indie Publishing
PO Box 2728
Rowville, Victoria, 3178
www.tatindiepublishing.com.au

Chapter 1 - Reunited

Nicole Wexford took her daughter to the US Embassy with a great deal of relief. With fierce protectiveness, she had fended off all the efforts of the police to question her little girl. She knew her daughter, and knew Rachel was not herself. It was normally a battle to keep her quiet, but since being found, she hadn't said a word.

"Mr Thomas, where is Mrs Martin, we want to thank her."

She was carrying Rachel, who was hiding her face on her shoulder.

Neil Thomas knew exactly where Wanda Martin was; the embassy staff were buzzing with the information, although no one was discussing it with outsiders. Not only that, most were in shock at the discovery that Nicole's husband was a Russian.

"Mrs Wexford, why don't you settle your daughter in your room and put the TV on for her. We have US stations here, via satellite, and I will have Mr Browning have a word with you."

"I don't wish to interrupt the Ambassador, and Rachel doesn't want to let me out of her sight. Is Mrs Martin here?"

"No, Mam, not at the moment," Thomas told her politely.

"Is she still in Austria?"

"Yes, Mam, but I don't know when she can return here."

"Then I want to go and see her," Nicole insisted.

"I will endeavour to discover if that is possible, Mam."

"Let me know as soon as you find out," Nicole directed, as she began to head for the lift to go up to her room.

Neil Thomas watched her until she was out of sight and then went into an empty office and dialled the hotel where Jim Phillips was staying. When the phone was answered, he explained Nicole's request.

"Does she know about her husband yet?" Jim asked. It hadn't made the media yet, but it was sure to be leaked soon.

"I don't think so, Sir. At least, she said nothing to indicate that she did – unless that was what she wanted to talk to Mrs Martin about. She has refused to let the police talk to her daughter as well."

"She has that right," Jim admitted. "Do you know if the police spoke to Mrs Wexford since they found her daughter?"

"I don't know, Sir."

"It would be best if we tell her about the suspicions before the police do," Jim decided. "Do you want me to come over?"

"It would be helpful, Sir, since you could also explain about Mrs Martin."

"Yes, I'll come straight away."

As Jim began to tighten his tie, his attention was caught by a knock at the door. He glanced at Nicholas, who stood to answer it. He didn't fully open the door, but spoke to whoever was there, and he sounded perplexed.

David's head suddenly swivelled from his perusal of Grant's laptop screen. He pushed the chair back and trotted to the door.

"It's okay, Nick. I know them," he assured his friend, as he pulled the door open wide enough for three women to edge in.

Nicholas saw Jim smile, as David explained, "These ladies are Wanda's private army." He shrugged and moved aside.

David closed the door and rounded on the well-dressed blond woman, demanding, "If you are here, where the hell is Davy?"

"Calm down, David," Elisabeth Willard insisted. "He's fine! I left him with my father. I told Davy that my father was the closest thing he'll get to a Grandpa. Dad is loving it!"

Nicholas blurted, "Don't tell me you are all sisters."

"Cousins," one of the two brown haired women claimed. "Wanda is our cousin. I am Erin Rand, and this is Tanya Krinsky. Elisabeth Willard is arguing with David."

"I see," Nicholas commented. He glanced at Jim who seemed to be resigned to the invasion.

"I have to go out," Jim announced. "Tanya, Erin, will you stay here with David. See if you can help Grant with his search. Elisabeth, since you are here, how well do you know Nicole Wexford?"

"Well enough. Why?"

"I'm on my way to talk to her. She might appreciate a friendly face."

"Have you found Allan?"

"Not yet. What do you know about him?"

"Vera mentioned he was still missing, but that Rachel was okay."

"What else do you know? I mean know because someone told you, not know because you have been getting mixed signals from Wanda."

"Not much. I know Dad asked Wanda's help, and he has had calls from the police here about Wanda and Wexford and someone named Carson."

"Ok, come on," Jim directed, grabbing his jacket.

"So what has Wanda got herself into?" Elisabeth asked, once Jim was driving his hire car towards the Embassy.

"Do you know where she is?" Jim asked, expecting an affirmative.

"Yes, in prison...again."

"So, how do you think she is?"

Jim knew Wanda and her sister shared an odd but strong mental link.

"At the moment, well enough, but twitchy." Elisabeth couldn't quite describe the impression she was getting.

"Ill-tempered and difficult?" Jim suggested.

"Yeah, like I said, twitchy. I haven't tried to think at her yet."

"She believes she is pregnant."

"O.....kay," Elisabeth murmured. "Well, that was well planned wasn't it? So what is happening about Allan?"

Jim knew he could trust Elisabeth Willard to keep the information to herself. "It looks like he is conspiring with a Russian crime group."

"The same one that took Vera?" Elisabeth deduced immediately.

"I don't think so, another branch maybe. David saw him at the airport with one of the high ups, and he wasn't going against his will."

"And Nicole doesn't know?"

"No," Jim agreed. "I don't know how she will take it. Now I don't know if Allan was replaced by one of them, and is dead or disabled somewhere. Or he willingly joined them." He went on to tell Elisabeth all he knew of Wexford's movements since he arrived in Austria to talk trade. In the process, he revealed the charges Wanda faced.

"Damn it, Jim. She didn't kill anyone," Elisabeth was shaken.

"I want to agree," Jim assured her. "However, she was under the influence of some potent drugs at the time, possibly hallucinating... but Wexford was there too."

Elisabeth felt ill. She knew some of the dark memories that lurked in her sister's mind. "How is David taking it?"

"Holding up," Jim told her. "Wanda told him to go home once she is sentenced."

"I will see that he does," Elisabeth promised. "Meanwhile, we came to help Wanda, even if it is only by keeping her mind busy. You have spoken to her?"

"Several times. She is holding up, in her own way."

Elisabeth relaxed back into the passenger seat and tried to reach her sister's mind. She sensed only that her sister was concentrating on something, and was not aware of her gentle nudge.

Jim recognised the car that was parked in one of the visitor's spaces. "The police are here," he warned Elisabeth.

"To see Nicole?"

"Possibly," Jim agreed as he pulled in next to the car Donau was using since his own car had been wrecked. "Before we go in, I'd better mention that they believe that Wanda's real name is Tatiana Carson, and Wanda Martin is an alias."

"And you are...?" Elisabeth though she should ask.

"James Phillips. I came to confirm Wexford's report about possible criminal intent involving the people he was talking to."

"And I will be me, come to help Nicole," Elisabeth said, and it was only a slight deviation of the truth.

Jim rang the bell, and a junior aide answered. He explained that the Ambassador was in a meeting with Mrs Wexford and the police, but that Mr Thomas had left instructions, to bring them through.

As they neared a closed door, they all heard screaming. It became ear piercing when the door was opened.

Both Jim and Elisabeth took in the scene immediately. Nicole was visibly upset and Rachel, who was clinging to her was screaming and refusing to be calmed down. Elisabeth didn't wait for introductions, she went immediately to Nicole and plucked Rachel from her arms.

"Come on pipsqueak, let's go find the kitchen and I will tell you what Maddy did the other day."

Suitably distracted, Rachel stopped screaming, to the relief of all present.

Nicole gave her a grateful look that was mixed with surprise at her presence.

Jim took note of the others in the room as Browning escorted Nicole to a seat, now that she didn't need to try to calm her daughter. He nodded at Mont Pelier and Donau, and was ignored by Wagner, who probably wondered why the new arrival had joined the meeting.

Neil Thomas followed Elisabeth out the door, having been instructed to bring coffee. He led the way to the kitchen.

"What brought on the ruckus?" Elisabeth asked, once they were away from the meeting room. Then she realised that the man with her probably didn't know who she was. "Sorry, I'm Elisabeth Willard. Nicole is my step-mother's sister-in-law. That makes the pipsqueak here, my cousin."

"Neil Thomas, diplomatic attaché. It is very fortunate that you are here."

"Seems so," Elisabeth agreed. "Do you have anything that Rachel might like?"

Neil grinned at the little girl, and when they reached the huge kitchen, he went off to find one of the chefs. While a trolley was prepared with the cups and the coffee brewed, a second chef brought out a glass of chocolate milk and offered a tray of cakes to Rachel and Elisabeth.

With Rachel making herself comfortable on a chair near the table, Neil finally answered Elisabeth's question. "The police gentlemen had questions for Mrs Wexford. Unfortunately, she had not long been back from the hospital."

From what Jim had said, she guessed that the timing of the police visit, was decidedly off.

Neil Thomas departed with the coffee trolley, and Elisabeth gave her full attention to Rachel. She pulled a chair up next to her, and as promised, began a tale of what her mischievous younger sister had done to "Uncle Charles".

She actually had Rachel laughing when the tall, distinguished looking policeman entered the kitchen.

"I see you are good with children." Derek Mont Pelier remarked casually.

"It is probably because I have seven younger siblings and my mother is working on an eighth," Elisabeth exchanged a grin with Rachel before looking at the new comer. "It seems that my father doesn't know when to stop."

"And your father is?" Mont Pelier asked, implying his interest.

"Charles Willard, and my step mother is Allan Wexford's sister."

"Ah, then I have had the pleasure of speaking to your father. He must be like my father. I have eleven siblings. Though most of us have escaped to the corners of the globe."

"Eleven!" Elisabeth echoed. "Ouch!" Rachel, noticing the tall stranger, climbed across to her lap. She decided to stand, and hoist Rachel onto her hip. To distract her from the policeman, she asked, "So, what have you been up to?"

She made the question seem casual by swinging her around on her hip.

"Nothing," came the answer in a barely audible voice.

"Seen much of you Dad while you have been here?"

Rachel shook her head.

"Ain't that the pits," Elisabeth consoled. "Your Uncle Charles is as bad. So, were you with Mummy?"

Rachel nodded solemnly and spoke in a whisper, "Until she got sick and Daddy took me to his Daddy – Grandpa Theo."

"Oh, I don't think I have met him. Is he nice?" Elisabeth kept her voice neutral and interested.

"He's horrid and mean and so was the nurse."

Elisabeth was aware that the tall man was listening intently as she teased the story out of the little girl. She hid her anger at the way the nurse punished her for every little thing she did wrong or out of ignorance. And she inwardly winced when the little girl innocently described how the 'ghost' cousin had come and got her, after knocking the nurse on the head, tying her up and putting her in the cupboard.

"Serves her right," Elisabeth said firmly. "Then what?"

Rachel said she went and drank her milk so that Grandpa Theo wouldn't smack her, and went with her 'ghost' cousin. "I think I fell asleep," Rachel admitted.

Derek Mont Pelier spoke up, but kept his tone friendly. "You have a 'ghost' cousin?" He ducked his head at an odd angle to see Rachel's face. She laughed and hid her head again. "I wish I had one. Did she give you her name?"

"No, but she is like Maddy said. A ghost sister that no one ever sees, but she said her mum saw her."

"Well, I think you are a very lucky girl to have seen her too," Derek said. "How would I know if I saw her?"

Elisabeth gritted her teeth as Mont Pelier managed to get a very good description of Wanda from the little girl and then moved on to Grandpa Theo and the nurse. She had to admit that he was good, and uncomfortably good looking as well.

"Want to go back to Mummy, pipsqueak?"

"No."

"Why not? Don't you want to know where Daddy is?"

"No."

"Okay, I guess we can stay here a bit longer." Elisabeth glanced at the tall man, hoping he was not going to ask more questions.

"Maybe we can talk again later," Mont Pelier suggested to her. He seemed to be studying her.

"About what? I just came here to help Nicole."

"About that," Derek said, giving her a slight bow before walking out.

Elisabeth returned to Nicole after Neil Thomas told her that the policemen had gone. Jim and Browning were still with her, and she looked like she had been crying. Rachel wriggled from Elisabeth's hold and went to climb onto her mother's lap.

"Mama, I had chocolate milk and a cake," she said, happily.

Nicole, held out her hand to Elisabeth and said, "Thank you so much for coming. Everything has been perfectly horrid."

Jim spoke to Browning for a little longer before the Ambassador retreated from the room.

Nicole looked from Elisabeth to Jim, and blurted, "Allan is not some criminal. They're crazy if they think he is."

"Mrs Wexford, there may be an explanation," Jim suggested quietly. "That is why they needed your help."

"That fat one, Wagner. He all but said that Allan had killed some woman. And that he had been living with her before that. They must have him confused with someone else."

"One thought that I had," Jim said slowly, "Was that someone might be impersonating him."

"Oh, you mean my Allan might be a prisoner somewhere?"

"Yes," Jim agreed, not wanting to suggest he might be hurt, or dead.

"But what more can I do to help?" Nicole looked distraught.

"We'd need some way to identify Allan," Jim told her. "So if they think they have found him, they can make sure whether he is your Allan, or a fake."

"What if Allan has done something wrong? He could go to jail."

"Aunt Nicole, if he has, and wasn't forced into it, it's his own fault," Elisabeth said bluntly, with thoughts of Wanda intruding into her mind.

Jim inserted, "He walked into a mess here. Some of the men he was to meet are believed to be involved in criminal activity, like he thought. There is a group, like those who took you, who seem to be protecting the criminals. They have managed to get Tatiana Carson in trouble. Arrested."

It wasn't the exact truth, but it illustrated the point Jim was making.

"They might be doing the same to Allan?" Nicole asked, frightened now for her husband's safety, but relieved that he might not be guilty of a crime.

"It is a possibility," Jim admitted. "So you see, we need to know."

"I have a photograph of him," Nicole volunteered. "It's in my handbag." She tried to reach for it, but had to hold onto Rachel, "The policeman with the dog brought it back. He said that Tatiana helped him find it."

"That's a start," Elisabeth encouraged, but she noticed Jim's frown.

"What about things he might have handled," Jim suggested. "Looks can be imitated, but fingerprints, or DNA, would be better guides."

"I've got nothing here," Nicole said, shaking her head in frustration. "What about at the apartment? Tatiana was going to look around there."

"She did," Jim admitted. "But someone came in later and cleaned the place out – fingerprints and all."

"What? You are not saying it was her?" Nicole protested. "She helped to find Rachel. The policeman said so."

"No, I am not saying it was her. She had no reason to," Jim said bluntly.

Nicole looked on the verge of tears again as she said, "I don't know what else to suggest."

"Was he ever in the armed forces?" Elisabeth suggested. "Or did he have dentist back home. Sometimes dental records are useful."

"Do you think he might be dead?" Nicole asked sharply.

"No, Nicole. A person doesn't need to be dead for that," Elisabeth said firmly.

"I don't think that Allan ever needed a dentist, or a doctor," Nicole said. "And while he talked of joining the marines when we were in high school, he said he went to university instead."

"What about scars, birthmarks, moles, spots," Jim suggested.

"Nothing really, A couple of little ones. One on the back of his left hand, and another on his shoulder. He said he couldn't remember where he got them." Nicole spoke quickly, and then asked a question.

"What about at our place back home? Vera has a key."

Elisabeth glanced at Jim, wondering if he shared the feeling that Nicole didn't want to mention some other body marks. She decided that he had, so she acted on the instinct.

"Nicole, why don't you and I take the pipsqueak up to your room and work out what we need to get for her. You will both need some more clothes and personal stuff."

Jim said, "I will get in touch with Senator and Mrs Willard."

He glanced at Elisabeth and she quickly said, "Jim, I'll get a taxi back to the hotel if you have other things to do."

"Fine. I will talk to you later," Jim agreed. He was willing to trust Elisabeth Willard to find out what Nicole hadn't wanted to say."

Later, once she was back at the hotel, she took Jim aside and explained what she had learnt.

"So that's what it was, Jim. Allan has a blob shaped patch of pigmented skin – a birthmark - on the left side of his groin."

"And she didn't want to say so," Jim said with raised brows.

"She's a bit of a prude, like Vera. Allan was pretty sensitive about it. She called him body-conscious, I'd say image conscious. I never saw him in anything less formal than a suit, and his idea of casual is to remove his tie and take his jacket off."

Jim asked a question. "I don't suppose she mentioned if Allan had that mark in high school?"

Elisabeth stared at him, wondering what he was thinking.

"I did kind of get to asking about Allan back in high school, like how he compared to when he came back, widowed and with child. But to answer your question, I don't think she ever had sex with him back then, though I think she fantasised a lot. Are you trying to figure out when a switch might have been made – if there was one?"

"You have the same disconcerting habit that Wanda has," Jim remarked. "But yes, that is exactly what I was trying to do."

"Do you really think there was a switch?"

"Wanda saw Wexford at the house where Rachel was found. She heard him called Aleksi. Other than that, there is no proof. It is most likely, that any switch was recent. Allan went off and was out of touch for three days before Nicole and Rachel were taken – perhaps that was so she wouldn't be aware of the switch."

"Could be," Elisabeth agreed. "But how would that help Wanda?"

"I don't know," Jim admitted. "Perhaps you can help me unravel her mind?"

"Huh! Don't ask too much of me. Can I ask you something though?"

"Sure."

"Those policemen, what do you think of them? Except for the tall one, I only had a glimpse of the others, but the vibes in that room were definitely hostile. Nicole said she liked the one with the dog, hated the fat one, and thought the tall one was creepy because he just stood back watching and listening. What's the deal with them?"

"The fat one, as you describe him, is Rudy Wagner. He leads the team that are investigating the double murder, the death at the house where Rachel was kept, and one at the airport," Jim explained. "Otto Donau, the one with the dog, was investigating the jewel theft, and he is working to help us find Wexford. Wanda helped him find where Nicole and Rachel were taken, even though he is the one who arrested her. She got away from him the first time. She is not helping Wagner at all."

"After listening to Nicole sound off about Wagner, I can't say I am surprised. So you think she likes this Donau? I am surprised that she isn't insisting on helping to find the truth."

Jim's grin was genuine. "I managed to find a lawyer who convinced her to shut her mouth. There is a lot she can tell them about the criminal conspiracy that they don't know yet. We are trying for a plea bargain."

Elisabeth hoped they were doing the right thing, but refrained from commenting on that. Instead she asked, casually, "And the other one? The tall guy?"

"Derek Mont Pelier is from Interpol. He has limited authority here – he's involved in investigating the jewel theft and the Russian connection."

"He came out to the kitchen, just as I succeeded in getting Rachel to laugh. I was trying to find out why she was so petrified, apart from the aura in that room. She told me things that I think the police should know, but that Mont Pelier got an excellent description of Wanda from her, as well as one of the nurse and Grandpa Theo. She called Wexford 'daddy' and very calmly told how Wanda hit the nurse on the head, tied her up and dragged her into a cupboard. Is he going to tell that man Wagner? I came here to help Wanda, not make things worse."

Jim saw real fear in the blue eyes of Elisabeth Willard.

"I think the police already knew, and not from Derek," Jim warned her. "He actually knows everything that Wanda did, and remembers. Although there are a couple of periods that are a total blank, probably when she was drugged. Wanda and David totally trust him. We have worked with him before. He's using his discretion. He cannot interfere in local investigations unless it relates to his own. He can choose to stay quiet if speaking out will adversely affect his own enquiries."

"I have such a bad feeling," Elisabeth admitted, she wiped a trace of moisture from her eyes.

"I am doing all I can to help," Jim promised. "Nicholas, Grant, Max and Casey, shouldn't still be here, but they stayed to help. Derek has co-opted us to be 'confidential' informants. If we find anything to help Wanda, we pass it on."

"I do appreciate it, and I guess I had better go down to our room and let Tanya and Erin know how things are."

"Have a go at trying to reach her," Jim suggested, meaning Wanda. "And don't give up hope."

Elisabeth tried to smile. "I will get the others to help me."

Chapter 2 - Unsubtle threats

A week had dragged by, and Wanda was learning the routine that remand prisoners lived by. She had learnt the timing of meals, and exercise, and lights out and wake up. She was behaving herself, but not being completely docile. Of the other eight women currently on remand, she knew very little, and they did not share an exercise period with her. Her own guess was that their crimes were minor compared to those she was charged with.

She was not letting her mind brood on the looming future, because that was the way to despair. Instead she was preparing herself to survive, observing everything she could. Though she suspected the guards were watching her more closely than the others in the section.

Her lawyer came every second day, bringing news from her friends, but she did not let her hopes for freedom become paramount.

Hauser had visited the previous day, and she was not expecting any other visitors when the guard arrived and went through the routine of ordering her from her cell, and directing her towards the visitors' room.

She thought it odd that they didn't snap on the hand cuffs, as was usual when she had a visitor. They didn't do it for exercise periods, but she'd been out already that day. Still, she was out of her cell, able to move more freely – she would learn what was up soon enough.

She found herself outside – amongst the regular inmates, and turned to the guard.

"Hey! I'm not meant to be here!" Wanda called to him, but the guard kept walking off.

She was attracting attention – a new face, non-prison clothes. Within moments she was surrounded by a circle of inmates.

A woman, tall and lean, in her forties and with a twisted face, spoke in a rough voice. "I hear you are going to join us soon, for a very long time."

"You heard wrong," Wanda responded instantly. "The charges

are phony."

"They all say that. But I just wanted to introduce myself, Brigitte. I'm the person who is really in charge around here. Do as I say, and things won't be too bad."

"So, you reckon you are the toughest," Wanda shrugged, betraying nothing. "Congratulations on your primacy."

"You're going to have to learn respect," Brigitte warned.

"I'm no arse licker," Wanda gave her own warning. "And if you or any of your lesbian crowd try to make me, you will find out that I am no pushover."

"Fine words...for now." Brigitte smirked and gave a gesture that make the crowd disperse.

She hadn't given any hint that the guard had returned, but her little crowd had. The eyes of several in Wanda's sight, had flicked to someone behind her. So she was not startled when she was grabbed from behind and her wrists cuffed.

Brigitte strolled off as the guard spoke with his lips close to her ear. He was almost an echo of Brigitte with his words, "You're going to have to learn, Carson, that there are penalties for trying to escape. Especially if you are too stupid to succeed."

Wanda had been having a horrible day. She had been hit by an intense bout of morning sickness, and the feeling still lingered. This sham 'escape' was none of her doing. It had been deliberate, designed to demoralise her, and the knowledge that the inmates knew about her was worrying.

The woman's veiled threats were not an immediate problem, but it pissed her off.

"I wasn't escaping, you bastard. You took me out there!" Wanda hissed at the guard.

His reaction was to shove her roughly, almost making her stumble.

"Swearing at a guard...that can get you into real trouble."

Wanda didn't need to see his smirk, it was in his voice. He was enjoying his power over her.

"What are you suggesting?" Wanda asked, although she thought she knew. "Whatever it is, I am not going to do it."

"Offering a bribe," the guard stated. "I am going to have to report this to the Governor."

"Bastard," Wanda switched to American, but her tone was evident and she was shoved again.

"You've got a visitor," she was told then, and she was hustled to the visitors' area.

The man that waited in the room was oldish, but expensively dressed in a pale coloured tailor made suit. His features were sharp, his eyes a piercing blue. He was a complete stranger to her.

Wanda had been pushed into the room, and the guard had not entered. The door had been shut behind her. It seemed that this man was not afraid of her, since she wasn't cuffed to the table.

"Who are you," Wanda demanded rudely. She had not moved closer than where she had been pushed, and the man moved from near the window, and came to study her.

"I am in a position to potentially help you," the man stated, not answering her question.

"Really? Are you god or something?"

"Or something," he agreed, and his accent was tantalising.

"You haven't told me who you are!"

"Who I am, is unimportant," the man said calmly.

"It is to me," Wanda said, turning her back on him and going to the door. The guard had his back to the door, and looking both ways along the passage.

"I think you should hear me out," was the deliberate warning. "I have something to show you."

Some instinct warned Wanda that she needed to see what it was. She turned back to the man, and caught a flash of blue in his hands. He opened his hands, and she saw he held an American passport. The hairs on her neck began to rise. He flicked it open, and even from the distance of six feet away, she knew he held her diplomatic passport. When he knew she understood, he palmed it out of sight like a magician.

Wanda felt her legs wanting to turn to jelly, and slowly walked to the table and pulled out a chair.

"How did you get that?" Wanda asked, without the deliberately rude tone. "Are you one of Theo's or Aleksi's flunkeys?"

It was a stupid thing to say, but it had the effect that she had been trying for with the previous comments. She saw a flash of anger in his eyes, before he masked it. Now she knew that the man was dangerous.

"I was going to ask you how you got it," the man had a hard edge to his voice.

"What's in it for me if I tell you?" Wanda retorted. "Not that I have anything to say, since I don't know who the hell you are."

"Never mind. The question can wait."

The man began to study her as if memorising her every feature. All during that uncomfortable scrutiny, Wanda stared back at him. She didn't need more than an instant to commit his features to memory.

Then the man shocked her. "I know who you really are."

The comment was so unexpected that her stomach seemed to fall to the floor. Wanda sat very still, controlling the shivers of panic that the comment had caused.

"So who am I?" she challenged.

Whether he really knew or was guessing wasn't the point. He had her passport and that was trouble enough.

"A problem with a big mouth and my grand-daughter."

She had not expected such a comment, and didn't completely hide her reaction. The man smiled, but she found no comfort. It was like a shark's grin.

"I don't have a Grandfather!" That was the truth – at least it had been. She sensed the man truly believed what he claimed.

"I am sure that your mother never mentioned me. She was a stupid little bitch, ungrateful and useless."

Wanda was confused. He had to be mistaking her for someone else, because her own biological mother had died when she was four years old. The man kept speaking.

"She married a mousy genius, who could have chosen to be rich, working for me, but who had some inconveniently strong ethics. How are your mother and father?"

"My mother is dead!" Wanda said flatly.

"And your father is a traitor and a defector, not to mention making himself an American door mat."

Wanda's mind felt like an icy wind had entered the room. With sudden clarity, she realised, "He thinks I am Tanya."

"You made a mistake, coming to Austria, and a worse mistake in stealing from me."

"I didn't..."

"Don't lie to me!" the voice came like a whip crack. "Six purple tinted diamonds, from the safe in Alpha Prime. How did you know they were there?"

There was no safe answer to that. He would never believe it was mere fluke.

"I think you should come back when my lawyer is here," Wanda diverted the question.

"I will find out," the man promised.

"So, haven't the police returned them to you yet?" The question was not important to her, just a means to indicate that he wasn't terrifying her as much as he really was.

"In time," the man assured her. "And then they will not be so easy to steal again. That's if you live long enough to try. Do you know, those stones are cursed?"

Wanda thought to herself, that she had no intention of trying to take those damned stones again, but she then wondered why he thought she would try. As for curses, she didn't believe in them.

"Superstitious crap," she told the man. "You're still alive."

"Yes, naturally. The stones rightfully belong to me."

"Inherited, I presume," Wanda said, not sure why she had that idea.

"Yes. When I married Anneliese, they became mine, but she cheated me."

Wanda suddenly decided that she had heard enough, and decided not to try to push the man any further. He did not realise that she had not known any of this until now. He, however, was not finished trying to frighten her.

He spoke his tale, his version of what he assumed she knew already. Well, she did know it, and knew he was lying. That man, who must indeed be her maternal grandfather, had never married Anneliese Mosellan. He had been long gone when her children were born. If these diamonds were hers, he had to have learned of them many years later – from where, Wanda had no idea. There had been no mention of them in the research that her sister and cousin had done.

Wanda sat back and yawned, suggesting boredom. When he finished, she stood up and told him, "My ten minutes is up. You will have to come back later."

As she began to walk to the door, the man's voice snapped at her. "Sit down!"

Wanda sensed his supreme confidence, that he had her in his power. She stayed standing, but every warning sense she had was screaming at her to obey him. She turned and inched slowly back to the table. She would have preferred to have fled, but it wasn't possible.

Those eyes bored into her, as the man said, "Do not think that you are safe in here. Your mother isn't dead. I had her taken out of that death cell, just before they were to give her a lethal injection. I was coming for you and your bastard sire, but the coward had run away."

"Where is she then?" Wanda demanded in a low voice. "Where is she?"

"Be careful what you ask for," the man warned with a savage smile. "Your mother, the ungrateful, disrespectful bitch, tried to sell me out. She is learning that I will not be disobeyed."

"Where is she? Tell me!" Wanda tried a mental trick she seldom used, to force someone to obey her.

The man's expression became a snarl. "My daughter tried that freak's trick on me, and she won't do that again. Neither will you. When I learnt that an interfering US agent was sniffing around in Vienna, I said I would deal with the problem. My cousin gave me your passport. You are the image of your Grandmother, and since we are all responsible for our offspring, it was my duty to collect my daughter's trash."

Wanda couldn't control the shivers any more. This man had people in here. They had overheard her conversation with Jim, and the guard must be one, to have let her stay in here so long. How many more were there?

"I see you are beginning to believe me, so I will get to my point. I can get you out of here and all you have to do is pledge to obey me."

"If I do, then what?"

"When you have learnt obedience, and respect, I will let you indulge in your criminal skills. I find that you have real talent, even if you are a female."

Wanda hedged, "All this has been really interesting, but I work for myself. And the charges are faked. I will be out of here as soon as they put me in front of a judge. So, no, I am not interested."

The man didn't seem surprised, "You are no better than your mother! I will return when you have learnt your mistake. However, you will regret it if you say anything more to the police."

Wanda stayed by the table, as the man walked to the door and pressed a button. The guard opened the door immediately and let the man out.

She was thinking furiously as the guard came and grabbed her arm. She knew who the man had to be, Pieter Tatarovich, and he had admitted that his cousin had given him her passport. That meant he was related to Theo and Aleksi, who controlled the masked thugs.

As she was dragged out into the passage, she was thinking, "Oh, mother of gods, this has to be a nightmare. He's part of the goddamned Family. What would he do when he realised that she was not Tanya? Did he even know that his daughter, Ivana, was one of triplets?" Then a worse possibility occurred to her. "What would he do if he found out that I messed around with another 'cousin' last year? She'd be damned if she would let him anywhere near her sister or cousins."

As for working for him, being obedient and respectful, she wasn't going there anymore. She'd been there. No way would she let some freak who claimed to be her grandfather, and who hadn't given a damn about his daughters, order her around. But she needed to think on all this, back in her cell.

She looked at where she was going. It wasn't back to the cells.

The guard seemed to anticipate her question.

"The Governor wants to see you, Carson."

Wanda was reminded of the false claims that this one was going to make about her. She kept her mouth shut, intending to make her complaint to the Governor.

A voice called for them to come in, when the guard knocked on the door of the Governor's office. Wanda had been in there when she first arrived, briefly. She had thought he was a reasonable man, but this time he gave her no chance to speak, nor to speak against the fraudulent claims. Simply swearing at a guard was a punishable offence.

He told her, in a very severe voice, that the prison charter encouraged politeness and dignity.

When she tried to say, "Surely the truth is important," she felt a solid blow on her back, and she decided that she was not going to be given the dignity of being able to refute the charges. Instead, she would lose her hour of outside exercise, for a week, and only have basic rations for meals. And visitors would be restricted.

As much as she wanted to say more, prudence finally won. They wouldn't stop until she backed down. So she parroted the apology the Governor insisted on, which was, effectively, admitting the guards accusations were totally true, and let the guard shove her back to the cell room.

Then, when the guard should have removed the hand restraints, he left them on, daring her to complain. In was intended as a subtle humiliation and a huge inconvenience, which she suffered in silence, until a full five minutes had past and the guard returned to release them.

It was enough to tell her that he could do it for as long as he wished, and she didn't want to give him even the hint of a reason. It would mean she couldn't eat, and would have great difficulty using the hygiene facility. She consoled herself with the knowledge that she was not yet pregnant enough to need to use it frequently.

When she was sure the guard had finished having fun at her expense, she began to pace the small room and mentally vent her annoyance. But she had barely started when her silent vituperation, was interrupted.

"Wanda?"

She instantly stopped pacing, and thinking, and the sense of a voice came again.

"Lisbeth?" she thought tentatively. Listening for the mind touch that had been her line of sanity so many years back when she had been in prison before. Her anger turned to malicious glee. Between her and her sister was a means of communication that Pieter Tatarovich could not possibly believe. It felt like a weight had lifted from her.

"You're in Vienna," she marvelled, sending her thankfulness as an emotion. The residual shivers of fear and hopelessness receded, and she seemed to have strength coming back into her whole body.

"Are you okay?" Elisabeth Willard asked, or rather she thought it in her mind, knowing that her sister would sense it.

"Yeah, nothing I can't handle...now," she sent back, then added urgently. "I need to talk to Jim."

"I will tell him to come," Elisabeth promised.

"They might not let him visit," Wanda admitted.

"What have you done?" was the resigned question.

"Fell into a set up and got pissed off. Don't worry, I'm fine. It's putting me in the right frame of mind. But I do need to talk to Jim."

"I will tell him. If he can't come, surely they can't stop your lawyer talking to you."

Wanda hadn't thought of that, and she should have.

"How's David? Have you seen him?" It had been a very long week since she had seen him.

"He's...driven," Elisabeth summarised. "He's like he was just before you came back that time."

Wanda knew when she meant and understood. "Tell him I'm fine."

"I will. Jim is keeping him busy. At the moment he is off with one of the policemen, following a lead to someone called Heinrich. He is being that Interpol guy's assistant. Tanya and Erin were keeping him occupied for a while too."

Wanda tried to hide the dismay she felt at having all her cousins here. What if Tatarovich saw them?

Her sister sensed her dismay and said, "We came to support you. Did you think we wouldn't care?"

'No, it isn't that. I didn't expect you all, but it's not that I am not grateful, but tell Tanya and Erin to keep out of sight. You should too. Please, you must."

"What is the matter? I haven't felt you to be so scared before."

To anyone else she would have claimed not to be scared, but

Elisabeth knew her too well.

"It's complicated, Lisbeth. Oh, gods, it's complicated. Is Tanya nearby?"

Of the cousins, Tanya was the next strongest at sending and receiving thoughts. If Lisbeth was linked to her, and Tanya was near, she might pick up on the conversation.

"No," came the hoped for answer. "She and Erin are with some of Jim's friends, looking through old newspapers. So what is going on? Are you just pissed off?"

"No. I just had a visitor here. I don't know what he is calling himself, but it had to have been Pieter Tatarovich – and he thinks I am Tanya."

"He's dead!" was Elisabeth's immediate reaction. She and Tanya had done a great deal of research into their mothers' background. No trace of Pieter Tatarovich had turned up in the past forty years.

"Okay...so he thinks you are Tanya. Do you think he knows about the rest of us?"

Tanya and Wanda could pass for twins, so the misidentification was not unexpected.

"I am pretty sure he doesn't," Wanda sent, but went on quickly, needing to pass on a lot of information as soon as she could, in case she was disturbed.

"Listen. He claims to be the owner of those cursed stones I took. He claims to have inherited them, and not from his Russian antecedents."

Wanda allowed herself to be amused by the rude words her sister was thinking. She never actually spoke them aloud. She realised that Wanda meant he had taken them from Anneliese Mosellan, their grandmother.

"Lisbeth, enough. I need you to tell Jim something, and it's very important. Tell him that Tataorvich has my passport. He got it through his Family, with a capital F, connections."

"What do you...?"

"Just tell him. He will know what I mean and all the implications."

"I'll try to call him now," Elisabeth promised. Horrid thoughts were occurring to her, as she recalled when her stepmother had been missing, before Wanda had found her. "You mean, they belong to that group...?"

Wanda knew what she meant to say. "Yeah, but guess what? He doesn't know I know who and what he is. He doesn't know I've bested some of his relations, and best of all, he doesn't know I am not Tanya. And he doesn't know I am passing on things he thinks he has scared me into silence about."

In fact, knowing she had outsmarted the man, allowed her to relax. Anger gone, and her mind back to normal efficiency.

Chapter 3 - Cousins and connections

Elisabeth paced around the hotel room she was sharing with Tanya and Erin, she should have been out getting more things Nicole needed, but now she was too uptight. Every five minutes, she tried the number for the room Jim Phillips was using. She wanted to speak to him before her cousins returned. They would know at once that something was wrong. Finally, her call was answered.

"Jim? It's Elisabeth. I need to talk to you…"

"I'm sorry, Fraulein Willard, its Derek Mont Pelier. Perhaps I can help you? Jim is out at the Embassy with Mrs Wexford."

"No, I really need to talk to Jim. I'll try the embassy number."

Without realising how rude it was, she hung up the phone and tried to find the number in a phone book. She could speak German, but she was not very skilled at reading it.

A knock on the door distracted her. Thinking it was Jim, she went to answer it, but was wary enough to check who was there through the spy hole.

At the door was Derek Mont Pelier. With misgivings, she opened the door to let him in.

"You wouldn't happen to know the number for the US Embassy, would you Agent Mont Pelier?" Elisabeth asked, feeling her face flush. "I'm sorry I hung up on you like that but…"

"I understand," Derek assured her. "As it happens, I do know the number it's…" He spoke the numbers, and watched as Elisabeth backed off, saying. "I will just make the call."

He watched her, watching him, as she asked for a message to be given to Jim Phillips. He went to perch half on one of the heavy padded armchairs, and waited for her to finish the call before speaking.

"I apologise if my coming is intrusive, but you sounded upset and I came to see if I could help."

"I'm sorry, but you can't really," Elisabeth tried not to sound rude. "I mean, I appreciate your offer, but …"

"No, I understand. It is not my business," Derek backed off graciously. "However, perhaps while you are waiting for Herr Phillips to call back, you could help me for a while?"

"How? I mean, if it's about what is happening here, I don't know a lot."

"This is about learning more about Allan Wexford. You obviously know the family," Derek suggested. "What can you tell me about him?"

"He's my step uncle or something like that. I told you that last week."

"Yes, I do remember. I also wanted to complement you on your deft questioning of young Rachel. My Austrian colleagues want to question her officially. Her mother is being fiercely protective. What do you think?"

"I think they need to be careful," Elisabeth told him. "Seriously. Rachel seems okay at the moment, and she's recovering from her ordeal, and that's because I didn't make it out to be a big deal. If they start questioning her, it will become a big deal. Kids pick up on emotions, you know."

"Go on," Derek invited.

"At the moment, seeing this ghost cousin hit the nurse on the head, and so on, is a bit like a cartoon – not real. The ghost cousin came and rescued her...like in a fairy tale. She is too young still to appreciate more than an unpleasant nurse, who was going to punish her again, was stopped. Do you understand what I mean? Questioning her will make her realise that it was all too real."

"Yes, indeed. For now, I passed on what she said," Derek caught the slight tensing of the American woman and wondered at it. He went back to his original topic. "Tell me about the Wexford's – before they came on this trip."

"I only really met him when he came to visit Vera. Nicole came around more often."

"He lived in Austria for a time, didn't he?" Derek said to give her a starting point.

"Yes, he came back after his wife died. Rachel was a toddler, just starting to walk. He seemed nice enough, and Vera was glad he was back, for a while."

"Did she say anything to imply that he was different?"

"Only that he used to be arrogantly full of himself, and often insufferable. Mind you, he was much my age then, and I don't think he and Vera were really close. When he came back, he seemed to need her and she felt nicer towards him. It got a bit annoying after a while. He left Rachel with Vera for hours each day, and she had young kids of her own and another on the way. I heard her complaining to Dad, once or twice. He told her that fatherhood and grief can change a person. I mean. Dad got on well enough with him. I think that was about when she got tired of grieving father and decided to match-make by encouraging Nicole to come around."

"How long has Vera been married to your father?" Derek asked.

"Oh, ten, eleven years. Mind you, Allan didn't come to the wedding. Did you speak to Dad about him?"

"I did. He gave me the man to man view. I also wanted to get a woman's view."

Derek smiled, and he seemed both charming and friendly. "You know, you look familiar."

Elisabeth tilted her head and challenged, "That isn't the start of a pickup line, is it?"

"No. I was being serious. You remind me of Fraulein Carson."

"I always thought I looked pretty ordinary," she commented, trying to sound relaxed. She was aware that the outer door of the room was opening and who was coming in, and she kept her attention on the tall policeman.

"I meant no disrespect. I have a great deal of respect for both Wanda and David."

A voice distracted Derek from wondering at the sudden tenseness in the American woman's manner. He turned abruptly and saw two other young women behind him.

"Who is he talking about, Elisabeth?" Erin Rand spoke with a deliberately audible voice.

She was subtly balancing on her toes as if she was prepared to attack the tall stranger. Tanya, off to one side was imitating her manner.

Derek took the sudden arrival of two potentially hostile newcomers quite calmly. Then he took a good look at Tanya Krinsky and couldn't help staring.

Tanya stared back and asked, "And who is this?"

"This is Interpol Agent Mont Pelier," Elisabeth introduced.

"Derek," Mont Pelier insisted. "Jim didn't say there was three of you."

"Need to know," Erin stated. "Is this the reason you were so bothered, Elisabeth?"

"No," Elisabeth said quickly, although having Mont Pelier so close was troubling in another way. "That was a relatively urgent matter that I am not at liberty to discuss." Elisabeth felt herself relaxing and forced a smile. She sensed that her cousins both understood the reference and would wait for details. They didn't ask more questions.

"May I at least have the pleasure of knowing who I am meeting?" Derek asked pleasantly.

The phone began ringing, and it gave Elisabeth a reason to delay answering, and neither Erin nor Tanya offered their names. They simply kept watching Mont Pelier as Elisabeth answered the phone.

"Yes, I do. I do need to talk to you. It is very urgent, but I cannot explain now. I have Agent Mont Pelier with me. It borders on high up confidential."

She listened to Jim talking for a while before hanging up. She was more relaxed now, and gave her cousins a quick smile. They in turn relaxed from their provocatively belligerent stance.

"Agent Mont Pelier, this is Erin Rand," she gestured to the sturdier of her two cousins. Erin smiled, as Elisabeth introduced Tanya. "Jim says Wanda trusts you, but I still can't tell you things. But I thank you for being concerned. Was there anything else?"

"I was going to be ask you about this ghost-cousin reference, but I think I am beginning to understand."

"What are you talking about?" Erin asked looking from Derek to Elisabeth.

With a shrug, Elisabeth explained. "It was originally the 'ghost sister'. My second brother, Paul, made it up for the younger kids when Vera was missing last year."

"Yes, I heard that Wanda and David helped there, and that was why Vera asked their help for her brother," Derek admitted. He had a sudden irrational idea that the three women in the room with him were subtly communicating. They all seemed to relax their tense stance at the same time.

"You are all related," Derek said. "And you, Fraulein Krinsky are the image of Wanda Martin. You could be twins."

"I'm not," Tanya stated.

"Cousin?" Derek persisted.

Elisabeth decided to admit, "We're cousins."

"I wish you would trust me," Derek suggested.

"Sorry, you're Interpol...police," Tanya gave her opinion, and Derek wondered how she had known, when they had just met.

"True," Derek admitted, not affronted. "I will be off. I hope we can speak another time."

Jim arrived back ten minutes later. He put his case on the low coffee table and began to loosen his tie. "What is so important?"

"Wanda," Elisabeth summarised and then explained. "She had a visitor at the prison, a little while ago. The man was not police, and not her lawyer. He didn't give his name, but he claimed to be the owner of those damned diamonds. Wanda is convinced that it was Pieter Tatarovich."

Jim looked at her sharply, he recognised the name, and had not expected to hear it.

Elisabeth went on, having the complete attention of her cousins as well. "She also wanted you to know that the man had her passport, and that he got it through family, with a capital 'f' connections. She wants Tanya, Erin and me to keep out of sight."

"That is an extremely good idea," Jim agreed. "I do not like this development at all."

He glanced at the three women and saw Tanya had gone quite pale.

Erin asked, "Why is he such a problem?"

"For one, he thinks she is Tanya, and she thinks he is trying to dominate her into working for him," Elisabeth explained.

"And those people who had Vera Willard last year, are probably related to that man," Jim added. He saw the women glance at each other and said. "It seems that he is not aware of the three of you, and that Wanda is not going to be forced. I will go out and talk to her."

"Uh, you will probably have no luck. Wanda got into some trouble. A set up she said. I think they revoked visitation privileges."

"Let me find out," Jim suggested, moving to the phone. "If I can't, I am sure they will not stop the police seeing her."

While he was on the phone, Elisabeth spoke quickly to her cousins. They all knew their maternal grandfather was Tatarovich, but didn't have all the full impact of the problem. They stopped talking when Jim returned.

"You are right, and it does sound like a set up – based on how she was behaving before she went there."

"Which explains a lot of her cussedness," Elisabeth decided. "I think, though that the man scared her."

"Yes," Jim agreed. He didn't say that he had never known Wanda to admit to being scared. "I think that we need to bring Derek Mont Pelier in on this. He is interested in the Russian group – that must be related to Tataorovich and he is on Wanda's side."

Tanya and Erin gave nearly identical shrugs, Elisabeth only said, "If you think so." Privately, she wasn't averse to being around the man.

Jim made a call down to Derek's suite, and invited him back.

After listening to what Jim had to say, and accepting that the source was confidential, he proposed, "I will find out from the prison authorities the name the man gave. I will also start some enquiries into this Pieter Tatarovich and Pierre Taunton who I was told is the owner of the stones."

Tanya suddenly blurted, "He is meant to be dead! I never met him, but my mother hated him, because he never wanted anything to do with her."

"Could you be very discreet when asking questions?" Elisabeth asked. "Don't mention any of us?"

"Indeed," Derek assured her. "And I will arrange a way for you to talk to her, Jim. Even if I must have her brought to the police facility."

Chapter 4 - Small details

After Nicholas dropped his helpers off at the hotel, he proceeded to the police complex and asked to see Inspector Donau. The officer at the contact desk called up, received an affirmative and had a junior officer escort him up.

He saw David sitting to one side of Donau's desk, gave him a nod and handed Donau a USB storage device. "That is all we found about Wexford in the newspapers. Most of it is from just before he took his daughter back to the States. It does say that he was questioned about the death of his wife."

"I will look up our records," Donau promised. "This will be a great help, my thanks for this." He looked at David and suggested, "Why don't you go off? I will call you if I get anything else."

After staying seated for a moment longer, David stood, tacitly accepting the suggestion. He made a parting suggestion. "I'd ask that gardener more questions. I saw him eavesdropping."

"Why didn't you suggest that while we were still at Heinrich's house?" Donau asked, startled.

"So they will think we have learnt nothing new. If you challenge him when he is away from the house, you might find drugs on him. He's a smoker, and he smelt of marijuana."

Donau grinned, "I will do as you suggest."

David nodded a goodbye, directing it at both Donau and his colleague Bauer, who still had healing cuts on his face. He walked out with Nicholas.

Donau listened to the footsteps fading as his helper and the other American walked towards the steps to the lower floor.

"The Americans can certainly train good investigators," Donau remarked. He was thinking of Wanda Martin, though he would not admit to the ambivalence he felt. This David, who had not given him a last name, had the same knack for getting to the heart of an issue. Taking the American with him when he went back to Heinrich's place had been an impulse, but it had paid dividends. David had seemed to be a mere subordinate, intent only on what his superior was doing, but had actually been observing everything around him.

To Bauer, he said, "Give Christian a call and find out if anything has been happening."

He had arranged for his other team member to observe the place after he had left.

Bauer transferred the call to Donau's phone after getting onto Christian.

"The gardener went down to the payphone at the corner of Graberstrasse and Wassergasse and made a call. I have the box number," Christian reported.

"I'll get that from you," Donau reached for pen and paper. "Excellent. I will get the call records from there. Keep watching."

He ended the call and gave the still recuperating Bauer the job of getting the records, explaining the reason.

Bauer had to wait for the call to be answered, and while he waited, he commented, "That young man of Mont Pelier's is sharp, right enough. Intense though."

"I agree. I would say he has a personal interest in the case. Perhaps Carson is a colleague. However, Mont Pelier must think he is an asset. Certainly his insights have been spot on."

Alex woofed and stood up, as if he agreed with the statement, as well as to remind his person that he had been ignoring his pet.

"I don't know if I can trust your recommendation. After all, you like jewel thieves and accused murderers,"Donau commented.

Alex woofed again on a different tone.

Donau answered, "Oh, so you don't agree. We'll see who is right. You just keep your opinions to yourself at the meeting this afternoon."

Bauer chuckled at the exchange; he'd heard many similar one-sided conversations. "I have found a record on that gardener. Two convictions for petty theft, in Germany."

"What about phone records?" Donau asked.

"I am on hold with a stern sounding lady," Bauer shrugged. His attention suddenly switched back to the call, he listened, then covered the mouthpiece and said, "They will send them over before four o'clock."

"We need them as soon as possible. See if they can email them to you. If she gives trouble, I will call the chief. I really want to trace that call right away. Finding Heinrich is a priority."

Jurgen Hauser called at the hotel to see Jim, and the two men went into Jim's sleeping room to talk privately. It wasn't because he didn't trust Grant, David or Max, the only three who were around at the time, but so that David didn't hear certain things.

"The police have scheduled a progress meeting this afternoon. I expect to hear the outcome of our request for reduced sentence after that."

Jim watched the young lawyer, who was concerned about his ability to help his American client. He waited as he gathered his thoughts.

Hauser finally went on, "This crime cartel is becoming a huge can of worms. They want everything done by the book." Again he paused, then asked, "How much information can my client give them? I know she visited many of the business premises."

"She downloaded information from the business computers, and sent it to David. He hasn't had time to go through it all. She had a program to get her through the security programs and firewalls. So, allowing for the fact that her information was obtained illegally, at least it should be able to give them avenues to investigate. At best, she could testify to what she saw and found. The catch is, that the police have her android tablet, which is the means to accessing the copied data."

"So the police could bypass us and use it to get the information?" Hauser suggested.

"No, all her files are encrypted, using a very high level encryption algorithm. And the passwords to decrypt them are different for every file and consist of random characters," Jim told him.

"Then she would have to have the passwords somewhere?"

Jim shook his head. "She has a photographic memory – a rather amazing one. So there is no written record of passwords. What concerns me about the police having access to the tablet, is that there might be information on it that they can use against her."

"What sort of information?"

"Maybe nothing. She pays attention to detail, but I doubt she expected to lose the tablet."

"I will take that into consideration," Hauser promised. "What does she know about these Russian criminals? I have the impression that now they seem to have left the country, no one is concerned about them."

"They should be," Jim said. "No one knows what they were intending, or how entrenched they are. The leader might have fled, but there were those masked raiders, who I believe are part of that group, not the cartel. The fact that Wexford, our trade consul, left with that leader, makes it of interest to the US. In fact, Ambassador Browning is going to pressure the Police Chief, to get results on finding him. Our current theory is that someone is impersonating the real Wexford, who is either dead, or imprisoned somewhere. Carson, might be able to throw some light on that, since they have placed her at the house the Russians fled from."

They discussed many points, and many possible ideas to help his client. Finally Hauser told Jim, "I am going to ask for a maximum of ten years for the murder charge, and the minimum term for that jewel theft charge. I will also insist on a stipulation that any admissions of criminal activity made during subsequent questioning, be exempt from charges."

"Carson didn't murder those men," Jim restated his belief.

"I am talking worst case," Hauser said. "I know what the police are saying, but there are other interpretations, especially if you believe that she had no memory of that time. I can make a strong case for being framed."

Jim subsided, and asked instead, "Have they set a trial date?"

"Not yet, and I did not intend to hurry it up, I could if you think it better."

Jim shrugged, uncomfortable. "No, the further off it is, the more time we have to work in. However, I am not sure how safe Carson is in there. I had word that someone visited her today. A man who claimed to own those diamonds."

Hauser looked startled. "I should have been there. Would Carson know not to say anything?"

"You can be sure of that," Jim knew. "I asked Mont Pelier to make enquiries, and he was told that there was no visitor. They claim that Carson infracted several rules, and as a result has lost visitation privileges."

"That is very odd. However, they cannot deny me the right to talk to my client. Do you want me to find out what it is about?"

"Yes. My source could only give me the bare outline," Jim told the lawyer. He wasn't ready to mention the apparent relationship between the visitor, and Carson. "I suggest that you take a tape recorder, for there may be things she needs to tell me that are classified. I am not suggesting that you can't be discreet, but I am concerned about how private your talks with Carson are. This way, if she needs to talk at length, she can use one of a few odd languages that she knows, and I can have David translate."

"I was planning to go out this afternoon, anyway. I need to prepare her for the hearing about the plea bargain."

"I won't answer any questions here," Wanda insisted softly. "They can and do listen in."

"They?" Hauser asked, as if he thought her paranoid.

"Someone at least. That visitor that I had this morning used a term that I had spoken when talking to Jim."

"They tell me that you had no visitor," Hauser told her quietly.

"They're playing mind games," Wanda said soberly. She waved her hand to dismiss that problem. "I can deal with that. The man that came here doesn't want me to say anything else to the police. The mind games may be the start of them trying to discredit me."

"Do you still insist on telling the police everything? Even if it is dangerous?"

"I know things that they need to know, and I didn't come to Vienna for the purpose of personal gain."

"Those diamonds...." Hauser reminded her.

"When I went to Alpha Prime, I had absolutely no idea of their existence, although my visitor cannot believe that."

"So, your purpose was?"

"When I realised there were jewels in that safe, I decided it was a perfect way to deflect suspicions from my real intention. If they thought I was there for them, they would never conceive that I was hacking their computers."

"If you hadn't taken them, I doubt they would even have known you were there," Hauser stated. "I am told that you are really good."

Wanda had a flash of a memory – the sense of being drawn to that safe, hidden as it was in a storage room. Only now, after her morning visitor, she had the inkling of a really crazy sounding reason.

"I still can't tell you why I took them, and didn't just leave them on the floor the way I meant to. So you may as well consider it an act of insanity. Or perhaps it is the curse that bastard reckons follows those damn diamonds. I didn't even look at them."

Hauser frowned, then commented, "I heard some things about them. They are called blood diamonds, even though they are mauve tinted, not reddish..."

Wanda felt an icy chill, and she turned pale. Her visitor had claimed they had belonged to Anneliese Mosellan, her maternal grandmother – she knew things about her that very few people on Earth did. Those diamonds had to be alien. Blood diamonds...they had called to her!

"Are you all right?" Hauser was saying.

"Yes." The answer was automatic. "So, Donau has me tied up for that aberration. I will accept the time for that crime, but I didn't murder anyone. So what is happening there?"

"The murder charge is still looking solid."

"If I tell them all I know, they will have to realise that I couldn't have done it."

"If they agree to a bargain, we will negotiate a better deal," Hauser advised her.

"I won't admit to a crime that I never committed. So why don't you start from 'drop all charges' if they want my help?"

"They won't go for that," Hauser protested.

"Probably not, but I won't go for what they want either."

"Why don't you let me handle the legal work as I am being paid to do?"

Wanda controlled her frustration, and waved one of her cuffed hands again. "Go ahead."

"How about telling me how Mr Phillips knows you had a visitor, if you have no communication privileges."

"That's classified," Wanda stated flatly.

Hauser wanted to dispute that, but the American had implied that. "Fine. I have a recorder. I believe that you know some odd languages. So, start talking and I will ask for sensible answers from Mr Phillips."

Wanda sat straighter, buoyed by the brilliance of Jim's idea. She took the pencil sized microphone and began speaking rapidly. Her mind was focussed on recording all the facts, the conversation almost verbatim, and all the thoughts on it since.

Hauser tried to identify the language, and decided it sounded like nothing he had ever heard. It made him think the idea would work.

When Wanda was finally finished, he turned off the digital recorder and put the palm sized unit back in his case.

"I don't know if they will want you to be there, or will only discuss things with me. However, if you are to be there, I do not want you saying anything."

"Fine," Wanda agreed. "So if they don't want me, when will you be back to give me the decision?"

"As soon as I know the outcome. I will also pin them down to when they will want to question you."

Wanda sat back in her chair, "Right."

"Was there anything else you needed to say?"

"No. I'm done."

Hauser rose, picked up his case and indicated he was ready to leave. The guard opened the door leading to the visitors section, then relocked it after Hauser had passed through. Only then did he release her from the table and grab her arm in a painful grip. He grinned when she grimaced but stayed silent.

It was the same guard who had caused her trouble that morning, and this time he didn't speak, just hustled her back towards her cell like room. Wanda knew he was making her walk fast on purpose.

At her cell, he shoved her in, but instead of releasing the wrist restraints, he deliberately tightened them, to the point where the circulation was restricted. He held her that way for five minutes, during which Wanda made no comment, and allowed her posture to slump, just a little.

"I see you have learnt your first lesson, Carson," he sneered as he released her, with a shove that forced her further into the room.

Wanda waited until the door was closed before swearing at him. She knew what he was doing – giving her insidious reminders that she was a trapped rat. No doubt these annoyances would escalate and she already knew complaining would have no effect. No doubts existed in her mind that this was the start of 'learning about your mistake'.

Well, those bastards didn't know her. She might be limited in how she could defend herself in this prison, and have no apparent place to run to hide, but she had been in such positions before. What did scare her was how far the man she believed to be Tatarovich, would go to stop her talking to the police.

Well, they would have to be very creative to kill her in the prison, Wanda decided as she went to sit on her bed and hug her knees. Once there, it didn't matter that she looked to be staring at nothing. An observer would think she was agonising about her situation. In fact, she was thinking hard on what she might expect from the guard or any others that obeyed Tatarovich.

She could pretend to be subdued, and she would not use her combat skills to get back at her tormentors. They would never learn how capable she was, and how many times that guard had been lucky. If her life was in danger, she would have some advantage.

If it came to that, Wanda felt sure she could escape from this remand section. Her skill at opening locks bordered on magical, except that it was a well-honed skill and the understanding of how every type of lock worked. She could make the most innocuous looking junk into a lock pick, and she decided then to keep her eye out for anything she could use.

Still, escaping was not an option. Not while they believed her to be a murderer, and even without that charge, it still wasn't. She had been stupid and she had to pay the price.

Chapter 5 - Can of worms

The progress meeting was chaired by the Chief of Police and the Senior Prosecutor in the first district of Vienna.

On top of the deaths of Wessler and Lunn, the investigation into the business dealings of a number of prominent men was causing an uproar. The men being investigated were doing all they could to cover their tracks, and much of this had been done by the time they were ordered to cease trading, and submit to a search and seizure of business records and computers. The business premises had been sealed and would stay that way for the foreseeable future. The innocent employees, were unfortunate casualties in all this.

Of the men being investigated, five had already fled the country, and the lesser ranked members of the alleged crime syndicate were not talking.

The first reports were requested from the leader of the new task force. Mostly this was confirming the seizure of records, and telling of the need for IT experts to help open the files or to recover erased data.

Derek Mont Pelier was present, as the overall investigation touched on his own enquiries. He listened to the tone of frustration, and noted ways in which Wanda/Tatiana might help them. He had no intention to help them yet.

Inspector Wagner was called on to update everyone as to the status of the murder investigation. He made no bones about believing that they had the killer of Wessler and Lunn in custody. He outlined the evidence that supported his contention, and omitted the pieces that didn't fit.

The task force leader, an officer of higher rank that Wagner, asked, "Have you located Lunn's computer? It was not at his office, or at his house."

Mont Pelier saw the slight jerk, as Wagner heard the question. "We have not," he admitted, sharing the lack of progress with his team. "We searched at the murder scene and in the rest of the house. Lunn's residence was not located until after your team took over. May I ask if Wessler's records were intact?"

"We have no way of being sure," the taskforce leader admitted. "However, as you reported, neither man had time to get away, nor did your prisoner have any records on her when found."

Wagner was about to speak again and thought better of it. Mont Pelier wondered what he had thought of…that his murderer might have taken things and given them to someone else?"

Possibly, and then realised that if there was a confederate, his case against Tatiana would be weakened.

Wagner's face tightened as the Chief of Police brought up Heinrich and Wexford. He knew that both of those men had been placed at the house just before the murder. Heinrich had fled and his family had no idea where he was. Wexford, had been seen at the airport. In each case, they could be construed to be fleeing from the murder scene.

Mont Pelier knew that Wagner didn't believe that the man at the airport was Wexford. But the question of how a bag like the man had been carrying when he got there, was found to have a suit inside with the blood of the two dead men on it was one of the contradictions he had not mentioned.

He didn't look happy as Christian, Donau's team member put up two photos on the large white board, and invited the assembled experts to compare the image of Wexford provided by his wife, with the image taken from the airport cameras.

The Police chief commented, "The US Embassy is insisting that we find their citizen. They believe that Wexford was abducted, not fleeing."

This resulted in some heated discussion, and eventually led to the murder of Heidi Lowenbach at the airport, because she was a known associate of Wexford, and the lab results on tests done on the dumped suitbag. Wagner faced some pointed questions. He stuck to his theory, that Carson was guilty, but seemed to concede that Carson and Wexford might both be involved.

Donau spoke of the investigation of the house where Rachel Wexford had been found, that had been let to the man seen at the airport with Wexford. He gave the evidence that Carson had been a prisoner there, prior to the murder of Wessler and Lunn, had been in the house and taken the child out before it was torched to hide any remaining evidence.

"What do we know about this man, the one with Wexford?" the police chief asked.

Mont Pelier chose to speak up, sensing that the Austrian was prepared to dismiss the man as unimportant.

"Sir, you should have had a report that the man, the one with Wexford in the image provided by detective Christian, is a Russian criminal known as Father Theo. It is my belief that a group of masked thugs that have been operating in Vienna are used by that man."

That created more questions, and the revelation that such men had abducted Nicole Wexford and her daughter, helped Carson escape, had made an assault on Carson's hideout.

It cannot have been missed that Carson's name was mentioned in all aspects of the trouble, and that, Mont Pelier decided was the reason why few people even considered the idea that Carson could be innocent. If he hadn't met Carson in a previous investigation, and known her skills and affinity for finding trouble, he would have found it hard to believe she wasn't guilty.

He had made suggestions to Donau about how to bring up the hobo that had been rescued from the burnt house. Now he added the suggestion that this man needed to be helped and questioned, in case he could add to the information about the men at that house.

Having all the information set out, the Chief of Police gave instructions for further investigation, and the Prosecutor stressed that correct procedures should be followed to prevent the guilty being freed on technical points. Then the assembly was dismissed, and the Chief invited Mont Pelier to join him in his office.

Mont Pelier had questions of his own, and agreed to the suggestion. He was not surprised when the Chief asked him to clarify his interest in Carson.

"I am sure you did not miss the way Carson's name kept cropping up at that meeting," Mont Pelier said as he made himself comfortable in the visitor's chair, since the Prosecutor decided to stay standing.

He had the feeling they were treating him as a suspect, but that did not surprise him. Many policemen considered Interpol a useful resource, but one that should not have a visible presence.

"I have my mandate, which I have explained to you already. However, Carson seems mixed up in the investigations I need to make."

"Well, I want to question that woman about a few matters that came to light at the meeting," the Police Chief said with annoyance, explained by, "Except that her lawyer has gagged her."

He turned to the Prosecutor. "We need to find out what she knows."

"And I think that is the point. She wants us to feel that so she can try to get away with murder. Hauser called me and has stated that his client won't say a thing unless we drop all charges against her. That is quite unacceptable. I have examined the evidence in those murders. I do not want to let anyone capable of such brutality loose in Vienna. I cannot envisage what she could possibly tell us that we cannot find out ourselves."

Mont Pelier let the two men consider that point for a while before insinuating, "She infiltrated Alpha Prime's security. That reveals a great deal of skill. Donau admits that catching her was only due to a freak power outage. You might stop to consider if that was the only place she infiltrated while she was trying to find Wexford."

Both men stared at him, as they considered that possibility. At least they were now thinking beyond the diamonds. They had fallen into the assumption that Wanda had intended, a person caught with jewels, was presumed to be interested only in them.

"What are you suggesting, Mont Pelier," the police chief asked pointedly.

"Much the same thing as you, I imagine. I am sure that Carson could help us remove a threat that is a greater threat to law and order here than a group of misguided business men."

"Very well, I will talk to Carson's lawyer, but I will not drop all the charges."

The police chief made a phone call, instructing his aide to bring Hauser in to see him.

Derek was impressed by the young defence lawyer, Hauser. The final deal was hard won, and although the Prosecutor did not like it, he was convinced that Carson knew things that would help with the major investigations. The man should lose his regrets once Carson began to speak, but for now, having to agree to a maximum of ten years on the murder charge was griping him.

It was understandable, Derek admitted, for if he truly believed Carson guilty of the murders, he would have whole heartily agreed with the prosecutor.

The part of the deal about not adding to the charges based on what Carson admitted, seemed to be a lesser concern. Perhaps because the Prosecutor could not envisage the full scope of what he would hear. He did add a rider that Carson had to front for trial.

When Hauser had left with the signed agreement and the Prosecutor had seemingly forgotten his presence, the man spoke to the police chief.

"I will draw up warrants for the extra charges. Escaping from police custody, accessory to causing injury while escaping, abduction of a minor, involuntary manslaughter. I will have them ready to serve by morning."

Derek had control of his face, and forced his body to seem relaxed.

"Isn't that contravening the agreement you just signed?" he commented neutrally.

The Prosecutor turned abruptly, his face was flushed, but his voice was calm. "No. I am acting on information already known. I will not be creating charges based on what she tells us in the future."

"I see," Derek nodded, as if tacitly agreeing, but the idea made him feel ill. "When will you be advising Carson's lawyer?"

"We will see him tomorrow when they attend for the first questioning session. That will be soon enough. I expect that you will maintain our confidence and not tell them sooner."

He almost seemed to be daring the Interpol agent to object, but Derek had no authority to interfere.

"I have no reason to speak to either of them. I will wait until they come to ask any further questions I have." He rose, bid both men farewell, and calmly left the room.

His own words had been as duplicitous as the Prosecutor's deal. He wouldn't be speaking to Hauser or Carson, but he would be speaking to Jim, who would have a way to get the message through.

One thing still puzzled him, and that was the stipulation that Carson had to front for trial. Of course Carson would attend the trial, did the man think she would escape? She probably could if she wanted to, but she knew that escaping would only confirm her guilt in everyone's mind. But what if, someone else, stopped her?

Hauser went to the prison for the second time that day, only this time he had representatives of the media following him and asking insistent questions about the deal the Prosecutor had done. He refused to comment, and made a firm resolution to discuss privacy with the Prosecutor's office, and hurried to the gatehouse.

It was late, past the time that prisoners had their evening meal and final mingling time. Though the prisoners in the remand section had a different schedule, they would be approaching the nightly 'lock down' time. The night admin staff were reluctant to allow his client to come to the interview room. He insisted, and Carson was fetched.

He paced the room while he waited, ready to sell his deal to her, knowing that she would still not be pleased. The door was opened, and Carson was led in. She was clad in a dull orange prison frock, and had a long jacket over it; her hair was loose, and since she was looking down, it hid her face.

Her whole demeanour was out of character.

"Are you feeling well?" he asked as the guard secured her to the table.

"Well enough," was the reply, but the tone was lifeless.

He waited for the guard to leave, and when her head came up he saw her face was nearly colourless.

"I don't think so," he contradicted her, as she seemed about to be sick. "What happened?"

"I got a touch of gastro, I think. I was fine until I had the insipid basic rations this evening."

"Will you be able to answer questions tomorrow?"

"Probably," Wanda failed to sound convincing. "Did they agree to the deal then?"

"Yes, but there are stipulations." He began to explain, but Wanda interrupted him.

"Not so loud, they listen in remember. Where do they plan to grill me?"

"Here. They are not willing to risk transporting you."

"Last time nothing happened. They used some kind of armoured car, didn't they? I don't really remember."

"They will be here at ten tomorrow."

"I won't talk to them here."

"They will take that as you trying to renege on the deal."

"I'm not, it's just...."

"What?" Hauser noticed Wanda swallowing hard.

"I was warned about saying more to the police. That man that came. He's letting me know that he can get to me here. I was feeling fine until ten minutes after I finished my tea."

"So you are saying that someone deliberately dosed your food to make you sick?"

"Gastro doesn't hit that fast," Wanda said carefully. "I don't care if you believe me or not. They don't expect anyone to. You are supposed to think that I am faking, going mad, or paranoid. But it's like I said – mind games."

Hauser sensed no belligerence in his client's tone, and believed she was serious. "The trouble is, I don't think the police complex is any less secure from eavesdropping. I had the media following me here to ask about a deal only four people should have known about. Security wise, they could keep you in the holding cells there, but I don't think you would be any safer there."

Wanda stared at the table, and was starting to shiver. "Ok, whatever. I am still going to do it...but I really want to get back to my room."

He hadn't finished going through the expectations of the deal, but he could see she was in no condition to pay attention. "Alright, I'll come back here about nine and explain everything then."

Wanda nodded, and with misgivings, Hauser pressed the bell to be let out.

She was trying very hard not to be sick again, but the guard was not making it easy. He was trying to hurry her along, and even though she had asked politely for him to slow done because she was feeling sick, he paid her words no heed. Half way back, as her shaking intensified, she threw up.

The guard was disgusted, and even though he had been warned, he blamed her for the mess. He radioed for a mop and bucket, and when the cleaner arrived, made her clean up her own mess.

While doing that job, he released the handcuffs, judging accurately, that she was in no condition to make a break for it. He left them off for the last part of the return, allowing her to pull the jacket around her more tightly, and this time let her move at her own speed.

He closed the door behind her, but watched through the window and saw her head straight for the toilet, to throw up again. He was convinced this was not self-induced, and, fearing it might be contagious, called the prison doctor.

Wanda had crawled back to her bed when he arrived, but she recognised him from her arrival, and sensed that he was not antagonistic towards her. But then, he had been around when Renee was treating her and would have sensed that the foreign doctor believed her innocent.

He checked her out, found that she had no fever, but that she was dehydrated. The signs did not indicate gastro.

He went off briefly, and returned with a full plastic jug of an unpleasant tasting rehydration drink, and a plastic mug.

"I want you to drink that over the next hour," he told her. "After that, drink plenty of water, especially if you are sick again."

An "okay" was the only answer he received. He added, "Once you've finished that jug full, try to sleep.

He had misgivings about leaving her there, but the worst of the vomiting should have passed. He requested the guard to keep an eye on her, and accepted the agreement.

As to her condition, Wanda had enough medical knowledge to realise that whatever affected her, wasn't a simple virus that she had picked up. It had come on her too soon after the meal, and she had been perfectly fine before that. It had been so sudden that she had not had time to get to the toilet bowl. Her clothes had caught a lot of it, and the floor as well.

The earlier guard, who would be off duty now, had made her clean up the mess, and had found some prison issue clothing for her to change into. While that might be meant to make her feel like one of the sentenced prisoners, it was at least clean and didn't smell of anything but laundry powder.

Wanting to feel better, Wanda made the effort to drink the hydrating drink, but it seemed as soon as she drank a cup, she was throwing it up. She tried to sip it more slowly, and that seemed to help, but she was exhausted, and really wanted to sleep.

Chapter 6 - Private communications

When Hauser came the next morning, he insisted on accompanying the guard to fetch her. This guard was a woman, and she rapped on the door with her baton and called out, "Wake up Carson, you have a visitor."

Hearing no answer or sound of movement, the woman looked through the window. "Carson!"

She moved to look into the room from a more oblique angle, and then swore. She had the door open, and baton ready for trouble within instants.

She let Hauser go to where Wanda lay on the floor near the toilet, watching in case this was a trick.

"She's unconscious," Hauser said, after gently shaking her, and checking to feel for a pulse.

The guard radioed for medical assistance, and still didn't approach the prisoner. Perhaps the smell in the room had a part in that.

When the doctor arrived with a trolley, pushed by one of the trusted prisoners, he told Hauser to move aside, whilst he checked the condition of the woman. His eyes checked the room, took in the almost empty jug of fluid, and the puddle on the floor.

"I'll need to get her to the infirmary," the doctor directed, and he and his helper lifted Wanda onto the trolley, and the guard secured one wrist to it.

To Hauser, it was quite clear that she would be in no condition to be questioned and he firmly quashed any thought that he had that his client had contrived it. He needed to tell the Prosecutor of the problem, and did so once Wanda was lying on a proper hospital bed, having her vital signs checked and a drip inserted.

He rang the Prosecutor, who was explosively incredulous, and demanded to know what had caused the situation. When Hauser admitted that he didn't yet know, he had to endure the claim that it was self-induced.

A short time later, the task force leader entered the infirmary, with instructions to get a report from the doctor. The lack of a reasonable cause, for the doctor had checked for all the most probable causes, did not placate the man, who proposed and was disabused of the idea that she had drugged herself. Angry, he cancelled the morning's session, but agreed to consider a more secure alternate venue, not realising he was betraying his thought that an outsider had made Wanda ill.

Hauser didn't mention the previous day's visitor, or the treatment Wanda had described from the guard, as he was sure both incidents would be strongly denied. However, he was starting to lose all the reservations he'd had about the threats Wanda had claimed.

He paced just inside the door, while the doctor tried to revive his client. The task force leader had gone off to contact the others who were due to attend. His own attention was on Wanda, who was starting to move around, when a guard escorted two more people into the infirmary.

"Mont Pelier, David," he greeted with relief. "They have cancelled the session."

David had gone straight to his wife, leaving Derek to talk to the lawyer.

"I can see why," he said succinctly. He quickly made his own diagnosis, after glancing at the doctor for permission. As he held her wrist to check her pulse, he knew she was conscious again.

"Is she functional?" Derek asked.

"Yes," Wanda tried to insist, but her voice was weak.

"No," David overruled her in a firm voice.

"Get them to let me outside for half an hour," Wanda tried to insist.

"There's about as much chance of that as there is of it snowing in here," David said tartly. He was aware that Derek and Hauser were talking, but could not make out what they were saying. He was more concerned with getting Wanda feeling stronger.

"Are you still feeling ill?" the doctor was asking Wanda.

"Yes, but I can't have anything left in me to throw up."

"I'll give you something for nausea, and some electrolytes in the drip. You need to rest and try to sleep for a bit."

The doctor moved off, and David moved closer and felt Wanda gripping his hand. "What is Derek saying?"

"I don't know," David admitted. "He just said he had something to tell Hauser. Why?"

Wanda shook her head. "Something is going on. I heard him say 'more charges'. The bastards. Hauser feels like an active volcano."

David turned to look at Derek, with a look of accusation.

Derek brought Hauser over.

"What are they trying to pull?" Wanda demanded, though her words had little force to them.

"Later," Derek advised, for the doctor had returned. "I wanted to ask you a couple of questions."

"It's okay, they are not related to local matters," Hauser told her.

"What?" Wanda looked at Derek.

"Do you know of a Yuri Tatarovich?"

"Yes, he's Ivana's grandfather, Tanya's great..."she had to stop and take deep breaths.

"Why don't you ask Tanya?" David suggested. He felt Wanda suddenly tighten her grip, he leant closer to hear what she was whispering.

"Tell the others to link to me, like they did that time...energy."

David understood immediately, but Derek looked askance and David simply shook his head. "What else did you want to know?"

Derek looked directly at Wanda for the answer to his question. "Do you truly believe that Ivana is still alive?"

David looked at his wife and stared as she considered the question and stated unequivocally, "Yes."

"She can't be..." David blurted. "We..." He stopped himself saying that Jim and his team couldn't be wrong.

"Is this relevant to the immediate problem," Hauser asked before David could quiz Derek or his wife.

"An Interpol matter," Derek claimed, not attempting to explain.

Hauser was tense. "I don't know how the Prosecutor will react to the delay. He was angry."

Wanda spoke up, "Derek, that ...." She stopped when he shook his head. Now was not the time to introduce the recorded interview.

"We will work something out," Derek assured Wanda, as well as Hauser. To the former he added, "You concentrate on feeling better."

After hearing from the doctor that he would not allow questions until the next day, Derek gestured the others from the room. David managed to give his wife a quick kiss.

Later that day, when Wanda was once again back in her cell like room, she lay down, facing the wall. That way, no one would be able to see her face, and read her unguarded thoughts from it.

She was feeling better, the nausea had receded, thanks to the three litres of glucose solution pumped through her. Even better, she had been able to keep down a snack of dry biscuits and cheese.

Now she was able to consider what had happened to her. Except for the man who had visited her and any guards he had paid off to do his dirty work, the authorities didn't know her and only knew what she was charged with. So the wrist restraints and the occasional use of foot restraints was to protect themselves. It was standard treatment, impersonal, and it didn't bother her.

She had learnt to hide her true feelings from everyone, to show the world an uncaring façade. It was a survival skill but it meant that people misjudged her, and might make people think that maybe she could have killed people and was blasé about it. It didn't prove she was a callous, murdering beast.

However, this deliberate malice, directed at her by people with no faces, the indirect attacks that she couldn't predict or guard against, was different. She had nowhere to run and hide, no way to fight, made her feel that she was not in control of herself.

Wanda let herself cry silently, admitting to herself that she was afraid of being in prison again, and terrified of being found guilty of murder. Hauser seemed confident that she would only be found guilty of the jewel theft, but she could not believe that. And she hated being confined, and having to rely on others to do the work of finding evidence to help her, and being totally dependent.

"No wonder you were a brat of a child," a thought came into her mind, abruptly halting her spiral into despair.

"Lisbeth?" Wanda thought back desperately.

"All of us," another thought came back, and it was a blend of Erin, Tanya and Elizabeth. It came with a sense of nothing less than total acceptance of her, absolute unswerving support and complete willingness to share and ease her fears.

Her sister, and her cousins knew her as well as David did, knew she committed crimes, without a qualm, had once done it for personal profit, and now, for other reasons. They knew she abhorred injuring others, even when necessary, and then she did it impersonally, efficiently. They knew that she could not murder, because she would sense the blankness where a mind had once been.

They did not think less of her for being caught, being in prison, for being less than perfect, for being human.

"Wanda, I promised I would be here for you, no matter what," Elisabeth's mind voice reminded her.

"We are all here for you."

The outlook no longer seemed helplessly grim, and Wanda felt her resolve returning. It had been Elisabeth who had kept her sane during that past time when she had spent a year in a training centre. She had shared all the humiliations, all her fears and anger, and never seemed shocked or thought less of her.

"I don't deserve all of you," Wanda thought back.

"That's the damn hormones talking," Elisabeth thought back, but it came with the sense of Erin, who had the most empathy of all of them.

"And why should you have all the fun," Tanya thought directly. Her thoughts were always clearer when she was with the others.

"This isn't fun," Wanda thought back forcefully. "When they leave me alone, it is damn mind-sapping, energy sapping boredom. And I am a sitting duck."

"Well, Jim has suggested a solution to part of your problem," Elisabeth thought at her. "A few knotty problems to think on, and to perhaps suggest avenues of how to investigate them. Are you game?"

"Anything," was the immediate answer, and in her cell, Wanda drew the blanket over her head.

"First though, I overheard Derek Mont Pelier sounding quite excited about the idea of our unloved grandfather being in Vienna. Apparently, he's a nasty piece of work."

"Who? Mont Pelier or Tatarovich?" Wanda was feeling better

and decided to tease her sister. She didn't need to see her sister to sense her blush…and other things.

"Grandfather!" Tanya sent, sounding like she was spitting out a piece of rotten meant. "How could he think that you were me?"

"The bastard is missing a few pertinent facts," Wanda sent back. "If he had cared enough about our grandmother to stick around, he'd have known he had three daughters. So, he doesn't know that there are four of us. I think, he decided that US agents got you and your father out of Russia, and probably thinks that the US government is controlling you both and fears that there might be ulterior motives for having Wexford investigated on the sly. So when he heard that a US agent, me, was nosing around, he added his facts up wrong."

They discussed the idea for a time, before Elisabeth asked, "My question is, did he think it was Tanya all along, or only after he got the passport? He couldn't know that you and she are like twins in looks."

"I don't know," Wanda admitted. "It depends on when he got my passport. I had the feeling that I was being followed from the hospital, the night I arrived, but that might have been the police. I really started being positive of followers after I helped Donau find the house where Nicole had been, and visiting Heinrich's place."

"And you think these later ones were Russian?" Tanya asked.

"Yes, Theo's crowd."

"So, why would they be interested in you?" Elisabeth asked.

"To find out what I knew, or what the people who sent me knew."

"But…" Elisabeth tried to hold on to a fleeting idea, "If it were Wexford who suggested this crime business, and he is being impersonated…why would he draw attention to himself?"

"A logical time for the switch would be after he went off, before Nicole was taken, during that period when he was out of contact. It makes no sense otherwise."

"That's the feeling of Jim and his team," Elisabeth supplied. "Though, surely Rachel would have said if she thought the man she was with was not her daddy. That contradicts the fact that agent Mont Pelier and David are sure of, that the Wexford you met was someone named Aleksi."

Wanda recalled when she had seen Wexford. "I am sure that the man I met was Aleksi. He is a good image of Nicole's husband."

"Do you think the real Wexford is still alive?" Elisabeth asked. "Since we are all agreed that Wexford couldn't have been the man David saw at the airport." There was a pause, and Elisabeth's mind voice came again. "Erin wonders if they had intended to leave the house at that time, or if they had to leave in a hurry."

Wanda had assumed the latter, but needed to ask, "How much stuff was found in the house? I know half the rooms were empty. And I saw a swank bedroom, but it had nothing of a personal memento nature. I tagged a second room as being used by Wexford's doppleganger, and occasionally Heidi Lowenbach."

"I haven't heard anything about that place. Assume either way?" Elisabeth suggested.

"My immediate thoughts are that if Aleksi was pretending to be Wexford, that he and Theo were trying to get an in, on that crime racket. The Wessler cartel might have been trying to pull one over Wexford, to screw the US."

"If that was so," Tanya added her thoughts, "perhaps they took over Wexford for a similar reason."

It was plausible.

"So if something unplanned occurred..." Elisabeth thought slowly.

"Like me turning up and taking Rachel," Wanda added.

"And someone murdered Lunn and Wessler," Tanya added.

Wanda flinched at the thought.

"They might have needed to leave," Tanya finished the thought.

"Because they would not want anyone to realise Aleksi was disguised as Wexford," Elisabeth finished. Then she relayed another idea from Erin. "They set fire to the house, but Jim's people were nearby and they rescued a derelict from there. Perhaps that was so that everyone would think Wexford had been a prisoner there, and died."

Wanda felt a shiver of disquiet. "There was no derelict in the house when I searched it before taking Rachel out. I accounted for Theo, Aleksi, six guards, three servants, the nurse and Rachel. There was only that poor old man they had imprisoned in the shed, and he was either dead, drugged or in a drunken stupor when I got out."

"Could that have been the real Wexford?" Elisabeth asked, and Wanda considered it.

"He'd been there a hell of a lot longer than a few days. He was too dissipated. He said he'd been there five years, but I found that hard to believe."

They had come to a dead end on that line of thought. "Let's go back a bit," Elisabeth suggested.

"If Aleksi is impersonating Wexford, how did they know he would be coming here? Dad said it was a hush-hush trade mission. It wasn't exactly top secret, but it wasn't announced."

Wanda suddenly had a truly awful thought. "What if the switch wasn't done when he got here?"

She sensed her sister's reaction. "Oh my...that is totally scary. If that is true...he had to have become Wexford before Wexford returned to the US. Oh my...Dad is not going to like that idea at all."

Wanda heard Tanya think at Elisabeth, "When was that?"

"That was about five years ago. This makes much too much sense. It would have had to have been then. Since he had been away for so long, any changes someone noticed would have logical reasons."

"That would have been about when I got to America," Tanya pointed out.

"Five years? Yes! Elisabeth, that idea about the derelict. Get them to find out. I have encountered some of the Family before. One of their nasty little tricks is to make people think someone is dead by burning a dead hobo."

"How would we check though," Tanya asked. "They haven't been able to find anything to identify the Wexford who fled, so they won't have anything to compare the hobo's prints and DNA to."

"Erin just had an idea. Compare the hobo's DNA with Rachel's."

"Yes, that might tell us something, or nothing. The hobo may be a random victim, or the switch might have been before Rachel was conceived. Remember, I heard Aleksi refer to Grandpa Theo when talking to Rachel."

Elisabeth ignored that. "That doesn't have to be true. If Rachel thinks Aleksi is her father, it maybe because he is the only father she knows."

Wanda added with a trace of anger, "And they didn't take Rachel with them, didn't even intend to. I know I took her first, but they didn't do much to try to find her."

"Suggest the test then," Tanya said decisively. "See what the result is and work from there."

"The only trouble about that will be to get Nicole to agree," Elisabeth sighed mentally. "She is going to assume that we have found a body."

"Sounds like they nearly did," Tanya said.

"Ok, say it is no match," Elisabeth thought. "No harm done; the hobo is a nobody. If it is a match, oh my, Nicole is in for a hell of a shock."

"Might be the best option. If she suddenly realises that she married a stranger, not her high school crush, she might open up and tell everything she knows," Wanda sent the thought.

"Maybe," Elisabeth agreed. "They did send a forensic team to Nicole's house in LA, and that place where you found him, but both places were as good as wiped clean."

Another dead end.

Wanda suddenly announced, "I think I am about to have visitors."

Elisabeth thought back, "I think I should call Dad and give him advance warning of this possible piece of dung...just in case."

Chapter 7 - More charges

Wanda let her mind drop from the link, no longer feeling out of control. It was just as well, for two guards banged on her door, and one of the demanded as he entered, "Up and face the wall, Carson. Hands behind you."

Pretending to be weaker than she now felt, Wanda rolled over slowly and made getting to her feet seem to be a major effort.

"Hurry up, Carson. You have visitors."

Considering that she was still supposed to be restricted from visitors, whoever it was had to be official. Still, she didn't let that thought drag her back into depression. The contact with her cousins had energised her.

They must have been told that she had been ill, for although they seemed impatient with her slow progress, they didn't give her any nudges with their baton. It didn't stop them from applying both wrist and ankle restraints. They didn't use the ankle restraints for her personal visitors though.

In the interview room, Inspector Wagner turned from his perusal of the yard outside, and stared at Wanda. She had stopped on the threshold, and was shoved further in, and pushed towards the table, where her hands were secured to the bar. The arrangement was meant to force the prisoner to sit, so that they were in the inferior position, but she was short enough that she could stand.

Her own reading of the body language of Wagner, and the sense of his attitude, gave her a damn good idea of what was coming. That, and having heard the quiet words that Derek had spoken to her lawyer, intending her not to hear.

Wagner wanted to see her fear, to feel he had won and that he had power over her. She did not intend to give him that pleasure.

"Shouldn't I have my lawyer here?" Wanda spoke in a reasonable tone, but wishing intensely for a miracle.

"He will be notified," Wagner assured her with an insufferable gloating smile. He moved towards the table as he took a folded document from his inside jacket pocket.

Wanda made herself an image of stone, while her mind was furiously thinking, "You are going to regret this, you bastard, you will regret gloating at me, and savouring this moment."

Something in her icy, intent gaze, made him hesitate.

"This is just a formality," he said carefully, trying to sound as firm as his last statement.

"No," Wanda stated sharply. "This is harassment. Your higher ups want me to help them, and this is how I get thanked. If they can't lock me up on one pretext, they try for another."

When Wagner stopped unfolding the paper, from surprise at her words, Wanda continued, "The whole lot of you can go to perdition!"

Wanda stopped before continuing on to say that the authorities could whistle for her help. Wagner was only the messenger, he might not even know about the deal, and would probably misrepresent her attitude in his ignorance. Fortunately, she sensed that her lawyer had arrived and was hurrying to the room.

He was slightly out of breath when he entered and took in the scene. His client's belligerent stance, warned him that she knew what was coming, or had Wagner served the new warrants already?

Wanda clarified the matter. "I am just about to hear the latest from the perfidious and unethical Viennese justice system."

Now that Hauser was here to speak for her, she made a performance of seating herself in a polite listening pose, and meeting Wagner's gaze. It had the desired effect, Wagner's posture slumped slightly, and he looked away from her gaze first, using the need to read from the paper as a reason. He read the new charges from the document, but Wanda sensed he knew the details by heart. When he finished, she continued to look expectantly at him, as if she had expected something more interesting or important. There was nothing in her expression to suggest the fury that bubbled within her mind.

Wagner asked if she understood the new charges, and Wanda politely agreed that she did. When he retreated immediately after her reply, she knew she had won that encounter.

Hauser told the guards to leave, and only after the door was locked, did Wanda let her reaction show.

"The dirty rotten bastards," she exploded, but in a low voice a she leaned across the table to where Hauser had moved a chair to sit. "You made them agree to a reduced penalty for the charges they had, so they more charges to make up the difference and they want to encourage my help? When you made that deal, did you have any idea they'd be as underhanded as to do this?"

"No, I was negotiating in good faith, and thinking only of what extra charges they would want when you tell them everything that you did."

Wanda slumped as far back as he restraints would let her. "I am not blaming you. I know you will do your best to deal with this load of crap. I expected better of the Prosecutor. But do you know what really pisses me off? It is one thing for me to be caught and charged with things that I did, and by that I mean I don't think ill of Donau for catching me. He was just lucky though. What I really cannot accept is to be charged with things that I did not do."

"Well then, why don't you tell me your perspective of these new charges?"

Wanda took a deep breath and began. "I did get myself free after Donau caught me near Alpha Prime. I still had a job to do, and two missing Americans to find. The second time, coming here from the hospital, I was in no state to try anything. That wasn't a rescue attempt, that was an attempted abduction, and I damn well got away from those thugs as soon as I could."

"You could have given yourself up," Hauser suggested.

"Like I said, I still had people to find," Wanda emphasised, with a glance around the small room that said, "I couldn't do that from in here."

She shuddered then, as she went on, "As for that third piece of crap, that diabolical wording! I was not intending harm to Rachel. She had decided to drink her damn milk. She had fallen asleep before I even got her out of the house. I couldn't carry her and run; I had to make sure she was safe. I wanted to lead the guards away, make them think we had got away. It was while I was planning that that I realised that Wexford was a fake. I needed to warn Jim."

"Okay – we've been over that already. What about the nurse?"

Wanda looked away from Hauser, and then back to meet his eyes. "I told you what she was going to do. I knocked her out and tied her up, so Rachel and I could get away without her raising an alarm. I was going to take Rachel to the police and tell them where to find the nurse. How could I have predicted that those bastards would try to burn the house down?"

"You couldn't," Hauser agreed. "If you hadn't acted when you did, she might have been really dead, not nearly so. Where did you slip up after hiding the child?"

Hauser had heard this part before too, but he wanted to hear it again.

Wanda pictured the events in her mind. "I got into the boot of Wexford's car, since I didn't know where he was going. I think the delayed reaction to whatever drug they'd given me – started to set in. I didn't sense danger when I decided to get out – and I should have done. I was caught as I got out of the boot, and dragged into the house. I think by Heinrich. Then I blacked out."

"Think carefully of that short period between the car, and that moment," Hauser challenged her. "Jim tells me you have an eidetic memory...what did you see?"

After concentrating for a long minute, Wanda began to answer. "I was trying to get free, and my eyes were going funny. The light was leaving afterimages on the back of my eyes."

Hauser persisted. "Where did you have your knife? Did you try to use it?"

"No, it was in my pocket. I didn't think of it."

"Who else was in the room?"

Wanda tried to make sense of the chaotic images, and snippets of sound. "I think, Wexford. Heinrich said something about my crawling out of his car. I can't swear to it, I was starting to hallucinate, but I think my hearing was still okay."

Hauser let out a breath, that was slightly more than she had told him before, and if they had knocked her out, she would not be able to remember any more. Someone could have found the knife, if they searched her, and then used it. And she had put Wexford on the scene. However, if she was hallucinating, she might have done anything. They needed to find Heinrich.

"It looks bad," Wanda knew, as some of her earlier hope vanished.

Hauser didn't disagree. "Are you still intending to stick to the deal?"

"Yes," was her simple answer, but she added, "Even if I feel like kicking it into their faces."

Even if they crucify me, she thought bitterly. Then she stopped herself – this wasn't like last time, when she didn't care what became of her, because she didn't believe she would live much longer anyway. Now she had David and Davy, and another child on the way. She had a lot more to lose.

But she wasn't going to let that skunk Tatarovich win either. Nor the little crooks that were running like scared geese.

"I will show them what honour really means," she promised her lawyer.

In that moment, Wanda locked herself into survival mode. She had to forget everyone but herself. She had to work at keeping active, even in close confinement – or she would get sick again. She had to armour her mind, so she would only betray reactions that she wanted others to see.

Hauser studied her expression and body language, using the little tell tales that Jim Phillips had mentioned to him. He was satisfied with what he saw, felt sure she was holding up to the uncertainty of her future.

Now wasn't the time to fight, Wanda told herself as she was shuffled back to her cell like room. Now was the time to lull everyone into thinking she was docile, resigned, helpless. Now was her chance to observe those women in the prison side of the complex, who thought they were supreme, because they didn't care who they hurt so long as they felt they had some control.

If, when the inevitable came, they tried their tricks on her, they would not find an easily dominated, totally crushed newbie.

She also needed to identify Tatarovich's paid off servants, be alert for more subtle harassments, and betray no sign of weakness.

She was going to talk to the police, even after Tatarovich's subtle order that she should not. He had claimed she was kin, and had to be obedient. She denied that relationship and would do as her con-science dictated. So what if the damn 'Family' protected each other.

She did not like the price demanded by her alleged grandfather for that protection. She didn't need it. He wasn't invincible. He should have less concern about protecting Theo and Aleksi, and more about protecting himself.

He thought he was going to punish her, and would try to break her.

Creatures that would frighten him into a babbling wreck had tried to break her, and failed. He would fail. He would be ruined – if it was the last thing she did. They could confine her within bars and walls, but she had friends, and the secret mental communication with her sister and cousins. There was much that she could do from in the prison that he would never suspect.

Even if Jim could not, or would not find a way to free her, she would survive.

Wanda rubbed her wrists when the restraints were removed, and waited for the guards to retreat before turning away from the wall. Instead of going to sit on the bed, she went to where she could stare out of the window at the activity in the yard below.

Even without deliberate concentration, she had the rhythm of the prison. The extra guards in the yard were getting into position. Soon the mechanical alarm would sound the start of the exercise period.

As the inmates began to emerge, Wanda watched intently, thinking of herself as a hawk spying out her choice of prey, ignoring the slow moving sheep, waiting for prey with more life. The one who called herself Brigitte finally emerged and a bevy of hangers on gathered around her, like attendants on a queen or dogs waiting for scraps from the table.

Wanda observed every movement Brigitte made, noticing at the same time how some women saw her coming and backed away, others ignored her and some who simply cowered.

Even when she felt her sister's mind touch, she was watching the 'dance' of people below her.

"I don't think I want to be your prey," Elisabeth commented, though she understood what Wanda was doing.

"You don't have to worry. For you, I will kill you first and then eat you," Wanda teased. "Down there are some I would prefer to eat alive."

"I guess I don't need to worry then, you don't seem particularly hungry at the moment, and you still need your message relay."

"Always!" Wanda sent a burst of gratitude. "You are my strength and my conscience. What's up?"

"I finally got Nichole to agree to let us have a DNA sample from Rachel – after a bout of near hysterics."

"How much was she told?" Wanda asked.

"That Allan was seen getting onto a flight to Hamburg, and since then the authorities have been alerted to a male victim that needs to be identified. She's thinking plane crash."

"How long will it take to get results?"

"Several weeks, unfortunately," Elisabeth confirmed. "However, Nicole gave permission for the FBI back home to check her house for prints, hairs, etc. We should hear back by tomorrow."

"I can hardly wait," Wanda said drolly.

Elisabeth changed the subject. "Who is your subject of interest?"

"The self-proclaimed top bitch," Wanda admitted. "I hope that the guard who set me up for durance vile, tries to talk to her again. I want another look at him."

"When you find out who he is, tell me. Derek would like to question him about Tatarovich."

"I was going to try to wish him into falling down a well or something...but since you asked..." Wanda sent back. "So, how are you and Derek getting on?"

Once again, Wanda sensed that her sister was blushing, but this time with guilty overtones. She thought back, gently, "Lisbeth, he's a good man. Good at what he does."

"But he's a policeman," she thought back.

"Why should you hold that against him? I don't. Even if he had to arrest me, I wouldn't. Policemen have jobs to do, often thankless. Anyway, I have worked with him before, he knows what I can do, and I think he understands why I do it. If you want to get to know him, I think you should. Besides, your brother is a policeman, what's the difference?"

"Stu, as he now prefers to be called, pretends that you never existed."

Wanda knew that, though she hadn't done her brother the favour of disowning him. "Well then, by comparison, Derek is a saint."

She sensed her sister relax. "If you worked with him, can you tell me more about him? He says he has eleven siblings."

"Oh, yes," Wanda agreed, "but that business is kinda classified, and really, I think you should find out about him for yourself."

Elisabeth's mental presence went from her mind, and Wanda thought privately, "I am not going to scare you away from him just because his brother is a king and his father used to be."

Feeling strengthened by the mental contact, Wanda went back to watching those below her.

It took three more days of watching before she was rewarded. A guard matching her mental picture, inserted himself into Brigitte's circle. From her vantage, she could see the furtive movements of his hands, although the other patrolling guards and the ones in the towers, would see nothing. Small packets of something changed hands.

"So, he's the local supplier," Wanda thought to herself, as she switched her attention to him. She decided that he must have a sore, or lame, right leg, since he was favouring that side as he walked around. As he walked off, she noticed that he wore his baton on his right side, not on the left like the others. Did that mean he was left-handed?"

Wanda felt she had achieved another small success. Another, because the expected interrogation session insisted upon by the task force, had been delayed whilst her lawyer argued with the Prosecutor. She didn't expect the delay to last much longer, or that her lawyer could win any further concessions, but it was another day that Tatarovich had to delay 'making her regret talking out'."

Chapter 8 - Revealing knowledge

They came for her early – before breakfast, before the sun was even up. These were not the normal prisoner escort guards, but men that looked more like an army assault squad.

"WEGA," her lawyer explained.

Wanda translated that as some group like SWAT, but she couldn't decide if they were there to protect her, or stop her escaping. In the latter situation, she would hardly get very far with the foot and hand restraints. She didn't intend to try, anyway.

No one told her where she was going, not even her lawyer. They gave her orders, and made sure she obeyed. First it was to walk, and she was led outside into the chilly pre-dawn air, which smelt faintly of smoke. One of the army looking types had a firm grip on her right arm.

Once outside, she was hustled into an armoured van, up a fold away step and told to sit on a bench that folded down from one wall. The one who had led her out continued to watch her, alert for trouble – from her. However, she wasn't secured to any part of the truck. Inside the back there was dim illumination, enabling her to stare back at her escort, as she tried to get a sense of why he, and his fellows were guarding her. She could see very little of his face for the eyes were covered with goggles, and the rest, except for his mouth was covered by a black balaclava. Three other WEGA officers were seated nearer the door.

Wanda leant back against the side of the van and moved only enough to keep her balance.

At the end of the journey, she judged that she was in the basement garage of a building, for the sounds she was hearing from outside, seemed to be echoing. The door opened, and she was gestured out, her escort once again holding her arm, but that helped her to balance while stepping down. She had a brief glimpse of a row of police cars, between the solid forms of the WEGA quartet who formed a box around her. Then she was in an elevator, where Hauser joined them before the door closed.

When they emerged on the fifth floor, her guess that she was at the police building, was confirmed. The passages through which she was led, were oddly deserted. It might have been because of the early hour, but she decided they had been cleared until she had been along them.

Their destination was a large meeting or briefing room, and she was led to a place about halfway along a large table, and told to sit. One of her escorts released one of the foot restraints, and resecured it after passing the chain through a ring set in the floor.

Wanda wondered if the ring had always been there or was a new addition, especially for her. She stopped trying to decide when Hauser sat on the chair beside her.

"We have fifteen minuted before the police will be allowed in," he told her. "Have you a preference for how you want to do this?"

"Yes, I want to be able to tell things my way, not to have to answer questions piecemeal, from people who only know or think they know part of what I can tell them. They can record this, but not for public release. If they have questions, they can jot them down and ask me at the end. I want to get through this as fast as possible."

Hauser nodded, guessing that his client knew the kind of nit-picking questions that would arise.

"Now, I need to advise you of the questions that you do not need to answer," he counselled her. "Any question relating to the crimes you are charged with, I will deny them answers to. Any question that does not relate to the information you give them, will be denied."

Wanda considered that and asked, "What if I think there is something important that I must say – that I saw – at a place where one of my crimes was committed?"

Hauser considered that. "Will you be keeping your hands on the table in front of you, like that?"

Wanda glanced at how she had her hands, with the left hand cupping the right palm. "Ah, is it too provocative?"

"I'm not saying that, I was going to suggest that if such a question is asked, or that situation arises, that you put both hands flat on the table, and I will request a moment's discussion with you."

"Fine," Wanda agreed.

Hauser gave her a few more instructions, urged her to keep her temper, and encouraged her to 'shove it in their faces'. A comment that make her smile, as she recognised the sentiment as coming from David and her sister.

"Is anyone going to give me breakfast? I am going to need something before the morning sickness really kicks in. Black tea and toast would do."

Hauser stared at her for a moment, until he realised she was being serious. He used his mobile phone to make the request.

"Are mobile phones going to be allowed during this session?" Wanda asked, concerned by the potential security risk. She didn't want certain people to know what she was telling the police.

"No," Hauser assured her. "All this is too important and sensitive to be leaked. They will bring in a detection team in a moment and sweep for listening devices. All mobile phones will have to be turned off, and they assure me that all forms of eavesdropping will be blocked."

Wanda merely nodded, but twisted around to examine the room while it was still almost empty. She let her eyes slide past the WEGA men, each standing at one of the doors to the room.

"Who is monitoring the security cameras?" She nodded at the one facing her.

"They have no sound reading capability," Hauser assured her.

"Lip readers?" Wanda counter suggested.

"Unlikely," Hauser protested mildly. "I can request that hey be aimed to one side."

Wanda shrugged. It didn't really matter. Tatarovich probably already knew she was going to talk, and would mention things about Theo and Alexsi. He personally had little to fear.

When the men checking the room for listening devices departed, the first of the police and task force members streamed in. Wanda was sitting back in her chair, concentrating on trying to quell the rising morning nausea. To the people walking past, she looked to be feigning boredom.

An arm, clad in a sleeve of some expensive fabric, reached past her and placed a covered styrene mug and a plate of toast, biscuits and cheese in front of her. She glanced up, saw the faint smile on the face of Derek Mont Pelier, and nodded slightly in thanks. He walked around the table and took a seat directly opposite her lawyer.

Wanda lifted the mug and took several sips of the steaming liquid. She glanced at Derek in appreciation, for it was a herbal tea, and it had already started to make her tight gut relax. Soon she felt able to eat the plain buttered toast, while ignoring the increased activity around her. She was aware of the microphone and recorder being set up in front of her, but gave the man no overt attention.

The same could not be said for some of the people passing her to go to seats further down the table. Wanda was aware of their stares, as if her eating was an affront, and she had no right to do so. Hauser commented to one such affronted starer.

"I don't suppose that you got breakfast this morning either?"

The pointed remark sent the man hurrying on.

The large group settled as the police chief began to speak. He stressed the need for the utmost confidentiality and the instruction for all phones to be turned off.

"This session will be recorded, and several copies will be made," he went on, but Wanda's eyes had gone to where a woman was seated by the wall, typing a verbatim copy of the proceedings. She wondered if the word processor was directly attached to the main police computer.

Jürgen Hauser stood and introduced his client, and stated the parameters of the information that she had agreed to give. He followed up by explaining the format for the session.

Many of the people were moving restlessly, a sign that they disagreed with what seemed like the pampering of the prisoner. Wanda focussed on Derek Mont Pelier, who was sitting quietly, and still, and took courage.

Then it was her turn to speak. She took another mouthful of the tea, to lubricate her suddenly dry throat. Everyone was waiting for her, and there was a faint murmur of subvocalized commenting.

Wanda sat back in her chair, projecting her voice to the microphone, but at a volume that required the audience to be quiet to hear her. Those that leant forward, were the ones who were most interested, those that didn't were likely to give her trouble.

"You all heard who I am, but I am obliged to repeat it. I am Tatiana Carson, an American from Los Angeles, California." She gave the rest of the information that was on the passport being held by the police. "I came to Vienna to find two missing Americans. I am not going to justify my methods, but I am going to state what I discovered whilst seeking information of the movements of Trade Consul, Allan Wexford. This information will be of value to the ongoing investigation of the Adler Taskforce."

She heard the rustling of many bodies shifting to listen. Most eyes were on her now, and Wanda put her mind shields up full, so that the emotions of the gathering did not distract her.

As she began her exposition, from when she had gone to see Nicole Wexford in the hospital, she flicked her gaze along the row of faces she could see, and saw from their body language that they were listening. She did not have to think about what not to say, things relating to the criminal charges against her, whilst she concentrated on what was pertinent to the crimes of the cartel.

She used the visit to Nicole as a means to mention the follower she had sensed, although she made it seem like she had actually spotted the tail.

Police Chief Leitner, interrupted briefly with an aside to Donau. Had he sent on officer to follow her? He hadn't. Wanda was pleased to have had one point confirmed. It had been the Russians then.

As she went on with a detailed account of her actions over the next three nights, admitting to entering multiple premises, scouting them, hacking into the computers, the muttering of disbelief began. Many could not believe that she could remember so much detail, so exactly. Even with her admissions of only having glanced at samples of the records that she had downloaded. Others were honestly astounded by her emotionless summary of the security defects in each of the places she had entered, and left, undetected.

When she reached the point of how she had entered Alpha Prime, the volume of the murmuring reached a point where she would have to raise her voice to be heard. That was not her intention. She was dominating this crowd, simply by speaking calmly and quietly. She went mute and waited, using the respite to drink some more of the now cold herbal tea. Chief Leitner restored silence, but didn't stifle the growing hostility.

He asked the question that was probably in most of the minds at the table. "Have you proof of what you claim to have read in these places?"

Wanda glanced at her lawyer, saw his slight nod, and said, "Yes."

Hauser spoke quickly. "We will come to that later. Please allow my client to continue."

Wanda knew that Donau was somewhere behind her, and now she felt a warm furry body creep next to her legs and settle there.

She continued to speak of her foray inside Alpha Prime, omitting all reference to the jewels, and how she had left.

Instead, she began to correlate what she had learnt, with Wexford's proposed itinerary. She summarised the information that confirmed who he had seen and when, and who he had yet to visit when he allegedly disappeared. She noted that he had actually continued to follow his itinerary, even after that time, up to the day when his wife and child had been abducted. Her conclusions were based on the diary entries of the person he met, and that person's secretary.

She continued to give her observations and deductions, and worked up to her conclusion that the Wexford she had met in Vienna, was not an American, but a Russian.

Once again, the noise level increased, as the attendees discussed the possible reasons why a Russian was masquerading as an American, and why he was involved with a group of suspect businessmen.

Wanda did not try to force her own belief on them, for they wouldn't listen to surmise. They would have to come to the conclusion on their own. Once again, she waited for silence to return, glad to give her voice a rest. She had more to say, but the next part of her disclosure needed to be worded carefully, since she had to tip toe between details that related to charges she faced.

When she finally fell silent, it took a while for everyone to realise that she had finished. Hauser rose as the first of the listeners tried to ask a question.

"Let's all take a break now, so that you can think of the questions that you want to ask."

While the majority of the attendees stood to stretch, or do personal things, Chief Leitner reminded them all that nothing that was said in the room was to be discussed outside during the break.

Wanda waited until the room was a lot emptier before telling Hauser, "I really need to find a ladies room."

That was a production performance. First, someone had to come to release her feet. Then, two female police officers were co-opted to accompany her to the female toilets, and watch her there. Two of the WEGA men waited in the corridor.

The worst part, from Wanda's perspective, was trying to do what she needed with the restraints on. She was finally forced to ask for her hands to be freed, which required one of the officers to go find the key, while one of the WEGA officers replaced her temporarily.

Neither of the female escorts were sympathetic towards her, and seemed resentful at being required to watch her. She gave them an impersonal thank you, as they were released from that duty, but neither acknowledged it.

During her absence from the meeting room, someone had set a sandwich and another drink at her place. One whiff of the rising steam told her it was coffee, and her stomach began to roil. She couldn't tolerate coffee whilst she was pregnant. She lifted the plate to study the sandwich, saw only that it contained a thick slab of some unidentifiable meat that also smelt off to her, and put it back down and slid it away from her.

"Not hungry?" Chief Leitner asked, as he returned to the seat opposite her. He seemed to be insulted that she didn't want what had been brought for her.

"'I'm sorry," Wanda spoke politely, and looked directly at the police chief. "The meat smells off to me, and I cannot tolerate coffee these days."

Her direct gaze seemed to disconcert him, and he looked away to someone behind her.

"Inspector Donau, perhaps you could get someone to remove those items from here."

Wanda sat back in her chair, and let Donau lean past her to hand the Police Chief a satchel. He then drew the plate with the sandwich to the edge of the table, and the furry nose of Alex poked up beside her to sniff the sandwich. He woofed softly, and then sneezed. Donau lifted the sandwich and sniffed, then frowned.

"Is there something else you could manage?" Donau asked neutrally.

Wanda only sensed concern from him, and was about to speak when Derek spoke up.

"I'll organise something," he offered. He had been about to sit down, but he moved back and walked around the table.

Wanda glanced quickly behind her, and saw that he caught up to Donau at the door.

Chief Leitner was asking Hauser, "Who brought the sandwich in?"

"Some woman with an ID tag," Hauser told him. "Do I surmise that nothing had been ordered?"

"I wasn't told of anything," Leitner admitted.

"Perhaps you might have that sandwich checked," Hauser suggested, and he glanced at his client, who was listening to his quiet words.

The Chief nodded at the doorway. "I think the Inspector has already thought of that." Then he glanced at the prisoner who was sitting quietly, looking back at him with no trace of fear or subservience.

"I did protest that the precautions Mont Pelier insisted on were excessive," he mused. "What else can you say that is so dangerous?"

"My client is under no obligation to share her conclusions on matters other than those stipulated," Hauser reminded the Chief.

Wanda place both her hands flat on the table, with an audible thud. Hauser leant closer to her and spoke quietly. He nodded, and straightened.

"Chief Leitner, perhaps you should ask Agent Mont Pelier about 'The Family', and when you do, you should remember what I say now. You have absolutely no idea about the protectiveness of 'The Family' towards its members."

"So, you are saying they will try to get to you for implicating this Theo, and Aleksei?"

Wanda let Hauser answer. "I believe they are already trying."

The Chief was at least considering the idea. Though she had no idea how he was adjusting the facts he knew about her, with the alleged criminal conspiracy. He had been told about the Russian criminals; would he realise without being told, how much of a risk Wanda was taking by helping with the investigation? Or would the Prosecutor, who had sat beside the Chief all morning, studying her, stifle his concerns by reminding the chief he was worrying too much about a murderer?

Wanda hoped he would not think to mention it to the prosecutor, but at the same time, he needed to consider the danger of encountering those Russian thugs; perhaps even consider if the person delivering the sandwich was an infiltrator or a corrupted police woman.

Derek returned as the task force officers began to take their seats. He placed another cup of the herbal tea, and some more of the cheese and biscuits, in front of Wanda. As she started to eat, she noticed the startled look on Leitner's face.

"One of my staff could have fetched something," he protested.

"I did not wish more of the unsuitable fare, to arrive," Derek said without inflection. "I have a vested interest in having Miss Carson co-operate, for in case you have forgotten, once your Austrian justice has reached its verdict, I have matters that I need her to help me investigate."

For an instant, Wanda felt amazement from Leitner, that the Interpol agent was treating the alleged murderer as a fellow agent. Then his own bias told him that was absurd.

"Yes, of course," Leitner agreed gruffly. He glanced around the room, noted that most people had returned, and gave his attention to the satchel that Donau had delivered.

Wanda watched him remove a five inch tablet and guessed it was her android tablet. She made no comment as the man fumbled with it and eventually turned it on. He'd get no further, it needed her password. Still, he must have realised how awkward it would be to monitor what she did with it, if they let her have it in her hands. He summoned an officer, spoke quietly, and the officer went off. He returned with the last of the task force officers, carrying an armful of leads and equipment.

It was not hard to guess that it would be a data projector, and the means to set it up, attached to the tablet. She also identified a portable hard drive, and that gave her pause. If they wanted to copy the tablet's memory, there were files there she didn't want them to have, even if all her files were encrypted.

Chief Leitner initiated the afternoon session by asking Wanda a direct question. "You said you had proof of what you claim to have read in the computer records of the businesses you visited. Copied files. Is that true."

"It is," she said, looking directly at the senior policeman. "The files are on the tablet in your hands."

"This is your android tablet?" Leitner showed her the screen with its display of what looked like hieroglyphics. It had to be hers – they were like no glyphs created on Earth, and no one else in this room would understand them.

"Will you access those files?"

Wanda placed both hands flat on the table, and Hauser leant closer to hear her whispered question. He nodded and spoke to the assembly. "My client will unlock the files that are relevant to this discussion, but will not open any private files."

The Prosecutor considered that, and asked, "How will we know that you have opened all the relevant ones?" He was standing up as Leitner pushed the tablet across the table.

There were several particularly scathing comments that Wanda wanted to make, but she controlled herself. Hauser pretended he didn't hear the comment either.

When she lifted the tablet so that she could see where she needed to touch the screen to unlock the device, the Prosecutor said, "I want to see what you do."

Without comment, Wanda stood up, but that made reaching the device difficult. The joined hand and foot restraints didn't give her much leeway, so she sat down and did nothing.

"Well?" was the demand from the Prosecutor.

In a perfectly polite and reasonable tone, Wanda told him, "If you want to watch, you will either have to request that my hands are freed, or you will need to come around behind me."

The target of her comment scowled, liking neither option. Either way, it meant obeying a prisoner's suggestion. He chose to walk, rather than partially releasing her.

Wanda hid the tiny spurt of amusement that his choice gave her. He was afraid of her, didn't want her to be partially freed. He did however, watch what she did.

This gave her even more amusement. If he thought he could memorise the sequence, and open it without her help. The glyphs represented numbers, and the password was the date. Tomorrow, the glyphs would be in a different random order, and require a different number to unlock the device.

As soon as the normal screen activated, the tablet was taken from her and the technician connected it to the equipment. Soon after, the screen and its contents were being projected onto a screen that had lowered from the ceiling. Now everyone could see the neat rows of shortcuts to various folders. Each one was labelled with a term that she used to refer to the place where they were obtained.

What the watchers did not yet know, each separate file in each of those folders was encrypted with a different codeword, and opening them was going to take a very long time.

File by file, she opened the contents of the first folder, and she explained where each one came from – the boss's computer or the secretary's. Finally, one of the task force officers made the comment, "We have confiscated the computers from there, and haven't been able to access them yet. How did you do it?"

That was a question she was not going to answer. The program her cousin had developed was classified, and no one in that room had the clearance to learn about it. Still, she needed to seem to be cooperating.

"Have you taken the whole computer system or just the hard drives?" she asked.

"The complete computer from the director's office, and the personal assistant's desk," was the answer.

"I am not a complete expert," Wanda claimed, "but when I accessed the computers, I was inside the office, perhaps you need to access them when they are connected to some central server?"

The man shook his head, he didn't think that made sense. Wanda merely shrugged, making the statement that she got in easily enough, somehow.

Chief Leitner suggested, "Discuss it later, if it is that important."

Wanda said, with a touch of an apology, "I know that using this information is problematical, if you cannot access the source, but if nothing else, it might suggest avenues to investigate."

Some of the other men and women were indeed scribbling and glancing at the screen.

No one responded to that comment. Instead, they seemed to have suddenly decided to snub her.

Well, should she expect thanks? No, she decided, as they only noticed her when they wanted the next file open. While she waited between those requests, she alternated her attention between the Prosecutor, the Chief of Police and Derek Mont Pelier. Sometimes she caught those three watching her, the Prosecutor as if she were a nasty taste in his mouth, Chief Leitner, with grudging respect, and Derek with the faintest of smiles. The latter was probably the only person in the room besides her lawyer, that wasn't recalling that she was charged with two frightful murders.

As the afternoon wore on, and they had only dealt with two of the businesses, Wanda caught Hauser's eye, and leant closer. "How much longer today? I am really hungry, really thirsty, and really desperate to walk around and repeat the performance from lunch time."

"Let's finish this lot," Hauser suggested.

"Well, if they didn't bring the charger, that tablet will turn off soon," Wanda warned him.

"If that happens, what then?"

"I will have to unlock everything again. Perhaps you ought to suggest that they save all the files I have unlocked so far, to that hard drive they brought in. Sometime in the next ten minutes."

The suggestion was made and acted on, with Hauser overseeing what they did. He reported to her quietly. "They have copied all the files, locked and not, to the hard drive. Is that a problem?"

"The locked ones will still be locked, but while I trust the encryption, there may be ways around it."

There certainly was if they found the 'hack' program and managed to use it.

"Do you have a backup?" Hauser asked, with a degree of concern.

"Do you think they will try to hack it and wreck something?" Wanda asked. "Won't be my fault if they do." She saw Hauser frown, and added, "Oh, yeah. They'll blame me anyway, right?"

She caught Hauser giving the slightest of shrugs, and a glance at the Prosecutor.

"There is a backup. It is with my researcher."

"Good," Hauser said, and seemed to be waiting. He was, for when the screen went blank, he stated, "That will be enough for today. My client is willing to continue this in the morning. I expect you will need to find a charger for that unit."

The Prosecutor glanced at a clock on the wall behind Wanda and scowled, agreeing with ill-grace.

Leitner's comment put the afternoon in perspective. "We have a lot of information to sort through before morning, Herr …… What we have already will advance our investigations."

Wanda whispered to Hauser, "And he knows it the sod. He can't bring himself to be grateful to someone he wants to hang in the closet."

She looked at Derek who was standing and talking to the Prosecutor. He glanced her way, as if casually, and his tone changed to alarm. "Herr Hauser, your client seems quite pale."

Hauser stated with some belligerence, "My client has some urgent personal needs, if an escort can be arranged immediately. Also, a more substantial meal would be appreciated since she has hardly had anything to eat or drink all day. You would treat your pet animals better than you have treated her today. Prisoner or not, she is keeping her end of the bargain she made, saving the Austrian police a lot of effort, and you have yet to prove beyond doubt that she is anything worse than a jewel thief."

Derek murmured to the Prosecutor, who controlled a grimace and offered, "Perhaps your client will be willing to resume after a break, and a meal at the department's expense. We could get more of the questions from this morning out of the way."

Hauser insisted on having a break until next morning at nine, and Leitner dismissed the task force officers with the same reminders as he had given at the lunch break.

Wanda leant back into her chair with relief, but she was not ready to drop the façade she was presenting. She hoped the escort would come and take her to the ladies' room before she made a puddle on the floor or became too stiff to move.

Men streamed past her on their way to the nearest exit, not one of them spoke to her. However, a damp nose and a wet tongue pushed into nuzzle and lick her hands. It warned her that Donau was behind her. She had missed the comforting warmth of Alex during that long, boring afternoon.

"You may stay here," Donau told Hauser. "I have volunteered to be caterer. So what can I get for you and your client? I guarantee it will be eminently better than lunch."

Wanda twisted around and saw his face was serious. "Did you find out who tried to poison me?"

"Unfortunately, no one paid the woman much attention. She was in uniform, had a pass and everyone assumed she was meant to be there," Donau admitted. "As to poisoning you, I am amazed that you picked up on it? I couldn't smell anything, but Alex did – he sneezes when he smells certain types of compounds."

Wanda gave Alex a pat, and thought her thanks to him, as Hauser asked, "How do you think things went today?"

"Well, you probably noticed I was not here this afternoon, but this morning....I was impressed."

"Says you who has me tied up in a knot for robbery," Wanda said, without looking at Donau.

"Are you holding that against me?"

"No," Wanda said quietly, deciding to shut up.

"So, what can the department get for you?" Donau asked.

"Nothing heavy, nothing greasy, and either water or diet soft drink."

Hauser merely said, "Whatever you bring."

Alex gave a small woof, and moved to follow his master.

"So who is still left in the room?" Wanda asked without looking around.

Hauser looked behind his client and said, "The IT expert is disconnecting the hard drive, and your tablet. Mont Pelier is by the door with the Chief. The WEGA men are still guarding the doors."

Wanda saw the note taker packing up, and covering the portable word processor.

"Do you know where I am to sleep tonight?"

"I assume they will be taking you back to the remand section," Hauser told her. "Why?"

"Well, except for the fact I really need to relieve myself, all I feel like doing is trying for a powernap until the food arrives."

"Why don't you? I have a few things to discuss with you, but they can wait."

At that point, her female escorts arrived, not the same ones as before, and they released her feet and took her out of the room. Once again, one of the WEGA men followed.

Wanda found she could not move at the pace her escorts tried to force on her. She had been sitting all day, and even with the deliberate tiny muscle movements she had been making, her muscles were stiff.

"What's the matter?" she was asked.

"I have been sitting all day," Wanda apologised. "I'm just stiff. These decorations don't allow much movement."

One of the officers, chuckled. "No, I suppose not." Her manner was not hostile, and a pleasant change. Maybe she didn't know what her charge was believed to have done.

The other woman muttered, "They are not meant to."

While they allowed her some privacy in the cubicle, once again with her hands freed temporarily, Wanda stretched her arms up above her head, and flexed the individual muscles, and imagined she could see the blood starting to move around those extremities.

She didn't try to take too long attending her needs, as she was both tired and hungry.

Once she had washed and dried her hands, she allowed them to fasten the wrist restraints once more, and lead her back to the meeting room. At least, on her return, they did not refasten the foot restraints to the floor, and once they were gone, no one stopped her when she began to walk up and down the length of the table. The WEGA men were satisfied to watch her from their positions, and Wanda wondered if these men were the same ones that had been in the room in the morning. She couldn't tell, since they had not removed their face covering.

When Donau and Mont Pelier returned with the food, Wanda returned to her seat, feeling a great deal less stiff. She saw that they had enough food for four people and a dog.

"Who is looking after the tablet?" Hauser asked Mont Pelier.

"Chief Leitner. He found the charger with Fraulein Carson's possessions that they have in the evidence locker."

"I hope he doesn't take his eyes off it," Wanda spoke between mouthfuls of the chicken salad roll Donau had placed in front of her.

"The copy they made of it is in the evidence safe," Mont Pelier assured her.

"That is not what worries me," Wanda spoke with her mouth partly full, and swallowed quickly. She put the roll down on the wrapper, suddenly nauseous.

Alex, who had quickly inhaled three ham rolls, raised his head off his paws and looked at her.

"Who would try to break into the Chief's office?" Donau asked incredulously.

"Who would poison a witness in a police station?" Wanda countered immediately. She saw Donau go tense.

Mont Pelier commented, "Fraulein Carson has already received one credible threat, intended to warn her off speaking to the police."

"Why haven't we been told?" Donau demanded.

"According to the prison, the person who made the threat, was never there," Derek said mildly, and he continued before Donau could voice the obvious and intended belief. "However, she gave an excellent description of this non-existent man, who is a person of extreme interest to Interpol."

Donau now understood the reason for the WEGA guards. He took out his mobile phone and dialled a number. He walked off a few paces as he issued instructions. A moment later, two of the WEGA men suddenly dashed from the room.

He returned and asked, "So, who was it that threatened you? Someone related to this crime cabal?"

Wanda looked at Hauser and used her hands on the table gesture. Once again he listened to her whispered suggestions. Then he gestured to Donau and they both moved to where their faces would not be seen by the still active security cameras.

"Her notoriety here has drawn the attention of someone involved in other matters. It is a personal animosity."

"But you are implying that someone in the police department, who was here today, is working for a criminal!"

"It may not be one of the taskforce, just someone aware of what was being discussed here. And if that tablet holds all the information my client knows, then it is a dangerous piece of equipment."

Donau saw the implications, and instinctively scanned the room. He followed Hauser back to the table and stared at his now empty plate. He noticed that Carson had stopped eating, most of her roll still in front of her. He looked and saw his deceptively innocent looking dog and growled in annoyance.

Wanda took another bite of the roll to hide her amusement. She had felt Alex get up, saw him delicately grip the roll in his mouth, before dropping down to swallow it in two bites.

"I am sure your device is still safe," Donau told her. "The Chief knows how important it is."

"I hope it is. Though I am sure that many people wouldn't care if I have more to lose if it is stolen by the wrong people."

"They made a copy of the files though."

Wanda shook her head and put her food down again. She had a sudden irrational fear that she might not have encrypted everything. What if they found the 'back door key' program that she used to get through computer firewalls? Or the encryption program, that was also the means to unencrypt files. If they found that, all her personal files, her research notes, emails and everything would be vulnerable to scrutiny. Even if they didn't, hadn't her computer expert cousin once said that you could recover data on a hard drive, even if it had been erased?

"Are you alright, Miss Carson?"

Wanda didn't glance at Donau as she said, "I'm very tired."

Her mind was still envisioning possibilities, each one worse than the one before. David had sent a photo of him and Davy, by email. She had deleted it, reluctantly, along with David's notes on the searches he had done. The gist of those had been transferred to other files. But if the Russian bastards accessed those, they would know she was on to them. They would know she had encountered their damned family before – and survived.

It was Derek who said, "I'll see about returning you to the remand section." He used his mobile phone again, then told her, "They will be ready for us to go down in five minutes."

Wanda guessed what he didn't say, that the route was being cleared and secured. However, before that five minutes was up, he had a call and this time told her, "Your tablet is still safe and sound and under guard in the Chief's office."

During the short drive back to the women's prison, Wanda tried doing various calming exercises that she had been taught. And while she succeeded in pushing her fear to the back of her mind, she was aware that she was too tired to be fully alert for trouble. The guard here, or others like him, might be planning another not so subtle warning.

Nothing appeared amiss when she was back in her cell room. She studied the positions of the few items she had in there, the state of the bed – still in disarray from her rushed departure, and the neat pile of change clothes that had been brought for her. When she sensed that the guards had moved back along the corridor, she checked her bed very carefully, and didn't berate herself for paranoia.

Her sleep was not restful, since she was mentally primed to wake at the slightest noise. She became fully awake at five thirty when the food tray was pushed through the flap in the corner at floor level.

Knowing that she would probably be collected early again, she got out of bed and donned the long knitted jacket that Jim had provided for her. Then she began her morning ritual of using the facility, washing her hands and face with the icy cold water from the tap, and completing a series of exercises to warm up. Only then, did she move to examine the breakfast tray which did not contain the normal breakfast menu. Not surprising, she decided. The kitchen probably wasn't in operation yet. What she had was a sealed plastic beaker of juice, an apple, and six sealed portions of two crackers and cheese. She examined each item as well as she could in the dim light from the window, looking for signs of tampering, before she decided they were safe to eat. She decided to leave the apple.

It was only when she moved the cheese and biscuit plastic plate, now with the apple on it, to go to the small bedside table, that the shock was delivered.

While she was eating, the light had come on, so the seeing the photograph sent a jolt of terror through her.

"It's not possible! I erased that!" But the computer printed picture was of David and Davy.

Wanda shivered. They knew about her son! They had her tablet.

In the hotel, in the centre of Vienna, David Martin woke suddenly. He listened, but all was quiet in his room. He rose and walked out into the main room of the suite. The sound of breathing came from the room that Jim Phillips was using.

Just as he thought it had been a dream that woke him, he felt an indescribable terror. He immediately ran to his room, dressed and began stuffing his other clothes and belongings into his small travelling bag. He was unaware of the noise he was making until Jim spoke from the doorway.

"What's wrong?"

He finished packing and turned to his friend and mentor, who had at least donned a dressing gown.

"I have to get home, right now. I have to get to Davy."

"What brought this on?"

"I have to go, Jim. Can you get on the phone and organise a flight?"

Jim's instinct told him to comply, but as he went to the phone, there was an urgent knocking on the door. He checked through the peephole before opening it. When he saw Erin, Tanya and Elizabeth, he had half the answer to David's behaviour.

Erin immediately confronted David. "I need your tablet computer, now!"

Elizabeth explained to Jim, "Someone has got hold of Wanda's tablet computer. They managed to recover a photo that David sent her of him and Davy. A printed copy was delivered with her breakfast this morning."

"So what is Erin doing?"

"She is going to send a particularly nasty virus, by email, to Wanda's tablet. It should cause the unit to be re- formatted. She wants no chance that the firewall hack program or the encryption program will be useable."

"Might they have used them already?" Jim asked, his mind considering all aspects of the problem.

Erin answered even as she was quickly typing a program. "I am hoping that they had no idea such a thing was there. And even if they did, and tried to unlock the files, they would still need the passwords Wanda used, and they are all random, multi-digit strings, and are not stored in the computer."

"So, why the urgency?"

"Well, if they try to run the firewall hack program I wrote, they may realise what it does and use it on the files."

"Is that how they got the photo?"

"They may have used a program to recover deleted files, so they might have found the emails David sent to her, or copies of what she sent him. I'm doing damage control – and hoping like crazy they haven't thought to clone the memory."

"We have to get Wanda out of that prison," Jim thought aloud. He gave his mobile phone to Elizabeth and told her to organise a flight to LA. He went to the hotel phone and put a call through to Derek Mont Pelier. All he said was, "We have trouble."

Derek was dressed, but without jacket or tie, when he knocked and entered. He closed the door and asked what was wrong. Jim explained in terse sentences, and Elizabeth added detail as she waited for her call to get off hold. David had his tablet back and was stuffing it in his bag.

"Call me with the details, Liz," David said, as he grabbed his bag and made for the door. "Call down and arrange a taxi."

Erin, reached the hotel phone before Jim and made the call to the reception desk.

Once David was out of the room, some of the tension eased. Derek asked, "You claim it's the Russian crowd doing this. How can you be sure?"

"Because it is their filthy style," Elisabeth insisted, her eyes flashing.

Derek added ideas together and accused, "You didn't mention that Wanda had encountered Tatarovich before."

"Not him," Tanya spat. "Or he wouldn't be assuming she is me."

"His relatives, probably. Wanda didn't say much about the people that took Vera, but it happened after Dad got delivered a picture of her taken at some official function. All she really said was that speaking Russian helped."

Derek glanced at Jim, hoping he knew more.

"I wasn't involved in that investigation. Wanda and David do other work for the State Department."

"So was that affair official or personal?"

"She did it because I asked her," Elizabeth admitted.

"Fine. We assume you are correct, and I won't ask how you all know this. I am going to organise alternate secure accommodation for Fraulein Carson from now until the end of her court appearances. After that, my hands are tied. First though, I am going to confirm your theory that her tablet is missing."

Wanda sensed the agitation amongst the task force members, and the anger of Chief Leitner, as soon as she reached the fifth floor of the police building. The sensation was like being surrounded by a swarm of bees.

She had been joined by Hauser for the ride up from the basement, and was fairly sure that he hadn't yet heard the news. If that was the case, she was not going to tell him. He can believe it was all Derek's doing that the tablet switch had been discovered, and she trusted that no one would mention her part in it. The Interpol agent knew of some of her mental tricks, she didn't want the Austrian police to learn of them.

They were early again, but this time, the electronic equipment had already been set up, and a closed laptop was at her position. Hauser queried the difference, but the IT man was simply doing as directed. Wanda sat when directed, but this time, her police escorts did not insist on securing her feet to the floor, even if she did still have the hand and foot restraints on.

Derek Mont Pelier entered the room and Hauser gestured him over.

"What's going on?"

"We received notification of a threat against Fraulein Carson." Derek didn't look at Wanda as he spoke. "The nature of the threat indicated that the sender had obtained information from Carson's computer device. I insisted on checking the device in the Chief's office, and we found that it had been swapped with an identical unit with no data on it."

"It was taken from the evidence safe?"

"That hasn't been determined. There is no sign the safe was forced, but it may have been switched when it was out being charged. The Chief did step out of his office for a moment before the guard was put on. When he put it in the safe, he hadn't turned it on."

"I hope he is personally motivated to getting it found," Wanda said, allowing her anger to leak.

"It was fortunate that you suggested that they back up the files. Unless the backup disappeared too?" Hauser glanced at his client. Wanda simply stared back at him.

"It appears not," Derek continued. "But that is why the laptop is here. They will want Fraulein Carson to confirm that the backup is viable."

"If they trust my memory," Wanda spoke rudely, knowing the Prosecutor was approaching from behind her chair.

"I hope you are not going to make trouble, Carson," that man said.

Wanda did not stand, or try to turn around. She said carefully, "I am trying to help you, Mr Prosecutor. I am doing what some people wish I wouldn't. For my part, I expect to be protected as well as receiving favourable consideration from the judge when you are game to put me in court."

He didn't like her. Wanda could sense it, like a rash all over her. He would use her, and then delight in locking her up for good. He didn't respond to her comment, simply gave Derek and Hauser a muted greeting and moved on.

"SOD," Wanda muttered, just audibly. She stayed leaning back in her chair, watching the activity until the task force were all seated again and she had to examine the files on the laptop. As she was scrolling through, with Derek and the Police Chief looking over her shoulder, the IT man was checking the room for listening devices.

She was relieved to see that one particular file did not show up on the copy. The firewall hack had a copy protect on it. Erin had told her that it made the program invisible to copying processes.

"Looks like everything is there," Wanda confirmed, but she made no move to begin unlocking the files.

The Prosecutor insisted on a question session, to deal with the questions arising from the previous day's revelations. Hauser decided on an orderly system of one person at a time, which worked for a while until the people asking questions provoked more questions in others. Then it turned into a topic by topic question session.

Wanda easily fended off questions designed to trip her up or make her confused. If a question was repeated, she referred to her earlier answer. If they tried to insist that she had previously said something else, she repeated the earlier question and answer, verbatim, and challenged them to check her answer with the woman taking notes.

The verbal fencing amused her and distracted her from the morning nausea, and from wishing that Derek could have found her more of that amazing herbal tea.

At the lunch break, when she was able to walk to the ladies room, escorted again, she returned to find that Derek had indeed brought some of the tea, with the sandwiches.

She stood near the table to eat, rather than sitting down, and felt Alex come up and lean some of his weight against her. She slipped him half a sandwich, and listened as Donau spoke to Hauser. He didn't have much to say, except that he had tried to see if Alex could pick up a scent from the swapped in tablet, but hadn't had any luck.

Wanda was less amused during the afternoon when all she did was unlock files so that they could be saved in open format and made available to authorised people. She spent the time between each unlocking, while the contents were indexed, trying to sense the unguarded emotions of the Police Chief and Prosecutor. She was sure they could not use her unlocked files in court, unless they later obtained them from the confiscated computers. All they were really providing was the scope of the criminal conspiracy.

From snippets overheard as her information was discussed, Wanda knew that a lot of incriminating files had been found where Wessler had died, but Lunn's laptop office had not been found. She hadn't been aware of him at the house...

Wanda caught her mind drifting and returned it to the task in hand, that of sensing the emotional aura. Wessler's name was mentioned, and Wanda listened to a conversation in progress between the task force leader and the Police Chief, to which the Prosecutor was a party, although if they glanced her way she would seem to be staring at the ceiling.

It seemed that the police desperately wanted access to Wessler's computer from Alpha Prime. The two senior men were well inclined towards asking her how she had penetrated the fire wall in that building, and discovering if she could hack into the security on the confiscated unit. The answer was, she would say, that without her stolen tablet, she couldn't. But she'd like to say that they could whistle for her help there, as it wasn't in the agreement and since her last offer of help had resulted in extra charges against her, she didn't trust the Prosecutor to make further deals.

If she was offered a better deal and reduced charges, she'd 'recall' the passwords used by each of the cartel members.

It turned into a very long day, because they did not let her stop at the evening break, but kept on until everyone's' questions had been answered. When the session finally ended, Wanda felt like she wanted to fall asleep. She was too tired even to protest the lack of thanks from the police for her help.

Though, as if receptive to the thought, Derek came and placed a gentle hand on her shoulder. "That marathon session was well done."

"They could have thanked me. I've done half their job for them. So what now?"

"Now, you go to where I have arranged an alternate sleeping place."

"And wait there to see if they need more spoon feeding?"

Derek squeezed her shoulder again, as he spoke to Hauser. "Do you need time with your client?"

"A few minutes, that's all."

The policemen moved away.

"Mont Pelier was right. That was impressive, but at the same time our Austrian police are unsettled by your understated skill – both at how you obtained these records and by your astounding memory."

"I irritate a lot of people even without advertising my skills. They could have thanked me, but your prosecutor should realise I am on his side, instead he only sees the pack of lies I fell into, and the kudos for having caught a murderer. I am looking forward to you proving him wrong."

Hauser caught the edge in Wanda's voice, and the emotion she had been hiding well, until now when she was so tired. He pretended that he didn't notice, just quietly gave them his assessment of the way things now stood. He had been told that he didn't need to jolly this client. She would be more help if she knew exactly what the stakes were.

"If it is likely to be helpful, you can put me on the stand," Wanda suggested.

"That would be a course of last resort," Hauser told her, then asked, "Why?"

"Maybe I'd like a damn good argument," she said with a yawn. "Don't worry, I will do as you instruct, and enjoy the fuming when they can't make me say anything."

Chapter 10 - In limbo

The truck with the WEGA guards drove out of the police garage and took longer to arrive at its destination. Wanda was half dozing, but still alert to externals. She was prepared for trouble, but when the door of the truck was opened, Derek helped her out.

They were in a garage, not the prison compound, and Wanda glanced at Derek, silently signalling her amazement.

"I have organised for you to stay here for the rest of the time that you are in remand. However, I will have your promise of good behaviour and of not trying to escape. There will be guards of course, WEGA for now, but the duty will be shared by some of my colleagues who are on their way as we speak."

"You have that promise, Derek, and my thanks. Even though a large part of me wants to run and hide. Would I be correct in thinking that you have more questions?"

"Yes, indeed, but not tonight. You look like you need a good night's sleep. I will show you to the room you are to use, and you will find all your things from the remand cell."

"What little there was," Wanda yawned, then apologised.

"Jim said that you were using your time in remand to get into survival mode. I think I understand what he means, and hope that this doesn't change that. You might occupy your mind by following the media coverage of the various investigations."

"Okay," she agreed, but she was too tired to second guess his reasons.

Wanda found out what Derek meant by the media coverage when she was able to read the day's paper with breakfast. For that, she sat at a table in an austere but comfortable dining room and had Derek as company.

The tone of the newspaper reports was generally that Wessler of Alpha Prime was a martyr, and few people believed the allegations of his criminal activity. Lunn, lesser known, was washed in the same light. The double murder, and the allegations against the men had been relegated to page three, with the headline article being about some of the men being hunted by the police. She learnt little of interest.

After eating, Derek suggested a stroll and he took her around the two levels of her mini prison. He asked her to run her eye over the security that had been hastily installed in the rented house.

"Not so you can get out, mind," Derek teased. "But to stop others getting in."

"I really appreciate what you are doing for me, Derek."

"It's not all altruistic, I do need your knowledge of the 'Family'."

"You've heard all I know about Theo, Alexsi, and Tatarovich."

"You've met others though? Last year? With Wexford's sister."

"Did Elisabeth tell you that? I didn't consider Dimitri much of a threat, and I didn't say much about him."

"She said you mentioned a Russian speaker. But have you had a chance to consider the odd fact that last year, Elisabeth's step mother was abducted, and now there is the idea that he who she believed was her brother, might really be a Russian?"

"When I had that revelation, I had more immediate problems to deal with."

Now though, the idea suddenly assumed a great deal more importance, and ideas flashed through her mind, but her thoughts were not ones she could share with Derek. The one foremost in her mind was, "Why had Dimitri abducted Vera Willard anyway? It was a question that hadn't been answered at the time. Her next question was, had the false Allan Wexford, aka Aleksei, been a party to that? The 'Family' certainly stuck together and had managed to spirit Dimitri away. But the point she had just considered was that Aleksi, son of Theo, cousin to Tatarovich, could have known what Dimitri was doing. If he had, he hadn't stopped it, so he must have agreed with the reason. If he hadn't known...then what? She didn't have enough information. Now that Derek had pointed it out, it seemed too much of a coincidence that Tatarovich, who knew of Ivana and Tanya, and wanted to control both, had a cousin impersonating the brother in law of a man who had married Ivana's sister.

"Can you share your thoughts?"

Wanda shook her head and recalled Derek's presence. "I don't have enough information to base an opinion on, but your comment is raising the hairs on my neck. I promise, I will be thinking on that unnerving idea."

"Then can you tell me anything about that Dimitri you mentioned?"

Wanda paused to consider if that incident was classified. She decided it wasn't.

"I won't go into how David and I discovered he was the culprit, or where he had Vera, but at that time. I hadn't heard of the 'Family'."

She outlined the events that had occurred after Vera Willard had been found, how Dimitri had been sprung from jail and everyone was meant to think he was dead.

"So when did you hear of the 'Family'?"

"When I was talking to Dimitri's son. He told us, David and me, that Dimitri wanted him to join the family business. He, Dimitri, had abducted his daughter, Les's sister, and had her prisoner in the same building where Vera was."

That led to Wanda telling Derek about Les and his sister, and the information they had exchanged after that.

"So, you are saying that there is a branch of this perfidious family in Australia too? I must find out if the Australian police are aware of them."

"Some are," Wanda told him. "Les is trying to locate them."

"I see. So, was that your first encounter with Russian criminals?"

They were half way down the stairs, and Wanda stopped in her tracks, one foot about to step down.

Memories of completely unrelated events swarmed into her mind, her eidetic memory releasing them with the mention of Russian criminals and a first encounter.

"Maybe not," Wanda admitted, resuming her downward path. "When Tanya first arrived in the US with her father, Russian agents were trying to find them. I assumed they were Russian government agents. I don't have the name of the leader of that group. Jim might know, but the guy is dead. That was, five or six years ago."

They were at the door to the kitchen and Wanda stopped again. "And if Aleksei replaced Wexford before he came back to the US, that was about five years ago. Oh my…I hope that was a coincidence."

"You don't think so?"

"I don't have enough information." Wanda shook her head again trying to dispel new fears. She hoped, that the group that had been after Tanya and her father, had not mentioned a certain Wanda Martin to anyone else.

They entered the kitchen, and Derek told her she could help herself to tea, coffee and snacks. Her meals would be provided. Soon after that, he had a call and told her he had to go out.

"Watch television if you like," he invited as he left her with the WEGA guards.

Wanda had never been one to watch much television, and didn't feel like starting. She was feeling distinctly displaced. She wasn't free, but this house was not like a prison, not really, even though one of the WEGA men had her in sight from the moment Derek left. None of the four were talkative, they seemed to communicate with hand gestures. With an inward sigh, she walked to the room where she had slept and lay on the bed. She had left the door open so that her guards could check on her whenever they wished. She was glad of the protection, though she thought ordinary guards would be enough. Then she thought of the other side. To her current guards, she was accused of murdering two people. The thought depressed her. She decided to catch up on more sleep.

Over the next few days, she received news of the 'free' world by newspaper and TV, progress of the investigations through Derek when he returned from his own affairs, and from her lawyer when he phoned or came in person.

However, what she really wanted to know was that David and Davy were safe, but this was something even her sister could not yet tell her, and she had no way to call international from the house, even if she dared to try.

For the first two days, she passed the time by recalling in detail the events in her past that had involved Russians. That always led to her wondering what Jim and her cousins were doing. She had heard nothing from them for a while.

On the third day, Derek returned in the evening with a guest. Wanda wanted to run and hug her sister, but refrained, sending her delight via their mind to mind communication. They were left alone to talk in the formal front room, which enabled them to sit close together on an old faded floral upholstered settee. They both knew that the two Interpol agents, that were currently part of the duty guard team, were outside the door, but that didn't matter.

"The rules of this prison are much more civilised that the other one," Elisabeth said with an impish grin.

"Yeah, but...it won't last. So, have you come to stimulate my mind? I am going to die of boredom soon."

"No, merely to make sure you were behaving, and to reassure you. Dad called me. He said David and Davy are safe, not at his place, and not at yours. David has hired guards to check the farm and arranged for some of your neighbours to agist the animals, rather than just coming to feed and water them."

Wanda felt the tense inner part of herself relax. "Did your father say where they are?"

"Not on the phone, no. But he did say he has taken precautions too."

"Good! So what else can you tell me?"

"Well, Jim and his friends have gone off somewhere. He didn't say what for. Erin, Tanya and I are doing some more family history research, and I have been visiting Nicole and Rachel. Oh, and guess what? When the FBI went to check her house back home, looking for fingerprints or DNA of her Allan, they found absolutely nothing. Someone had been in there and done a thorough clean – wiped all surfaces, vacuumed so thoroughly that no skin flakes, hairs, etc. remain. Whoever it was even took the used hair brushes and toothbrushes, and replaced them with new ones."

"I'd call that a sign of a guilty conscience or ultra-protectiveness. Has Aleksei been found yet?"

Elisabeth shrugged. "He's probably gone to get his face changed again."

"What about the DNA tests?"

"Nothing yet. Do you have a date for your trial?"

"No, and they probably won't set one until they think they have milked me dry. That Prosecutor knows I don't like him for the two faced bastard he is, and once he's done his worst, he'll have to beg for my help."

Elisabeth knew her sister was dreading the idea of being in prison again, and decided to distract her. "Do you need me to bring you anything? More clothes?"

"I can wash my own stuff here, so no to that. I'd ask for a mobile phone, but they don't want me making calls out. I'd ask for a computer, but what I'd want to do involves the internet and this place doesn't have access. Magazines bore me, and I was never one to read books."

"What about an IPod? I could load it with audiobooks or music."

"Yeah, that might help," Wanda agreed. "I can listen while I walk around this place for exercise."

Derek returned to escort Elisabeth back to the hotel, and Wanda smiled at the feeling of happiness that her sister emanated when she saw him. She didn't make a comment, but she was glad. Her sister deserved a life of her own, away from the 'baby-sitting' duties and the need to cosset Vera when she was pregnant, which she was again.

"See you," Wanda promised her sister, as she turned to go back to her room. She hadn't missed the subtle movement of the guards towards the door as Derek opened it. They were not being paid to trust her not to escape.

The procedure didn't annoy her, and now she took amusement at thinking how her next child would have an aunt or uncle about her age, just as Davy did. Too bad, her children would not get to know them as relatives.

As much as she had been dreading her trial, she wanted it over. The worst part was anticipating the inescapable conclusion.

The Prosecutor had been presenting evidence against her for a full week, ensuring the events, according to his interpretation, were clear in the minds of the jury. Hauser raised doubts where ever he could, planting the seeds of ideas that would be presented during her defence.

For each of the charges, he seemed to have damning evidence, and Wanda wanted to cry out about challenge him, with "How can you possibly believe that?" But she had to stay silent, or it would go even worse for her.

The Prosecutor was skilled at his job, he presented the evidence in such a way that some of the jury might have thought she escaped from the police after the murder, not after the jewel theft, and have the idea she was guilty because of that. And then he made it seem like the Russian thugs had rescued her, not abducted her. Put that way it was easy to assume that she could be involved in the murders, and her actions of later were from remorse, not from some unbelievably odd drug reaction.

Wanda fought to keep her face impassive, despite the overwhelming knowledge that she was going to be sent to prison. At the end of each day she barely made it to her room in the old house before her repressed feeling erupted. She wanted no one to see her like that. That was the only benefit of being there.

She needed to be hard, to psych herself into the mode to survive. Yet this time, it seemed much harder, she had more to lose, and the changes in her body due to her pregnancy were making her mind weaker. Yet once she had vented her anger and fear by the physical action of kicking an old, heavy pillow around her room, she was able to go out and face her sister, and David, and Derek.

Not one of them thought less of her for being afraid; all knew she had the strength to keep to her commitment, without running off.

Each one of them knew that she probably could escape with very little help – if she had wanted to. They knew the temptation was there.

She knew that Derek was fending off a great deal of flak for keeping her at the house. Yet the WEGA and Interpol guards remained, and the latter were impressed by her intuition relating to the Russian criminals, and after a couple of days had stopped watching her suspiciously when she was in the room with them.

Derek may have told them of her, and how she had helped him before. Though it would not have been the full story, since he kept his royal status a secret.

However this respite was Derek's way of repaying part of the debt that he felt his family owed her. It meant she could have closer contact with her friends, who were her source of strength. But it would end, all too soon.

That day had been the worst yet, the last of the evidence against her had been presented, the jury of stolid Austrian men and women had been looking at her and she had not needed to feel their minds to know that they abhorred her.

Before coming back to the house, Hauser had spent half an hour going over his plan of defence. He had been bluntly honest with her, admitting that it looked bleak, but he felt confident that he could turn the situation around. Her clever and resourceful friends had done so much, and he intended to use every bit of skill he had to help her. He hadn't needed to tell his client that the general feeling of the spectators was against her. She had told him that there were only five spectators who mattered, the rest only believed the facts that were most sensational.

David was staying at the house; he had arrived the night before the trial started, and had been her pillar of strength each day. By mutual agreement, when they were alone together, they did not talk of the trial, but of the time when it would be over – the light at the end of the tunnel. At night, they clung to each other, until the early hours, when David would slip back to his room and she would build her defences for the day to come.

Wanda knew that whatever the final outcome, she was going to prison. She was going to be away from her family for some years, her daughter would be born in prison and then taken away from her. She would miss those precious infant years of her daughter's life. It was the uncertainty of how long she'd be imprisoned that tore at her.

Hauser had thought of clever ways to create doubt in the minds of the jurors, some had the hint of Jim Phillip's brilliant ideas. He intended to hammer away at the evidence relating to the worst charges, present his own compelling version of the truth about the damning facts.

Even the jewel theft, the one major crime she was truly guilty of, he intended to fight with the same intensity. He would work on the fact that the ownership of the diamonds that she stole, was in dispute, and imply she was recovering them. It would make little difference though, for whatever way you looked at it, she had entered Alpha Prime unlawfully, and taken them from a locked safe, and pocketed them. There was nothing she could say to explain why, in truth, for the truth was way too outré to be believed.

Her other reason for being there had come out with the Prosecutor's case – that she was looking for the American, Allan Wexford. He had used that as a further indication that she was in league with Russian criminals trying to get a foot hold in Austria. It had been a deliberate way to bring in the mention of her other illegal enterings, although no proof of these was presented and the judge had ruled that heresay. It would still be in the minds of the jurors, even if they were told to disregard it.

For the following three days, as Hauser presented her defence, Wanda locked her fears away and concentrated on a belief that the truth would win out. She listened dispassionately to Hauser's arguments, and questioning of witnesses, eyed the reactions of the jurors, and sensed the disbelief of the spectators. It seemed that the jurors simply had to realise that she could not have murdered Wessler and Lunn, or even been able to abet it. That she had saved Rachel's life, not deliberately endangered it, or intentionally disabled the nurse so that she would die in the fire.

Then it was time for closing arguments, for the jury to go off to consider the evidence, and she was led to a cell in the courthouse to wait.

Her mind was numb, she refused to hope, she listened to the promises of her sister and cousins that they were there for her, no matter what. She made them promise to make David go home, once the sentence was announced.

For five hours, Wanda paced the small cell, too tense even to sit or lie on the narrow cot bed. If they took any longer, she would have to wait through an overnight recess. Hauser had said that a long deliberation was what he wanted, it would mean they were not making a hasty decision. It didn't help.

Someone had brought her food, but she couldn't eat it. It was one thing to contemplate being caught, going to jail – when you still thought you were too good to be caught, but the reality was... too real.

She admitted that she could blame no one but herself. If she hadn't taken those diamonds...they would not have had proof. And despite ideas, she still didn't know why touching the bag of diamonds had made the damn pieces of carbon want her. They shouldn't have affected her mind...but they had.

Then, for a time she was shaken out of her tension as a shiver of atavistic memory travelled from her skull, down her neck and back. She remembered an old bracelet she had found in the farmhouse that she and David had later renovated. She hadn't known of it, until it had drawn her to where it was hidden. She knew now that the origin of that bracelet was alien, and her own links to it were a highly classified secret.

Her alleged grandfather had said those diamonds were once the property of a woman who was at most his mistress, not the wife he had claimed. She knew better, and if the diamonds had once belonged to the woman who was in fact her maternal grandmother, and had the same effect on her as the bracelet, then their origin had to be equally alien.

She shielded her mind from her friends as she thought, "Sacred mother of the Earth, please, don't let Elisabeth, or Erin, or Tanya near those diamonds." After a moment, she added a second plea, "Make a way to prevent Tatarorvich from getting those diamonds back."

For a brief moment, she thought she felt a faint breeze, as if some ancient power had heard her.

"Carson!"

Wanda spun around. The courthouse guards had entered the cell.

"Over by the wall, hands high and on it."

She knew the process, and complied without a struggle, although she truly wanted to run and hide.

It meant that the jury was back, it meant her fate was about to be sealed.

Had the guards seen her face at that moment, they would have seen the change that came over it. Jim had told her it was like shutters came down over her eyes. He had seen her do it in the past, when she had spoken out against her former criminal bosses. She was doing it now so that no one would be able to see into her soul, intuit her thoughts or gauge her reaction. She would not disgrace herself.

The restraints were snapped back on and the two guards each grabbed an arm, and pulled her out of the cell. Wanda sent a last thought to the unseen powers, "Let this not turn out too badly."

She stood by Hauser as the judge asked for the findings of the jury. Her eyes found David, edged into a position just within her line of sight. She stared at him as if he were her lifeline. She sensed her sister and cousins in her mind, quietly solid, repeating, "We are here for you."

It was all that kept her standing as the shock of the verdict struck her mind.

Guilty as an accessory to murder. Guilty of manslaughter. Guilty of grand robbery. Guilty of negligent conduct endangering a child. Two counts of escaping from police custody.

Her mind went numb. They were wrong! How could they think her guilty? Did they truly think she was working with those evil fiends who called themselves 'The Family'?

Her legs felt like jelly, her stomach like it was suspended over a gaping abyss. David's shock and horror hit her like a hammer blow, and her impassive mask almost slipped.

It could have been worse, but she wasn't the monster they were saying she was.

"David!" her mind reached out because her hands couldn't. "GO! GO home to Davy. Please go!"

He didn't move. She saw him standing there, resisting her sister and cousins, as if he had turned to stone.

The judge didn't call a recess to deliberate on her sentence.

"Ten years for accessory to murder. Six years for the robbery. Two for each count of escaping custody. Five for manslaughter and two for negligent conduct endangering a child. The terms not to be served together. Not eligible for parole for sixteen years.

The guards took hold of her, and she only had time to hiss at Hauser, "Twenty five years! That wasn't the deal. I had nothing to do with that murder. It had to be Aleksei."

Hauser gestured to the guards. To Wanda he said, "Calm down. I will come to see you about how we will proceed."

The guards began to hustle her forward. In her mind, she felt David's anger, and his burning need to do something for her. He was struggling in the grip of her sister and cousins.

"Please, Lisbeth, make him go home. Please! Make him go home, before I break down."

She was only vaguely aware, over the pounding of blood in her ears, and the feeling of being about to black out, that Jim, Nicholas and Max, were taking charge of David. That Elisabeth was telling him to calm himself, that he wasn't helping.

Then there was Erin and Tanya, sending to her mind the image of a tranquil pond, a feeling of calm and peace. In her mind it changed to a scene of a violently hot rock dropping into the pool and emitting clouds of steam and deafening bubbling hisses.

Still it eased the paralysing anger enough for Erin to remind her of the mantra's for calm that Jenha Mosellan had taught them. And then, the thought of that oddly young uncle of their grandmother, reminded her of her own strength, of how she had endured much worse than this moment, and how she was so much stronger than all those around her who were emitting satisfaction at the result.

Wanda was hustled past milling spectators. A wet tongue licked her hand as they needed to pause to unlock a door. She passed Donau, but her eyes were down and she only sensed his ambivalence about her.

Calm finally settled over her, imposed by the four-way link with Elisabeth, Erin and Tanya. Wanda was finally able to take a deep breath, as her kin sent her their strength. They had done this for her before, when all she had seen ahead was her inevitable painful death.

"This will pass," Elisabeth sent.

"But it is not a mere twelve months this time. It's 25 years," Wanda's mind wailed.

"Hauser is going to appeal. We will continue to pursue Theo, Aleksei and Tatarovich."

"Why him?"

"Didn't he tell you that you would be sorry? Erin feels that the judge and some of the jury were influenced."

"How?"

"That their initial thoughts about your guilt were strengthened by threats against their families."

"They will never dare admit that," Wanda thought helplessly.

"Maybe they would if Tatarovich is out of the picture," Tanya's thought was fierce.

"He won't let himself be caught."

"He thinks he won't," Tanya insisted. "Just as you didn't."

Wanda mentally flinched, but Tanya wasn't finished. "He has already made one major mistake – thinking that you are me. I am not as strong as you are, I couldn't have survived everything you have. He will come back to see you…soon. When you are supposedly most vulnerable. When the length of your sentence has you in shock and your mind has no room for hope."

"And we will be ready," Elisabeth added, a fierce promise. "Derek has refused to allow him to have the jewels back. He told the representative from Pierre De Coursey – the name he uses in France, that he has not been able to trace the ownership of them. He must be getting very annoyed."

Thoughts of vengeance stirred in Wanda's mind, something to focus on. "So, I am to be bait?"

"No," Elisabeth corrected her. "You are the shark! But you must be alert, wary of everything."

"I will be. To survive."

She was at the prison van now, but the sense of calm stayed with her as it moved away. The voices in her head were silent now. Her sister and cousins were with David. He needed them more now. Davy needed him, and he had promised her that he would go home.

Chapter 13 - Aftermath

A gathering of friends met in Jim's hotel room. It was nearly midnight, but not one of them was ready to sleep. Max and Nicholas had just returned from ensuring that David got on the chartered flight to LA. Derek Mont Pelier had joined them as they had come up the stairs.

He expected to see a scene of complete despondency. This group had all worked so hard, for weeks, and had failed. Yet no one was slumped in chairs. The three cousins of Wanda, were seated together, their chairs forming a triangle and they were leaning towards each other. Jim was pacing the room, going every so often to the dark skinned, Grant, and getting something noted on the computer.

Max went over to the drinks fridge, but Nicholas stayed with Mont Pelier.

"We put David on the plane, after giving him a few stiff drinks. Casey has gone with him," Nicholas explained. "He's had a severe shock, but he will be fine."

"Yes, I was concerned for him."

The three women broke from their huddle. Erin and Tanya stood up, but Elisabeth slumped back in her chair.

Erin said to Mont Pelier, "I told Gerry, my mate, to meet him. Gerry knows what it is like to be in a pit of despair, and he is a friend of David."

Tanya spoke to Jim, "We'll talk in the morning. Wanda has finally worn herself out and is asleep."

Derek murmured, "I would like to know how you could know that." No one enlightened him so he added, "Please, let me know if there is anything I can do."

Jim glanced his way and gave a terse nod, to indicate he had heard the offer.

Then Derek felt compelled to look at Elisabeth, still seated in the chair with her eyes closed. There was the suspicion of moisture about the eyelids, and a faint trembling around her mouth. He looked away, unsure whether he should intrude. He noticed Erin looking intently at him, saw her deliberately glance at Elisabeth and then back at him, as if she wanted him to do something.

"Miss Willard, perhaps I could escort you back to your room? You look like you need a rest."

Elisabeth opened her eyes. "No thanks. I'm fine."

"Then perhaps you might like a walk in the fresh air? It has been a long and emotional day." After a moment, Derek added, "There is a small garden on the roof of the hotel. I feel that fresh air might help me unwind."

Elisabeth held out her hand and let him help her to her feet. "You might be right. I doubt that I could sleep at the moment."

Derek led the way out of Jim's suite, and guided Elisabeth to the elevator. It came directly up from the ground floor, and when they pressed to go to the roof level, it made no other stops.

The lift opened within a glassed in area, and they walked from there to a sliding door that led out into the garden, where the air was crisp and smelt vaguely of wood smoke and car exhaust. Elisabeth walked to a parapet where she could look down over the lights of the city.

Derek went and stood beside her, saying nothing. When he saw the shoulders of his companion begin to shake he moved one of his hands to cover one of hers, where it gripped the parapet.

"I'm sorry, Derek. I am not good company right now."

He gently drew her around and moved closer. He wiped her tears aside with a gentle finger. "Even the strongest of us, sometimes need to lean on a strength outside our own. There is no shame in that. I will be that strength if you wish."

"I'm not the strong one, Wanda is." Elisabeth wanted to accept Derek's offer, but didn't quite dare.

"You underrate yourself. I think that in these past weeks, it has been you who has kept her strong. And I haven't missed how you helped David to be strong."

Derek pulled her gently closer, ready to draw away if she did not want him so close, but she moved into his offered strength and the threatening storm of silent tears and whole body tremors, broke.

He held her then, saying nothing, just being a safe haven, a source of support, as he would have been for his sisters or nieces.

When the tremors finally eased, he asked, "Is there a reason why you cannot admit that Wanda is your sister?"

He felt her tense, and then relax.

"Everyone thinks she, I mean Gwen Willard, is dead." Elisabeth looked at her companion, having felt that she could trust Derek Mont Pelier to tell no one else that secret.

"Ah, much begins to make sense. When I spoke to your father about her, it seemed that she was only an acquaintance. How does he think of her?"

"They don't meet that often, and they have reconciled. They can meet as strangers, since…it's just better that way."

Derek didn't press for more details. "It occurs to me that Wanda is a survivor."

"She's too damn stubborn to give up, and not too picky about how she keeps going."

"She does what she has to," Derek suggested, with no trace of censure. He too knew what expediency meant. "I think the worthy Austrian jury could not understand her. They would not be able to allow for her odd reaction to drugs."

"I expect that was part of it, but even so, I don't see how they could believe that she had any part of those murders. That Prosecutor didn't even provide a convincing reason. He's based it on her being covered in blood, and her knife being the murder weapon. Hauser made that point clear. They had neither proof of the deed or her intent. They may have dropped the charge to accessory, but even that makes no sense. It implies that she was working with the Russian criminals, but everything else suggests that she was against them."

Elisabeth stopped her tirade abruptly, not sure how this man from Interpol would take her criticism of the local justice system.

"Your faith in Wanda is based on more than that." Derek was fishing for a different kind of answer.

"I know her! She might have done countless criminal things, but she couldn't murder people, just like that, with no reason. She learnt marine tricks to disable people, so she wouldn't have to."

"She has killed," Derek deduced.

Elisabeth said nothing.

"I'm sure there was a compelling reason."

"It's part of something that I am not allowed to talk about. But, once it was so she could survive, and another time it was to prevent someone killing an innocent, and the first time it was a merciful death. Each time though, it is a diabolical shock to her mind."

"And you share it, too," Derek said, understanding.

Elisabeth only nodded.

"And you sensed nothing like that at the time of the murders here?"

"I was in LA."

"Yet you and David came here."

"Wanda and I are close, like twins. We both had the same mother. I just knew she was in trouble."

"And your cousins, did they sense it too?"

"To different degrees, but that awareness we share, I am not meant to discuss that either."

"Then you have my word that it will go no further. However, I am aware that Wanda has an ability to know how people think."

"From when you worked with her before? Wanda didn't tell me anything about that."

"It is enough to say that many good people of my country were cleared of criminal complicity, thanks to her. My brother owes his life to her and David."

"Which brother? Older or younger?"

"Karl. The oldest of us. He is from the first of my father's three marriages. I am from his second."

"He definitely sounds like my Dad," Elisabeth recalled an earlier conversation.

"So then, if Wanda likes to raise hell, what do you do with your time besides get her out of it?"

Derek wondered if he was being too intrusive, but the woman in his arms was not trying to pull away.

"I help Dad. I am sort of his administration assistant when he's at home. Sometimes I go with him to Washington. I gather you must travel around a bit too. So where do you call home?"

"I have a place in Paris, a modest apartment, but as you guessed, I am not there much. However, I am always welcome at home in Weisboden."

Elisabeth suddenly gave a huge yawn. "I think, that as nice as it is here, that I might be able to sleep now."

Derek was quick to release her and offer his arm. Elisabeth blushed at the old fashioned courtesy, but accepted his arm as they travelled to the elevator and down to their separate rooms.

Jim greeted Elisabeth sympathetically next morning, having deduced her sleep had not been restful from her dry reddened eyes.

"Can I take it that our mutual friend has not settled down in her new environment?"

"Jim, you have a way of politely understating things. But I think she was pushing the limits to see how far she could go, and working out a whole lot of anger. They stuck her in a 'time-out' cell, but I am sure that was her intention, although the authority there think they won that round."

Jim chuckled. "I shouldn't laugh, but if she is thinking and calculating, I am not so worried about her."

Elisabeth couldn't stifle a yawn. "I just wish she wouldn't cause trouble for herself. I worry about her."

"Then tell her that when she is intending to cause trouble to keep you out of it. She is not a naïve 15 year old any more. The two of you can block each other, can you not?"

"I can, but I don't want to...just in case, you know?"

"So, she should," was Jim's logical solution.

Elisabeth stood still and concentrated. Finally, she shook her head and said, "The bitch! You were right. She said 'sorry' and then shut me out."

"Good, because after you go get some coffee and food, there are a few things you could do for me."

"What?"

"Go and visit Nicole Wexford. I have heard that the DNA results are finally back, and Donau is going to talk to her later this morning."

"So...what were the results?"

Jim's look was thoughtful, "That there is a greater than 90% chance that the hobo we rescued is Rachel's father – the real Allan Wexford."

"Oh my...." Elisabeth felt sure that she could predict Nicole's reaction. "What was the other thing, Jim?"

"You to talk to your father. I had an idea, it's just an outside chance, but ask him if there is anything he can think of that Nicole's husband might have touched and left finger prints on?"

"O…kay, but if he thought to have their house cleaned so thoroughly, he's likely to have been ultra-careful all along." Elisabeth thought back to the few times that Nicole and her husband had visited. Mostly it had been Christmas and birthdays. "Even presents he gave to Vera, he probably wrapped with gloves on or had someone else wrap for him. Though she couldn't remember him ever wearing gloves. "Can you get fingerprints off paper?"

"Sometimes."

"I know that Vera keeps large scraps of paper to reuse, and lets the little ones play with the rest. And Allan, rather her husband, would always have something big and expensive for Vera. I will get onto that, and I will tell Dad that I intend to stay here for a while. David will probably have told him the rest."

"Let me know what you hear," Jim asked, and added. "After that you could help your cousins do checks on the jurors. Erin has managed to get the list already."

Elisabeth felt much better now that she had something useful to do.

Grant Collier waited for Elisabeth to leave before reporting his own findings to Jim. He had just arrived and was making himself a cup of coffee on the tiny hotplate, when she had arrived.

"I think we are onto something with that gardener. I went through the last lot of calls made at that phonebox, and compared them to the earlier lists. Each time the police have visited there on one pretext or another, he sneaks off as soon as he can to make a call. I have watched him do it four times now, and noted the time. The past three occasions, he called the same mobile number."

"Try and get the records for that number, we might be lucky and get a location. See if you can pal up with him. He might give us a link to Heinrich."

Wanda relished the opportunity to stretch her legs, as she was walked from the time-out cell to the main prison. The tiny cell had only enabled her to take three steps at most in any direction, and she had needed to keep herself active with other exercises.

She knew she was the focus of much covert and overt interest. From the way the more timid souls moved away from her, she knew that her reputation had preceded her. She only just had to stare for a second at them, for them to shrink into themselves. Yet she turned the same dismissive stare on everyone she saw looking at her.

She had decided, even before the shock of the sentence had worn off, that if she was going to be stuck in the prison for years that she wasn't going to endure the position of 'prey', for every longer serving inmate.

By fighting with the guards as soon as she had returned, and when she could during the first week, she had stretched a week in the time-out cell, away from the other inmates, to almost three. Really, though, it had taken very little to provoke the guards.

From the tiny window of that cell, she had returned to observing the prison routine, the guard rounds, the regular routes and the actions of the other inmates.

It also meant that she did not have visiting privileges, which was part of the plan. However, when her sister had told her that Hauser needed to talk to her, she had decided to stop being difficult.

Instead of going to join the outside exercise period, she was taken to the cell she was to share. Her cell mate was to be Josie Baum, but until the woman returned, she did not know who she was. While she waited, Wanda sat on the unused cot and took a casual pose leaning back against the back wall.

Their first meeting came at the end of the exercise period, for word of her appearance had spread. Josie came in, belligerent and determined to dominate her 'green' cellmate.

"I'm in for armed robbery, but I don't need no guns to keep you in line, bitch."

Wanda was ready for her. "Well, if you haven't heard what I am in for, you soon will." She turned her 'dead' seeming eyes, the shuttered eyes, on her new cell mate, and saw the woman stop moving closer. "I don't need guns either."

Now that she saw her cell mate in person, Wanda recognised her.

She was one of the cronies of Bridgette, the self-proclaimed 'top bitch'. That made her a follower, not a leader, and Wanda used that knowledge to manipulate her. She would, as soon as she could, report her feelings about her new cell mate to Bridgette.

In the interim, Wanda made no attempt to initiate friendly conversation, and only listened to her cell mate if she spoke of useful matters, like the jail routine. Even then, she asked no questions and gave no replies. It was Brigitte that she wanted to talk to, and her intention when she did, to force a mutual truce. If she could convince that woman that she was too dangerous to meddle with, that she should be left alone, all the 'lesser' beings would follow suit.

The place chosen for the showdown was the washroom, which Wanda was rostered to clean. She was half way done when the 'committee' entered and surrounded her. She continued her task, sloshing soapy, disinfectant from the mop onto the floor in front of Brigitte's feet, splashing her shins. One of the women standing to her left, deliberately kicked the bucket over. Wanda continued sloshing the mop around, deliberately ignoring the company.

"They will punish you for the mess, Carson." Brigitte told her.

"No doubt," Wanda agreed, amiably. She continued to look where her mop was going. "And I see that you still need your lesbian army to try to deal with me."

Brigitte took a step forward, and raised a solid looking fist at the woman who she saw as being shorter and slighter than her brawny six feet.

Wanda glanced up and warned, "Touch me, bitch, and you will regret it." She stopped mopping and appeared to rest her weight on the mop handle, as if she considered the bigger woman no threat. Yet she was watching the woman getting redder in the face, and was ready to react when the beefy fist lashed out at her. As fast as the jabbing punch had been, Wanda was faster. She was not where the fist was aimed, but Bridgette's stomach was where her kick landed. She had used the mop handle for balance, then discarded it. She watched impassively as Brigitte drew herself up straight again.

"Hold the bitch!"

Two of her cronies moved to obey, but before they could lay

hands on her, Wanda spun and kicked, and both lost their balance.

"Always knew you were a weakling," Wanda taunted her opponent. She was standing in a deceptively docile manner, whilst the taller woman was telegraphing aggression with every muscle.

"What's going on here?"

Wanda had been aware of the guards approaching, and had subtly inched so that she was between Brigitte and the fallen cronies.

"Wolf? Carson? You others?"

No one looked at the guards, Wanda was still watching her opponent.

"Carson, are you still causing trouble?"

The two fallen women were carefully getting to their feet, trying not to become the focus of the guard's attention. Yet, from their position, it seemed that Wanda was standing between them and the aggression of Brigitte Wolf.

The guards reacted as she had predicted. They put an arm lock on Bridgette, told the cronies to clear out and keep their heads down, and Wanda to clean up her mess.

Alone, after Brigitte had been marched off, denying any aggression, Wanda felt pleased enough to grin, but she kept it to herself. Instead she diligently continued to mop the floor using the spilt liquid, rinsed it down the drain holes with clean water and then swabbed the floor dry with mop and wringer. She felt like whistling too, but if she did, the guards might just change their minds about whose idea the confrontation was.

Their next meeting was out in the exercise yard two days later. This time, Brigitte gave her intended victim no warning. She went immediately into a fighting fury, lunging at Wanda from behind, believing that she was unaware of her approach. It was far from the case, for the woman's malevolence was like a storm front.

Wanda timed her defence, which was actually a solid counter offence. She spun and ducked, avoiding the fist to her back and used her opponent's momentum to toss her to the ground. That didn't end the fight, and Wanda had to use every trick she knew to avoid the full extent of the thrashing Brigitte intended to give her. She took damage from Brigitte's beefy fists, enough to show she was the victim, but her opponent was not the winner. She would have lost face by being thrown by a slip of a woman, who was inches shorter than she was.

When the guards finally forced their way through the crowd of cheering onlookers, by wielding batons and hitting those who did not move aside, Wanda was sitting in Brigitte's chest, with her knees on the other woman's arms. She had just finished saying, "If you want to be top bitch here, I don't care. If you want me to admit you are the boss, fine, you're the boss. Now, piss off and leave me alone, or next time you will see what happens when I am not just playing with you."

A baton struck Wanda on the back, when she was not quick enough to obey the demand to get off Wolf. Then she was grabbed and dragged away, and Wolf was dragged to her feet, and she immediately swiped her bloody nose when her arms were freed.

The watchers had quickly dispersed to join those who had wisely stayed away from the fight.

While Wolf was still breathing heavily, and glowering at Wanda, the latter subtly changed her manner, accepting the hand restraints without comment. Her opponent gave a token struggle and then realised that it would not be wise. They were both taken to the room the prison administrator used when he had to discipline any of the inmates.

A report of the affair had already been given to the chief warder, by the time he arrived in the room.

He demanded an explanation from Wolf, and received a tirade of lies from her, but they were disbelieved, for Wanda looked more damaged, and was only a fraction of the mass of Wolf.

In her turn, Wanda looked directly at the Chief Warder, met his gaze and said in a calm and reasonable tone, "I may be stuck in here for a long time, but I am not going to start by being a walkover victim of someone who likes to think she is your second in command. I didn't start that fight, but I sure as hell finished it, and I will do it again if she or anyone else tries that again."

It didn't get her out of trouble; prisoners were not meant to fight each other, and since she didn't let herself get beaten to a pulp, she was just as guilty.

However, whilst Brigitte Wolf got two weeks in the 'time-out' cell, she got one, for admitting she would fight again if attacked again.

It surprised her though, when she was taken from the warden's office, to the infirmary to be fixed up. Wolf was taken directly to the 'time-out' cells.

The difference was probably the amount of blood she had over her. Some was from Brigitte's nose, the rest was from cuts and scratches she had received. She learnt that she had an official visitor, and they didn't like prisoners with blood all over them.

After being stripped down and given a hospital style gown, the duty doctor – one she hadn't seen here before – examined her cuts, sutured one and directed an orderly to clean up the rest.

Wanda endured the process without complaint, there was enough evidence that she was the victim, to be reported back to the warden, and it gave her time to guess who her visitor was. She wasn't expecting her lawyer for another couple of days.

She was given a freshly laundered uniform before being escorted to the visitor's area. This was a different guard from the one who had dragged her in from the yard, but she sensed his heightened alertness, so she guessed that the word was already spreading about how she had taken on the solid Brigitte.

Hauser had his case on the table and was pacing the room when she was led in and secured to the bar on the table. He waited for the guard to retreat before sitting down opposite her. He studied her damaged face and asked, "So did the other end up worse?"

Wanda shrugged. "She gets two weeks on her own. I only get one."

"If I am going to have a chance to successfully appeal your case, Miss Carson, your record so far in here will not help."

"I'm still settling in and I have no intention of being everyone's doormat."

Hauser considered that statement, and made no further reference to the subject.

"I have a number of matters that I wish to discuss with you. The first is that I have the date for your appeal." He told her, and it was still two months away.

Wanda nodded, feeling a surge of hope that was quickly tempered by the realisation that the best he could do was cut down the length of her sentence, not eradicate it.

Hauser then handed her a printed page. She had to stand and lean over the table to read it.

"I want you to read that statement and note down any changes."

Within an instant of beginning to read, Wanda realised the strategy for outsmarting any listeners.

This statement was clearly what her sister recalled of the details she had send her mind to mind about Tatarovich. It was written in American, not German.

Wanda finished reading and reached for the pen Hauser had ready. He had to push it closer, and angle the paper so she could write while her hands were restrained.

"Will I request that you be freed for this?"

"Don't bother, I'll manage." Wanda was already writing quickly, all the other details of that encounter.

Hauser glanced at what she had written, saw it was in American, and simply slipped it into a folder. He passed her a second sheet.

Before she began to read, Hauser spoke softly. "I have obtained a properly notarised statement from the doctors who tested your reaction to certain drugs – however, the tests were done under the name of Martin. How am I to explain that?"

"I…" Wanda began, but stopped when Hauser pointed to the paper.

Wanda read the report from her good friend Dr Wells, and immediately realised that anyone reading it would get the implication that she was a covert American agent. She thought for a moment, recalling the details on both her passports. The Carson one was dated later, but the police knew of both. She wrote at the end, "Clarify my status with Jim P, US Embassy. I changed my name when I went into witness protection." She didn't say what name she'd had, or when it had been changed. She hoped Jim would get her idea.

Then she wrote, "What is the official US reaction to finding that Wexford was being impersonated by a Russian? Is there any evidence that impersonator was the man who returned to the US five years ago?

That was the crux of the problem. If her actions in helping to unmask the imposter was important for US interests, they might decide to give her actions diplomatic sanction. Although that might depend on her being cleared completely of complicity in the two murders.

Hauser glanced at her answer, that one being written in German for his benefit. But made no comment. Instead he shuffled through the papers in a folder and placed another one in front of her.

This one was the report of the DNA tests. It told her that the hobo she had seen caged next to her in the shed was the real Allan Wexford and Rachel's father. Before she could berate herself for not guessing, Hauser passed yet another sheet to her to read. This was a statement from the man who was still recovering from severe burns. It stated that he had seen a woman of her description, caged next to him for a short period, who had told him that she'd had a bad reaction to an illegally administered drug. He admitted tossing her a bottle, and seeing her using the broken shards to free herself. He said he'd passed out before she got out, and then woke up on fire.

There was another slip of paper attached to that one, which was the toxicology report from his admission to the hospital. Wanda, as a trained paramedic, read it and understood it. He had been drugged, it had to have been in the drink, and he'd been drinking heavily for a long time.

Wanda pushed those sheets back, she had nothing to add to them. "Does Nicole know?"

Again Hauser shuffled through papers to find a particular one. This one was written in American, but a translation was held behind it with a paperclip. Someone had questioned Nicole very skilfully. She wondered if it had been Jim, or her sister.

The tone of the answers told Wanda that she had learnt of the deception and was feeling used. Nicole admitted to a number of odd things that she had ignored – the differences between the childhood sweetheart and the man she had married. She had told herself that the intervening years, his experiences, becoming a father, losing his wife, were logical reasons for this. Then there were other things, that she had hidden from friends and relatives that were not so explicable.

His attitude to her, his possessiveness, and desire to dominate her, reflected those of 'The Family'. Aleksei had been smart enough to mimic American attitudes, and modify his own, but only to a point.

Hauser swapped that sheet for another, as Wanda's mind kept working. She read next of the complete lack of prints or any potential sources of DNA in his house outside of LA, and in his business office in downtown LA. The report mentioned a possible set of prints on some wrapping paper at the home of the real Wexford's sister. Though all that could be said of them were that they did not match the prints of any one regularly at the Willard house, and were on some paper that the ersatz Wexford had delivered a gift in. So far there was no match for them in any American fingerprint database, nor in Interpol files. Other police agencies were being queried.

A note, hand written at the bottom of the page, reported finding a set of fingerprints from the real Wexford, who had done a very short stint in the marines; he'd dropped out of basic training. Trouble was, trying to match them to the hobo's burnt hands would be next to impossible.

The stack of pages was getting down. Wanda found her eyes widening when she read the next sheet. Heinrich had been arrested in Germany and was in Interpol custody, pending a return to Austria. He was trying to push through a deal whereby if he gave evidence against Aleksi, aka Allan Wexford, he would have some of the pending criminal charges against him dropped.

"Hope he has better luck than I did," Wanda muttered.

Hauser spoke quietly, "He has already stated that Lunn was already dead when he dragged you in, and that Wexford, as he knew the man, said he would take care of things.

He saw Wanda's spurt of hope and dashed it. "The prosecutor's case against him is very weak. The IT people have been unable to access his files."

Wanda gestured for paper to write on, and he simply turned that report over to the blank back page.

"I had a file of all the passwords from Alpha Prime and the other places. They might not have changed them since they didn't realise I had been in their systems. Get Erin to talk to David."

Hauser asked quietly, "Why didn't you give them these before?"

"The Prosecutor was a double dealing skunk. He didn't deserve them. Anyway, I just remembered that I sent a back up to David."

"Have I met David?"

"He might have been with Jim."

Hauser thought, "Yes, and he is your partner in this?"

"He was my backup, but he was in LA until I was arrested. We communicated by email, and he checked things out for me. He went home when he discovered that my tablet had been stolen. He is my husband."

Hauser's expression went from thoughtful to enlightened. "He was at your trial. Is he still in Austria?"

"No, I told him to go home. Davy needs him." Seeing confusion at the reference, she added. "Davy is my son."

"And you risked all this when you have a son to consider?"

"Don't start trying to analyse my reasons. I was doing a favour for some people that I respect, and I had the skills that were needed."

Hauser sat back. "Very well, it makes little difference. You trust Agent Mont Pelier too, I believe? You've worked together?"

"Yes, and yes. Why?"

"He has a plan that I think he should explain to you. He thinks it will draw out a man named Tatarovich."

"I have expected that bastard to come back," Wanda said softly. "I half thought he was my visitor of today. It was another reason for me to be put in time out."

This time Hauser smiled. "I approve of that reason, if not the other. So, would you be willing to deal with the Prosecutor with these passwords?"

"What's in it for me?"

Hauser's mouth twitched, knowing that she didn't have any faith in the Prosecutor's integrity.

"What would encourage you to be helpful? More privileges in your cell?"

He didn't really know what he expected her to say, but it certainly wasn't, "I am amusing myself just fine at the moment. So, if he wants further help from me, I want an ironclad guarantee that no more charges of any kind will be laid against me, whilst I am in Austria."

Hauser's smile became more noticeable. "What made you say that?"

"Partly because, when he was forced to agree to a reduced sentence for murder, he added all those other charges to force the time in here back up."

"And partly because..." Hauser encouraged her to finish.

"He'll hate the idea like hell," was her next statement, but that was not all of it. "You mentioned Tatarovich. I don't know how much you know about him, but that bastard wants to use me...once I am suitably obedient and respectful. We all hope that won't happen, but it might and I have been down that path before and I am not going there again. As you pointed out, I now have a child to worry about."

"You're afraid of him," Hauser remarked, as if it was an unexpected revelation.

"I'm never afraid," she countered, but then admitted, "No, I can be. I just don't let it show. It tricks people. As for that man, I have some personal scores to settle with him, so if Derek wants me to be bait, I am the best suited for it. He wants me, and he doesn't know that the last bastard who thought he could control me is dead."

Hauser decided that he didn't need to know the details. "I have brought you up to date with everything your friends are doing. Is there anything else you want to add? Anything you need?"

A nebulous idea surfaced. "Yes, this is personal though, if you could speak confidentially to Jim P."

"I can do that."

"Find out if he can get..." she gestured for pen and paper, and wrote down "micro transmitter receiver".

"He'll know what you mean?"

"Yes, he's quick on the uptake. I need to talk to him confidentially."

"He won't be able to come until you are off restrictions," Hauser reminded her.

"That will do," Wanda assured him as she watched him stand up and get ready to leave.

Chapter 14 - New deal

Another benefit of time out was that you could sit on your bunk all day with a blank look on your face, if you wanted to, and no one would come and disturb you, simply for something to do.

Wanda waited for an hour to pass, since being locked up again, before reaching out with her mind for her sister, and when she did, she quickly withdrew. Her sister was occupied, and not alone.

A little while later, she sensed her sister's mind seeking hers.

"Is anything wrong?"

"No, just keeping in touch, since I don't plan to make any more trouble for at least a week. And I have just finished talking to Hauser. Could you let everyone know that I appreciate their efforts?"

"Of course. How are you doing? You seem less twitchy."

"I have been getting most of it out of my system. I just put the queen bitch into time out for two weeks, and sent my lawyer to twist the prosecutor's tail. And, I, um, didn't mean to interrupt you."

"It's okay," Elisabeth forgave her. "I kind of feel mean, having a good time when you are..."

"Where I probably deserve to be," Wanda finished. "And you have every right to be happy. I give you too much grief as it is. I know that you are there for me, for Vera, for a lot of people. If you ask me, it's past time that Vera learnt to manage being pregnant and having kids. Or you should tell your father to stop trying for a dozen. And time I learnt common sense."

"You really don't mind?" Elisabeth persisted.

"Lisbeth, how could I? You deserve a life, and Derek is a good man, and no, I am not match-making. Get to know him, see where it goes, and enjoy the journey."

"He is nice, not like any other man I have been out with."

"Yeah," Wanda agreed, and then hesitated about asking her something. "I suppose, if you and he were, um, talking. That the cousins were discreetly out of the way?"

"Yes, Tanya is helping Erin with a computer search."

"Good, because I need you to ask Jim something, in strict confidence."

'Ok, what?"

"I heard that Erin thought that the judge and some of the jury had been got at."

"We think that, and we are trying to get confirmation. What are you thinking?"

"That it might have been Tatarovich, trying to teach me a lesson."

"Go on..."

"I didn't want to broach this with Tanya listening, but that bastard claimed that he had rescued Ivana, just before she was due to die, and that she was still an ungrateful bitch and was being punished."

"You can't be sure she is still alive," Elizabeth protested.

"I know, and that's why I don't want to raise false hopes. But what do you think of the idea that she might have been set up for a long prison sentence too?"

"You have implied that they repeat their methods...How can we find out?"

"It is a long shot, since the guy could have been lying. But what if there was a way to get a list of all females sentenced in all European jails, from about the date that Tanya arrived, to now?"

"O...kay...assuming we can, and I doubt every jail has old records computerised, how would we know what she looks like? No, I do know. Tanya's father, the first time I met him, said I looked like her. But there could be thousands of women. How can we narrow it down?"

Wanda considered that. "I doubt it would be Russia. If Ivana was found there she would be executed at once, and the bastard wants her to suffer. If I had to guess, I'd suggest France, since he has a false ID there, but it might just as well be one of the countries in what used to be Yugoslavia."

"I will talk to Jim," Elisabeth promised. "Oh, I do hope that she is alive."

"And sane," Wanda added a prayer.

Hauser returned at the end of her week of solitude, with the document from the Prosecutor, granting her immunity from further charges in Austria. Wanda read it carefully, looking for loop holes, and when she was satisfied, she asked, "When does he want me?"

"Yesterday week, as you no doubt have already guessed. I have to admit to feeling quite pleased about winning this concession."

"I hope that defending me hasn't lowered your reputation."

"I am quite satisfied with my reputation," Hauser admitted. "However, I need to know how to get those passwords and how to use them."

"You don't need to know. I just need to have a computer with access to the internet and the decryption program that should be on the hard drive with the stuff I gave them. As to how to use them, I am sure they ought to be able to figure it out."

"It seems not, the police experts have had no success."

"I didn't think I was that much of an expert," Wanda said aloud. She wasn't but her cousin Erin was.

"I'll tell you what. I believe that there is a marine Private, stationed here in Vienna who is good at IT stuff. I will work with him, to show them how I did it."

Wanda said 'him' deliberately to mislead any listeners.

"I will make the request. Is there anything you need to bring from here with you?"

"Are you kidding? I wouldn't keep anything I value in this place."

"Come on then. Inspector Donau is waiting to escort you."

They must have organised everything before Hauser spoke to her. She was freed from the table and escorted downstairs and out to the van that was to take her to the police building.

As soon as the van doors opened at their destination, Donau and Alex were there, waiting. The dog woofed a greeting and ambled forward to lick her hands.

"So why did they make you come to get me?" Wanda asked by way of a greeting.

"I said that you had helped me before and might be disposed to do so again," Donau explained as he led her to the elevator and sent it up to the fifth floor. Even though the four guards from the prison followed them, she told Donau, "You're game. Last time I helped you, you ended up with concussion and might have died."

"Well if the person who hit me then is waiting to try again, we'll be ready."

Wanda glanced around, looking for the 'we' he mentioned. She was sure he wasn't meaning her, but if there were any more police around, she couldn't see them, but she did notice more security cameras than were in place the last time she was here.

A group of people awaited her. The Prosecutor glanced her way and then seemed to ignore her, but he was nursing a deep antipathy towards her. There were several business suited men, several police officers, but Wanda's eyes went straight to meet those of her cousin Erin who was looking capable and efficient in a borrowed Marine uniform. She had a laptop computer opened in front of her, and was pretending to be busy with it. Except for that initial glance, they would be acting like strangers.

Hauser hovered near her, but Donau pulled up a chair, further away near where the prosecutor was sitting, to listen to the proceedings. Wanda wasn't sure if either Hauser or Donau knew Erin, but if they did, neither were showing it.

The suit clad men kept their attention on Erin and her computer, and Wanda soon deduced that they were lawyers acting on behalf of some of the cartel members – the ones that hadn't fled. They were apprehensive, rather than hostile, as if wishing that no more evidence would be revealed against their clients.

Wanda was told to explain to the 'marine expert' what she had done to 'hack' into the computer systems. She in turn demanded to know why the men the lawyers represented, couldn't just tell the police how to get in anyway. None of the officials deigned to tell her, but Erin's mind revealed that the accused refused to cooperate and the police had obtained the warrants.

For the sake of being perverse, Wanda explained to her cousin that she had used the program Erin herself had given her, but spoke so no one else heard. She told Erin the passwords she had used to get into the computer of the boss and the PA of the first business she was asked about.

Erin playing the role of no nonsense marine with a job to do, nodded as if listening to a long winded explanation, asked questions unrelated to the supposed topic, and finally commented, just loud enough to be heard, the misleading, "Amazing, that wouldn't work unless you had a damn good memory."

Wanda intentionally smirked, and leant back away from her cousin and waited for her next command. By her body language, and the way she stared at the Prosecutor, she intended to irritate him, even as she was scrupulously following instructions and producing the agreed information. It seemed to be having more effect than she expected. The idea flitted through her head that he was acting as if he thought she knew he had a guilty secret, and she amused herself by thinking that she did. She knew he was an idiot if he believed her guilty.

Erin went to work, connecting to the first of the confiscated hard drives that were, for this session, networked to her laptop. It wasn't completely straightforward, the password got her part way in, but there were files that still wouldn't open, ones that Wanda hadn't tried to access. And, without letting on what she was doing, Erin used her 'quick and dirty' hack program to get in, so that it would seem Wanda had given her all she needed.

As soon as Erin announced, "I'm in," Donau rose and admitted one of the task force officers and the laptop was temporarily taken from Erin's control.

Wanda didn't care what the police did then, and while leaning back, switched her gaze from the prosecutor, to Erin, and asked, "So what did they bribe you with to do this?"

Her tone implied that no one should do favours for the Prosecutor, and that man seemed to guess she was obliquely referring to him, but her words were just innocuous enough that he could make no accusation.

Erin kept her attention on the man with her computer, and pretended to ignore the question. But her head scratch gesture was a hint for Wanda to read what she was thinking.

Wanda shrugged as if giving up trying small talk, and went back to staring, this time blank faced, at the prosecutor.

"I am extra protection for you," Erin was thinking.

The contact was much clearer than usual for when they weren't in direct physical contact. Wanda decided that it was the presence of the warm furry body between their legs.

Erin went on thinking, "If our so called grandfather tries anything, and if your reading of 'The Family' is correct, they don't expect much from women."

"He knows how good I am as a thief and wants to use me."

"And he probably considers you a freak," Erin thought. "But he won't be expecting two women who know how to fight. I took a leaf out of your book and learnt advanced unarmed tactics."

Wanda drummed her fingers on the table as if bored, and although she didn't actually think it, Erin was sensitive enough as an empath to pick up her resentment at needing protection. Aloud, she said, "Can we get on with this?"

The expected censure came from the Prosecutor, "Are you in such a hurry to go back to your cell, Carson? We could have saved you all this trouble if you had told us all this weeks ago."

"No one asked," Wanda said off-handedly. "And I wouldn't have got any credit for it, then. Besides, how was I to know I knew more than the best police experts?"

She had scored a point, she knew for the Prosecutor scowled.

Hauser leant over and whispered a warning in her ear. She slumped a little in her seat and went back to her game of staring.

When the computer was returned to Erin, she briskly checked a list beside her and asked for information on the next company listed there.

Wanda knew it was a trick question. "Lunn Imports and Exports was not included in my earlier information."

"And why was that Carson," the Prosecutor stood up and wandered to where he could give her his courtroom stare. "Are you saying that you failed to get into their computers? Or are you protecting someone?"

"That's a really stupid thing to say. Me? Protecting Lunn? When you did your damnedest to convict me of killing him? Which is it? Or don't you believe I really did kill him?"

"Answer my question!"

"I did. But if you mean the first part, yes, I am saying that I didn't get access to his records. The bastard operated his business from a laptop. His office only has a connection for the phone line, not for a computer. So don't expect miracles if the Austrian police can't find his computer."

Erin tactfully interrupted with the name of the next business. As Wanda switched her gaze back to Erin, she caught the faintest trace of a smile on Donau's face.

"KnV5467-omega" Wanda said blandly.

Everyone who heard her seemed ignorant of why she had rattled off random numbers, but Erin knew it was the next password, and set to work. When she had access, the previous procedure was repeated.

During that break, Wanda wondered which other companies were on the list beside her cousin. She thought her question to Erin, and the answer was sent by Erin seeming to study the sheet.

"Small fry," was her mental judgement, and she wondered why they weren't' trying for the bigger fish first. Then she asked Erin, "Do you know what the police are doing once you get access to the drive?"

"Looking," Erin thought. "I am using the confiscated hard drives, to help trick the server at the company itself. They are looking for further evidence, further culprits. Whatever. Does it matter?"

Wanda shrugged and turned it into a movement of easing her back and shoulders. She sat up straighter and thought at her cousin, "What do you make of the Prosecutor. He's really staring daggers at me."

Erin glanced past the man, and seemed to be watching the policeman using her computer.

After a while, she thought, "Well, he dislikes you, intensely – no surprise there. You have been subtly riling him since you came in."

"He disliked me the instant he set eyes on me."

"Well it's sort of like he thinks you are hiding evil behind a bland façade," Erin tried to explain what she sensed. "He thinks you are as guilty as hell…"

"Of murder?"

"I can't tell if it's that…"

Wanda concentrated on one name, "Wessler?"

"I think he was friends with him, same social circle…"

"Tatarovich?"

"No reaction."

"Theo?"

"I think he thinks you are one of his people, and he dislikes foreign criminals."

Wanda tried one more name. "Derek Mont Pelier."

"Oh yeah, that hit a nerve. He doesn't like the idea of Interpol interfering with you – undermines his authority, and he can do zip about it."

"Authority or credibility?"

Erin had to turn her attention back to her computer and the next part of her task, working more slowly than before because Wanda was still thinking at her.

"Do you know why only some of the business I looked at are represented here?"

"No, maybe we will find out when this lot is done."

Wanda's attention was suddenly riveted on the Prosecutor. She had heard the faint music of mobile phone ring tone, and the man had stood up and walked away from the group. She had been studying his body language while giving him misleading signals about her own. He had been tense before, now he was positively rigid. She focussed her hearing in his direction and ignored the nearer conversations, tried to read his mind, but there were too many others nearby. All she heard was, "I will have to call you back."

Wanda lifted one foot over Alex's bulk, and gently nudged Erin, their eyes met for an instant and then Wanda looked at the Prosecutor. She looked that way and saw the man pocketing the phone.

"He had a call…" Wanda explained.

"He's highly agitated," Erin confirmed. "Can you send to Elizabeth or Tanya from here?"

Wanda caught on at once, and put all her concentration into reaching her sister, and giving her the situation in a few terse sentences. She felt what she had seen was important, and hoped Elizabeth could get to Jim and he could do something to find out what the call was about.

After the fourth revelation Hauser drew closer and Erin moved aside to give him room.

"After these businesses have their websites opened up, the Prosecutor is intending to call a recess. Mont Pelier wants you to authorise David to send the password file to Donau so that the task can be finished."

"Okay...what's up? I do that, they don't need me."

"That call...the prosecutor received, it told him that his family has been abducted. He has to let you be taken, or his family will be killed."

"And, everyone is going to let that happen?" Wanda asked.

Hauser leant closer, "Put your hands under the table. We are expecting an attack aimed at getting you."

Wanda felt Erin pressing two hard, beadlike objects into her hand.

Hauser went on. "The round one goes in your ear, the capsule one is for you to swallow."

"Is this legal?"

Hauser nodded. "The Prosecutor alerted selected police to the threats he received. Since you have been in prison, a lot of things have been going on, that we could not tell you, but this meeting was arranged to draw certain people out into the open. Mont Pelier said you had agreed."

"Tatarovich," Wanda hissed, and Hauser nodded as the Prosecutor spoke.

"Let's keep this moving."

Erin resumed her place, and Wanda idly scratched her ear, and pressed the tiny radio receiver in as if it were an earbud. She had used these before.

"Am I allowed to have a glass of water?" she asked the assembly.

The Prosecutor merely said, "We will be having a break soon, Carson, and you can get a drink then."

When he finally stopped staring at her, to try to convince her of his authority, Wanda managed to slip the capsule into her mouth, and after sucking it for a bit, had enough saliva in her mouth to swallow it. This she knew was a tiny locator beacon.

After giving Erin the next password, Wanda heard a soft voice in her ear.

She recognised Jim's voice with a surge of relief.

His first words were, "If you can hear me, think at Elisabeth."

Once the odd communication was confirmed, she heard Jim's voice again. "Tatarovitch is convinced that he needs you to work for him and that his very life depends upon getting you on his side."

Wanda didn't ask how that belief had come into being, or how Jim had convinced him. "He has been sending threats to the Prosecutor for a while, but so far, what he was demanding has not gone against his core beliefs. He truly believed that you were guilty on all counts. However, having successfully convicted you, even if not on all counts, he has no desire to have a murderer go free. Yet, that is what he feels this threatener wants, and why his family is now hostage."

Wanda glanced at the Prosecutor, and for the first time felt something like sympathy for him.

The explanation continued, "Tatarovich believes that some files that you might access, could cause trouble for 'The Family'. He also craves the diamonds that you stole which are not being released to him. Rightly I may add. He wants them back and he wants information about them."

Through Elisabeth, she confirmed that she understood, but reminded him that, "I don't know anything about them, really – and I can't tell him my suspicions of their origin."

"That's for later," Jim brushed that aside. "He knows where you are and what you are doing, and like I said, the Prosecutor is working with us on this. The scene is to look like the police no longer think you are important or likely to escape."

Wanda interrupted through Elisabeth. "I am innocent of murder and still sentenced to 25 years, of course I want to escape."

"Exactly, and you are currently lulling any official suspicions by being good until the appeal."

"Ok, I agreed to this, so how grateful do I need to be to Tatarovich?"

"Up to you, just don't give him a reason to want to kill you."

Wanda sent to Elisabeth, "Wait a sec," when she had to give Erin some more information. Jim continued when she sent, "Go on."

"Tatrovich is acting on two needs. He wants your outstanding criminal skills, and he doesn't want you to access Heinrich's or Lowenbach's computers. He believes they have files on Theo and Aleksei with information that might lead to their hiding place – which I'm sure he knows. We want that information."

Wanda sent back, "And I want to know what he did with Ivana."

Jim went on, "We expect him, using Theo's muscle boys, to act when the break is on, since they expect you to need to use the ladies room."

"Dangerously predictable, considering I am nearly bursting already," Wanda admitted wryly.

"It works in our favour, since no one will think it odd, and he knows to expect it. And since he will be in a hurry, if you and Erin are tied together, they will have to take you both. She has some stuff to give you."

"Is that all?"

"For now," Jim confirmed.

When the Prosecutor called the recess, Wanda announced that she needed to use the ladies room. He looked like he wanted to deny her that privilege, but said, "Private Rand, do you think you can handle Carson if she tries anything?"

Erin gave a crisp, confident assurance, and Donau moved over and released one of Wanda's wrists and fastened the free restraint to Erin's wrist. He followed them from the room and watched the two prison guards, who had been lounging in the corridor, straighten up and follow the two women.

Wanda gave the guards a quick glance over her shoulder. It was all she needed, and she noted that these two men were not the two guards who had brought her to the prison. She assumed there had been a change of shift. She was alert for trouble, and in a gesture intended to make people think she resented her marine private escort, she moved further away from Erin. However, if there was to be an attack, it gave them both more room to move.

In an unusual move, the two guards followed them into the ladies room, and ordered two women who were just drying their hands to get out. Neither bothered to do more than throw the paper towel in the bin before leaving in a hurry.

They let the women enter a cubicle together, and in seconds, Erin unlocked the cuffs so that Wanda could do what she needed, while she leant against the door, taking things from under her dress tunic. The sound of water going into the bowl, hid the other furtive sounds.

Wanda removed her prison issue cardigan and scrunched it into a ball behind the bowl. Erin handed her a piece of synthetic skin, with a key and some metal wire pieces. The skin, she quickly stuck to the inside of her left thigh, while she made rude comments to Erin, for the guards to hear. While she was fixing her clothing, straightening the prison frock, the guards insisted that she hurry up, and Erin refastened the wrist restraint. They met each other's gaze and nodded. They were ready for the ambush.

Wanda studied the two guards as they emerged from the cubicle and went to wash their hands. She could see nothing wrong with the uniforms, or the body language. Still, Tatarovich had once had at least one guard in his pay.

She wondered if these men were part of Tatarovich's plot, as they gestured her out and told her to hurry. When Erin turned to head back to the meeting room, they were each grabbed by a guard and hustled in the opposite direction.

Wanda sent a thought to her sister, as Erin, acting the 'official escort' called out, "Hey, what are you doing?"

The man who held her, used his free hand to cuff her in the mouth. "Shut up or we shoot you," was the warning in German, but with a faint Russian accent.

A head poked out of a nearby office, but the sight of the guns waving about sent the man back inside. The guards hurried their pace to the stairs and started up, willing to drag their prisoners if they did not walk fast enough.

Behind them, Donau called an alarm, and began to run after them, Alex streaking ahead, ignoring Donau's command to heel.

One of the guards took a wild shot behind them, and continued to hurry towards the roof. He took a second shot at Alex when he came into sight. Wanda glanced back, wished Alex would keep out of harm's way, heard him growl.

Once out on the roof, one guard continued to drag the prisoners, the other quickly jammed a piece of metal under the bar that opened the door. Erin pulled on the wrist restraints to get her cousins attention. A police helicopter had its motor idling, two police offers were unconscious on the ground, and a masked man had a gun to the pilot's head.

They were lifted and thrown into the back of the helicopter, as loud banging began on the jammed door. Just as the side door shut, Wanda had a glimpse of Donau, and of Alex streaking across the roof. The helicopter lifted abruptly, leaving Alex impotently barking below them.

"Hey! Get these cuffs off," Wanda demanded. The guard was braced against the inner wall, and still covering them with his gun.

"Shut up, bitch."

"Hey, you took me out of that hole, so why do I have to stay tethered to a weight?"

This time, Wanda was the recipient of the vicious cuff across the face.

"We were told to get you, not let you go."

"Did you forget to grab the key then?"

Wanda received another equally violent swat.

Erin was thinking hard of one idea, hoping Wanda would pick up on it. "Don't provoke them any further."

She thought back, "I had already decided that. I think they know I am not cowed and frightened."

Erin's return thought was, "No, that's my role for now."

Both women subsided, huddling in the small luggage space behind the passenger seats. Wanda continued to stare at the guard that still had a gun aimed at them. Erin was trembling, her eyes also on the guard.

Her mind was telling Wanda that the man would kill them like bugs and not feel a qualm.

"Easy does it," Wanda thought calmly. "Between us, we will know when to act. We can let them think they are in control for now. They won't shoot us in the helicopter, for risk of damaging something."

"You're right," Erin's mind admitted. "I have been trained to handle all kinds of situations, but they haven't been for real yet."

"They don't know what they have picked up! You and I are the best suited for this. I wouldn't want Tanya or Elisabeth in this position. And I have no intention of letting Tatarovich have what he wants."

A buzzer began to sound, Wanda knew it was a warning – something was wrong with the helicopter. She glanced at Erin, sharing a moment of panic, then she heard a voice in her ear. The message reassured her and she thought at Erin. "There's no problem, Jim says they wanted to keep this close to Vienna. Just look scared."

The guard who was standing twisted to look down through the side window. "Land down there!" He pointed to the side.

The pilot made the helicopter circle the area of cleared land, and said calmly, "That should do."

Once again, Wanda heard Jim's voice. "They have the helicopter located. The nearest police units are on the way. Do nothing until Tatarovich comes. Tell us if you get moved onwards."

Wanda nudged Erin and passed the information on.

They could do nothing to help the pilot, once he had landed. The man who had held the gun on him had used the butt of it to knock him out. That one, with his face mostly covered, turned his cold eyes on the two prisoners while the other two guards hopped out and went towards the farmhouse that was only a hundred yards away.

After what seemed like an hour, during which Wanda had heard a faint scream that had cut off suddenly, the guards returned driving an old truck with a high canvas covered load bed. They stopped near the helicopter and came over.

As Wanda and Erin were hustled out, they saw the masked gunman trussing up the pilot. They had little chance to see more for they were forced to climb into the back of the truck.

The truck took off, carefully at first, for the ground in the paddock was soft. When they reached the road, it speeded up, but by then, Wanda had sent Jim details, via Elisabeth, of the vehicle's description and the part of the licence plate she had glimpsed. She also mentioned the state of the pilot and her fears for the family that lived in the farm house.

Erin kept track of the time as they travelled. After half an hour, the traffic noises had increased, suggesting they were nearing a town. Wanda recalled the map of the area around Vienna, and decided they were most likely returning to the city.

Jim confirmed her guess, making use of the tracking bead she had swallowed.

The truck slowed and made several turns in reasonably quick succession. The last stretch of road was rough, like it was cobblestoned, and then the truck stopped, and a noise like a garage door going up tormented their ears. Before it stopped, the truck moved into a building and the engine noise bounced off solid walls. The mechanical screeching halted and then started again.

The two guards in the back hopped out and a short conversation in Russian took place. Wanda translated for Erin.

"They called Tatarovich, before we came back here. He should be here soon. They will probably separate us, since I am the one they want."

She edged carefully towards the back of the truck, to try and see where they were. There was only a narrow slit in the canvas covering and all she could see was some piles of boxes, and chains hanging down from an overhead gantry. Some kind of warehouse, she guessed.

A new noise alerted her to the arrival of another vehicle. The engine hummed, suggesting a car. The engine stopped, doors opened and closed with a genteel thunk. More voices, a mention of, "in the truck" and "had to bring the other one, the woman guard."

"Get them out."

Wanda whispered, "That was him." She was still peeking through the gap, when the canvas was suddenly whisked aside. She took a step back as a slender man with his face masked, leapt up onto the rear fender, and almost walked into her. This wasn't the man who had terrorised the police pilot. That man had been more solidly built. This one moved with almost feline grace and balance.

He grabbed the wrist which was in the restraint, and his grip was like a vice, though he didn't feel like he was trying to break her wrist. He had the handcuff opened in a mere second.

"Get out and do not try to run."

A second masked man was standing a short way from the back of the truck with a gun aimed her way. Wanda moved with deliberate slowness, giving herself time to glance around as if assessing her chances of escape. She counted six men: Tatarovich, the gunman, the two fake prison guards, the man that had released her and another like him terms of the grace of movement. There might be more outside, or out of sight.

Erin dropped down beside her, but Tatarovich merely gave a dismissive flick of his hand. One of the fake prison guards grabbed her and began to drag her away. In spite of her marine uniform, he was seeing only that she was female, and assumed that his greater bulk was sufficient advantage to keep her under control.

Wanda glanced up and saw walkways high up towards the roof. An idea was already forming, of how she could keep all attention off Erin.

"You aren't going to be able to get away," Tatarovich told her.

Wanda ignored him, waiting for a moment's distraction to act. It came when the door next to the roller door opened and two more masked men trotted in, and headed for Tatarovich. She began to move, but the tall agile man grabbed her. She made no sound when he squeezed her arm, but he gave a quiet grunt when Wanda twisted and broke his grip, and kicked him in the stomach. She was running for the dangling chain and was only noticed when it rattled as she climbed.

It was a risk, but she did not think they would shoot. A gunshot would be heard and bring the police.

She felt the chain tighten as someone began to climb up after her. She didn't look down, but climbed faster and reached the walk way. From there she could see that the building was bigger than it had seemed from near the truck. Wooden partitions separated storage areas. She had a glimpse of Erin being hustled towards the back of the building, and the second of the slender masked figures running below her, and glancing up. She lost sight of him behind one of the partitions, just as she sensed Erin's satisfaction. In her mind was the knowledge, "One down," and the sense of her dragging the unconscious man out of sight.

She saw another man approaching from the rear, and sent her cousin a warning. Then she needed to watch what she was doing, for a dark shadow had reached the catwalk ahead of her, and was blocking her way. She spun around, but her original pursuer was between her and the nearest cross walk. Wanda was aware that a second gantry chain was dangling down just beyond the newcomer, and before they moved in on her, she began a sprint towards it, twisting and somersaulting – catching the chain to stop her fall.

Above her, the two men cursed in Russian. They were fast though. One clambered down the chain after her, the other threw something up at the roof. There was a small explosive thud, and a thin looking rope fell down beside Wanda, and the man seemed to slide down it. She kicked out at him, but he laughed.

"Look down, little girl, there is a big shark waiting for you."

Wanda didn't have to. She felt the malevolence of Tatarovich rising like the flume of a volcano. And if she had been trying in earnest to escape, she would have been out of options. Her feet reached the floor and she was grabbed by the rope climber. Moments later, the other man grabbed her other arm.

Tatarovitch walked up and glared down at her. "That was an incredibly stupid move – trying to escape from me."

Wanda spat at him, raising his anger even further. Other men were forming a circle around them, and were watching avidly. Tatarovich hit her across the face, but she had expected that and rolled with the blow, reducing its force.

"I owe you nothing! I didn't ask to be brought here..." Her defiant words brought a second blow.

"I got you out of prison, you ungrateful bitch. Or did you really want to stay there for twenty five years?"

Wanda squirmed in the iron grip of her minders, as if not wanting to admit he was right. "My lawyer is going to appeal."

"And you may have ten years knocked off your time. Fifteen years is still a long time."

Wanda threw herself forward as if trying to attack Tatarovich. He stood his ground, and her captors wrenched her arms. "Who says I couldn't have escaped by myself?" she shouted. "I can climb even better than your pet monkeys here."

"You are an undisciplined brat." Tatarovich stared at her coldly.

Wanda stared back. "Undisciplined, huh? I didn't get good enough to infiltrate Alpha Prime by being lucky." Somewhere nearby, was the sound of a scuffle, and Tatarovich turned to listen and gestured to one of the circle to check the noise. When he turned back, his voice was controlled, but had a deadly edge to it.

"No, someone taught you well. Who was it?"

His sharp question didn't force her to talk. It seemed like he had tried to command her, but he didn't have the talent needed to do it properly.

"If you know so much about me, you tell me," Wanda challenged, hoping he'd inadvertently reveal something.

"I will find out," he said with assurance. "I suppose it was the same person who told you about the diamonds at Alpha Prime."

"You have no idea, old man. None at all." Wanda knew he would not believe she had known nothing of them until she was there, or how they had called to her.

Wanda was aware of the two men holding her. They were not looking at her, or at Tatarovich, and might have been statues. Unlike the other onlookers, it seemed they didn't want to draw attention to themselves.

As Tatarovitch stared at her once more, eyes glittering with his anger, Wanda was aware that Erin had taken out a third man.

"You will learn respect. You will obey me."

Wanda felt herself shiver. She had no doubt that he believed he had ways to do that. But her reaction to threats, was to betray no fear. He had seen that shiver, so she said, "You expect me to respect you? When you didn't give a damn about my mother, or me? Now you are interested because you know I am a damn sight better than your monkeys here."

"I saved your mother from death."

"So you claim, but I don't believe you. And if you did save her, it was only so you could torment her even more. I reckon you set her up in the first place, convinced everyone that she was a traitor and a spy. I bet you did the same to me."

"Maybe I did do all that." Tatarovich's smile was evil. "Your mother is still alive. I can take you to her."

"You're lying! She's dead!"

"I will prove it to you, if you work for me."

Wanda had no intention of working for him, but to say so would be a death sentence. Tatarovich took her silence as a refusal to admit that she wanted what he offered. He dropped that subject, and switched to another.

"Why did you come to Vienna and how did you get to be working for the American Government?"

This was something that the man really wanted to know, and possibly another way he wanted to use her.

Still defiant, Wanda said, "What's the big deal? I could speak German and I needed to earn some good will points."

"The big deal, my dear grandchild, is that you interfered in Family business, and negated many years of planning, and many lucrative plans."

"And I was to know that how?"

Wanda thought intensely at her sister. "Lisbeth, how soon will help be here? This creep is getting very intense."

Like a snake striking at prey, Tatarovich shot his arm towards her and his hand gripped her by the throat. "Useless trash."

Wanda felt her airway being constricted, and turned her mental attention to him. She stared at his eyes and thought, "You will not kill me."

"Hugo, bring something to tie this trash up." He didn't break eye contact, and Wanda refused to let herself black out.

The two men gripping her arms, released her to apply tape to her wrists and feet. She did not try to wriggle free, but did try to keep her hands away from those trying to bind them.

Chapter 16 - Turning the tables

Aware of the situation that Wanda was in, Erin sought a way to create a diversion. She succeeded in pushing a crate off the top of a pile, near the rear door.

Tatarovich spun around, releasing his victim, and sending his men to investigate. In that instant, Wanda reacted, taking the two men nearest her by surprise. She kicked one in the groin, and the other in the knees. The first bent over, groaning, the second fell, but gave a warning. She didn't get far, for the man on the ground caught her ankle and Tatarovich turned and touched a small pistol to her head.

"Hurry up, Leo. This bitch your sister spawned is nothing but trouble. We will toss her in the garbage where she belongs, and if the police don't find her, the rats will."

Leo uncurled from the near fetal position and obeyed the command. He was still in agony, but it seemed that he did not dare disobey.

Wanda felt the gun press harder on her forehead, and saw the finger that was twitching on the trigger. She didn't need to read his mind to know that he was considering simply killing her.

A thought came into her mind and she spoke without thinking. "If you kill me, you will never know the secret of those diamonds."

The hand with the gun went rigid. "Tell me!"

Wanda saw one of the fake prison guards run into the edge of the doorway from the rear, and stumble into the room.

"Master Pietr, there are police all around here."

Tatarovich kicked Wanda's legs from under her, then lowered his gun and tucked it back under his jacket.

"Leo, Stephan, get going! Hugo, dump this trash down the chute. The police can have her. When you've done that, come after me. The rest of you, secure the doors, and go out via the cellar and disperse."

When Tatarovich strode off, Wanda began to struggle in earnest.

She sent a warning to her sister, that the police had been spotted and they were going to escape via a cellar. She didn't specifically say to her sister where she was, or what they planned for her, but she didn't need to. When she was desperate, as now, she received anyway.

Hugo was solid and strong, he tossed her on his shoulder and ignored her attempts to get free. Yet he still under estimated her, for when her cousins and sister joined their will to hers, the force of her command tone was irresistible.

"Put me down!"

The man obeyed without a thought, dropping her from his shoulder. He turned to her in confusion.

"Cut me loose!"

He drew a knife and immediately cut the tape on her wrists and feet.

"Go! Run! You have done what you were told to!"

Giving her one last look of confusion, he dropped his knife, turned and headed for the back door of the warehouse – the way Tatarovich had gone.

She headed that way, thinking at Erin, "Where are you?"

Erin was down near the river, having followed Tatarovitch along a tunnel that had originated in some kind of office near the back door.

"Did you see the rest of these rats?" Wanda sent the question.

"No, they were rushing around securing metal shutters on the windows and pushing steel sheets across the doors. Their leader didn't wait for them."

"So where did he go?"

"Some kind of bunker. If I didn't see where he disappeared, I would never have found the door."

Wanda heard Jim's voice in her ear, warning her that he police were around the building and about to move in.

"Erin, can you see the police cordon?"

"No, I'd say I'm well outside of it."

"Keep out of sight, try to keep an eye on the spot he disappeared."

"What will you do?"

"I'm coming out to meet you."

Wanda had every intention of confronting Tatarovitch again, but on her terms. That meant, she did not want to be in the warehouse when the police broke in. She would be instantly taken into custody.

She was heading for the tunnel Erin mentioned when she heard the sounds of some kind on ram assaulting all of the doors at the same time. When that failed, they would probably bash a hole in the wall of the building, or come in the roof. However they got in, it would be soon, and they may already know of the tunnels. She needed another way out....and thought of the garbage chute.

That wasn't hard to find. It was a hole in the rear wall, with a sliding door closing it off.

She pulled at the door and examined the metal surface, wondering what was usually tossed down there. It would act like a slide, and if she had been the helpless bundle Tatarovitch had intended, she would have had no way to slow her momentum. She wasn't helpless now.

Racing back to where she'd removed the adhesive tape, she grabbed all the bits she could, and returned to the chute. Before she climbed in, she wrapped some of the stuff around her prison issue shoes, with the sticky side out. The last pieces, she wrapped around her hands. She didn't care if it picked up dust and dirt, only that it helped her control her slide.

She stepped up and put her head and arms in first, just as she heard shouts front the front of the building. There was no time left to think, she pushed off with her feet.

The slide seemed to go on forever; with plenty of time to consider the possible dumping points. It was aimed at the river, and Wanda expected to shoot out into it, if she could not control her descent. But her taped hands were indeed slowing the slide, and she had some warning of the approaching opening, as a breeze began to cool her face. When the side of the chute ended abruptly, there was just enough light coming through a dense clump of trees, to see the chains holding the partly raised wooden flap at the end. She grabbed at them and held tight.

Her body was jarred by the sudden stop, and her head was dangling in mid-air, her feet still in the chute. A glance down, at the source of a foul smell, showed her the rubbish skip that was placed on a narrow wooden jetty that jutted into the river.

"Not today," Wanda told herself. Down was where her despised grandfather hoped she'd end up. She couldn't tell what was in the skip already, but an uncontrolled fall into the metal construction – if it didn't cause her to break something, would certainly cause cuts or grazes, and who knew what germs were breeding down there.

She kept hold of the chains as she eased her feet from the chute so they dangled over the skip. Then, swinging her body like she was on a trapeze swing, she swung out and dropped beyond the skip on the river side. She felt the jar of impact, but the wooden planks were old and gave a little, deadening some of the force.

Once she had eased her way around the skip, and reached the bank, she thought at Erin.

"I'm out. Where are you?"

In response, she heard a faint whistle. It was enough to give her direction, and she moved to her right along the sloping bank, forcing her way through thick underbrush.

As she was concentrating on placing her feet carefully, so as not to catch them on some hidden tree roots, she felt her sister. "Where are you? Jim has just been told the place is empty."

"By the river, but say nothing. I know where the bastard has gone to ground, and I plan on having a talk with him."

She knew Elisabeth had picked up on the type of talk she intended, but would not try to talk her out of it, or tell anyone her plan.

Erin was relieved to see her emerge into a tiny clearing, when a small amount of sun penetrated. She hid her apprehension by teasing, in a whisper, "What have you been crawling through?"

Wanda glanced down at her orange dress, and her legs. "I came down the garbage chute. It looked clean enough at the top. Then I slipped a couple of times on the bank. At least I didn't land in the skip. It smelt like it hadn't been emptied for months."

"You smell a bit," Erin warned. "How will you sneak up on him?"

"Where is he?"

Erin gestured to a group of trees. "There's a dirt mound just behind them, and the door has a coating of it, complete with growing weeds. There is a ring sticking out of it, and when you pull on it that bit lifts up. The joints are well oiled. Underneath that is a solid metal door, with a very modern looking lock."

"How close behind him were you?"

"He was in too much of hurry to get in, and too sure no one saw him get out, to see me. I was just back behind the tree here."

"What about cameras?"

Erin chuckled softly and pulled a device from her pocket. "He will think the connections are corroded."

Wanda recognised the jamming device and grinned. "They were breaking in when I did my slide, so we don't have a lot of time. I'll look at the lock, but I don't think that is the way I want to go in. I bet there is a back door, and a ventilation shaft. I'll have a look."

When she returned, she filled Erin in. "The back door is close to the river. There is only a very narrow section of the bank there. It looks like it collapsed there. The door is wood, still fairly solid, but the lock is an older type. The ventilation shaft is too narrow, even for me. Did you say you had some tools for me?"

As an answer Erin untucked her uniform and removed a wide linen belt.

"A gather that the police don't know about this?" Wanda spoke in a whisper as she opened the flap and found exactly what she needed, and made a mental note to thank Jim Phillips. Erin confirmed her guess and added, "I think Derek might, though. How are you planning to do this?"

"Like a sortie into enemy territory. I hope that he does not expect anyone to approach from the river, and I don't know if he has weapons in there or even if he is definitely alone. I will get that back door open, and we will sneak in."

"Do you always go in with so little preparation?"

"I am more than prepared. He's on the defensive now, I'm not. However, do you remember that little trick, of thinking 'Don't let anyone see me'? Now is a very good time for that."

"What if I project danger from the door he entered?"

"Maybe more of, needing to listen out for pursuit at that door? That danger will come from that direction. I don't want him cowering at the river end."

As Wanda led her cousin down to the river edge, they heard the sounds of cars moving beyond the nearest row of buildings, and occasional flashes of blue light.

She felt the touch of her sister's mind, "Jim wants to know where you are?"

"Tell him I have blocked you out, Lisbeth. Or that I am unconscious or something."

Wanda paused to show Erin a trip wire, and then pointed up to where another camera was mounted in a tree. The first time she had approached, she had crawled to be below its line of sight. This time, Erin's device would jam it, but it would be worth maintaining caution, and keeping to the overgrown vegetation.

She had Erin wait where the bank was still wide, and here she stopped and unwound the tape from her hands and gave the dirty fabric to her cousin. Then she approached the back door for the second time, already knowing what she needed to do. The trouble with the lock was not its design, but the fact that it hadn't been opened for a long time and muck had got into the keyhole.

The first thing she did was take a fine pointed tool and pick away at the muck, then she took one of several tiny plastic vials of sewing machine oil and poked a hole in the nozzle. She squeezed the vial sending oil into the keyhole. She pictured it moving everywhere within the mechanism. Then she selected her tools from the burglar's kit and set to work on the lock. Within a minute, there was a faint click. Wanda withdrew her tools, and put them in the linen pocket. She had all her senses alert, in case the noise had been heard inside. After a full minute, she took out a second vial of the oil and shared it between both hinges.

She gestured Erin to approach, and while she edged closer, Wanda checked the direction of the breeze. It was too little to disturb the bushes, and hopefully would not send any of the river smell into the bunker.

"Come in a bit after me and lock the door. Keep low and out of sight," Wanda whispered directly into her cousin's ear. Then she gently pushed open the door, but only enough for her to ease her head in to glance around. In that short moment, her mind registered boxes of supplies, stacked tins of food, torches, boxes of spare batteries, and plastic flagons of water. She passed the image to Erin, along with the image of the space further in – an open area with chairs, a low table, a TV, radio, a cubicle that was probably a portable toilet, and Tatarovitch pacing around, talking on his mobile phone.

She opened the door wider and edged in, immediately ducking down behind the nearest boxes. When Tatarovich was facing the other door, she sent the 'come in' message to Erin, who repeated her move after silently closing and relocking the door.

"Wait," Wanda thought at Erin, "Move forward, but let me keep this one on one for a bit. Keep thinking silent and invisible."

Erin nodded, and waited for Wanda to move.

Wanda took a moment to think through her intention. She preferred not to rely on invisible powers to help her, since they could be capricious. However, along with thinking the reasons for this intended confrontation, she thought of how this man was evil, and had taken objects that did not belong to him, and had knowledge that she needed of a life in jeopardy.

Tatarovich, was angry. How he stalked around the open area, and hissed into the phone, betrayed it. "I need a diversion so Kiril can bring up the boat. No, the fool was supposed to follow me. He didn't."

A break in the conversation was followed with, "He won't talk, if he's smart. He doesn't know of the tunnel, and even if it is found, it does not come out close to here."

Wanda crept forward, and emerged to couch on a crate, near to Tatarovich, and waited for him to turn and see her. In her mind, she chanted a mantra to focus her intent.

He turned, saw her, and snapped his phone shut.

"Good day, grandpa," Wanda spoke before he could. His reaction was one of utter shock.

He recovered quickly and drew his gun.

"How incredibly stupid of you to come here." His finger was tightening on the trigger.

"How incredibly stupid you will be if you discharge that in here. It will echo like a rocket launch and bring every one of the police from around the warehouse to here."

"How did you get in?"

"Through the door. I figured that if you thought you would be safe here, I would be too." Wanda was studying the tiny movements Tatarovich was making, and was ready to spring away from an attack if he tried one.

"I told Hugo to put you down the chute. You should have landed in the river."

"Oh, I did come down that way. But it doesn't come out in the river anymore. It wasn't hard getting free, and I didn't really want to be caught again. Besides, I have unfinished business with you, so here I am - one on one."

Wanda stayed crouching on the crate as Tatarovich moved closer, the gun still in his hand. She needed him closer, and he was taking the bait. Thinking that he could soon overcome her, he put the gun down and removed his jacket. He placed it over the back of a chair, and continued to approach.

"One on one," he repeated, looking at her as if sizing her up. He stared back at the blue eyes watching him, and laughed. "I could beat you to a pulp with one hand."

"Proove it," Wanda challenged, without a change of expression.

He lunged, and began to realise his misjudgement when he saw her leap across to the next box, and he landed on the hard wood of the first crate. He realised a moment later that he had cut his hand, and only then saw a knife tucked under a wide linen sash. He lunged again, full of anger, only to have his tantalising target slip out from under his grasping hands, and kick the back of his legs. He spun around, determined to catch her, and felt a weight land on his back as the woman kicked his legs from under him.

He lost consciousness as Erin delivered a precisely placed chop to his neck. She rolled off his back once he was on the floor.

"We have a few minutes before he is likely to come around," Erin said with satisfaction. "How do you want to hold him?"

Wanda searched her memory of all the items she had subconsciously noted. "I saw a hammer down the back, and some nails. We can take some of the metal strapping off one of the crates. We can use that and nail him to the floor."

They worked quickly, passing metal straps over their victim's chest, and nailing the ends to the floor. They took more and fixed his outspread arms and ankles the same way.

Wanda kept some of the metal straps close to her hand, and then sat cross legged on Tatarovich's legs, and willed him to wake up. Erin stood quietly behind his head, out of sight, but ready to add her special talent to the confrontation.

Wanda saw his eyes open, felt him try to struggle free, and when he glared at her, Erin sent to his mind the feeling of terror.

"As much as I like having you in this position, weak and useless grandparent, you know things that I want to know, and you are going to tell them to me."

He spat at her, the glob of spittle hitting her cheek.

Wanda casually wiped it onto her hand, rubbed both hands together so that it moistened the muck on them, and wiped her hand across his mouth.

She felt his shiver of revulsion, and she knew she had another mind weapon to use against him.

"You won't kill me," Tatarovich claimed.

"Won't I?" Wanda queried, her tone deadly. "They are already convinced of my complicity in two murders, thanks to your unlovable cousin. What is one more when I won't be caught again?"

"You haven't the guts! Ivana raised you to be a waste of..."

Wanda wiped her other hand on his mouth.

"Let's get one thing straight you useless turd. I am not...Tanya Tatarovich Krinsky."

"I don't believe you!"

Wanda wriggled forward so that she was almost sitting on Tatarovich's groin. "I do, however, know her. And no, she would not kill you...unless I told her what you claimed to have done to her mother."

"Kill me and you will never find her."

"You over rate yourself," Wanda said unruffled. She ignored the venomous glare of her prisoner while she rifled through his pockets. He tried to buck her off him, but she simply punched him in his groin as she drew out a soft leather pouch like the one she had found at Alpha Prime. They had the same effect on her as those others had, once she had touched his pocket with her knee.

"You are going to have to run for the rest of your life after this."

Wanda ignored him; something was making her open the pouch and she wanted to see the diamonds that had caused her so much anguish.

"Every single hand of the family will be turned against you."

Wanda barely heard him, as the six purplish diamonds dropped onto his chest. She drew in a deep breath, as they glittered in the light from a naked globe above. Then she touched one with the tip of her finger and it started to glow from within.

She sensed her cousin's awe, and the thought, "It knows you...us. I think you should put it away."

When Wanda didn't move, Erin forced a shield about her mind, and then Wanda shook her head and then eased the diamonds back into the pouch without touching them further.

Mentally, Wanda thanked her. "Keep your mind shielded, and put these in your pocket." Erin deftly caught them when she tossed them.

Only then, did she pay attention to the man she sat on. His shirt was singed where the diamonds had sat. She stared, and only then became aware of the 'presence' that Erin had sensed. In an instant of understanding, she knew what those diamonds were, knew they were from a far different world to Earth, and knew what had befallen them since they had been stolen from Anneliese Mosellan, her maternal grandmother, long before her children had been born.

"You are dead," Tatarovich promised, his voice still slightly shrill after her punch.

"Quiet!" Wanda commanded, and this time, he couldn't resist it.

She stared down and said, "It is not I who must be wary of the Tatarovich clan, but you who must answer to the Mosellan bloodline. Those diamonds have never belonged to you. Not by any right, not even by the marriage sham you claimed with Anneliese Mosellan."

Tatrovich shivered under her. He was staring at her eyes as if it were the devil looking out from her face. And perhaps it was, for she was feeling now, the way she had made herself feel when she had needed to torture, and to kill, to survive. Only now, it was one of her own that was imprisoned, in peril and despair.

"Where is Ivana Krinsky?"

"If you are not Tanya, what do you care?"

"I wonder if you would be so brave and defiant if I chose to castrate you – right here, right now."

"You wouldn't dare..."

Wanda drew the knife from between her and the tool sash, and showed it to her victim.

"You felt how sharp it was. And that will be fortunate for you. Do you know that I have killed creatures as vile as you by slashing their neck?"

She demonstrated, but judged it so closely that it only just broke the skin.

"And do you know that I killed others by thrusting a knife in their vile maleness?"

This time she moved it so that he could just feel the tip of the knife in his groin. She held the knife there, keeping him rigid, and commanded, "Tell me where Ivana is. Tell me what you did to her and how she is hidden."

Chapter 18 - Fighting back

Elisabeth sat next to Jim Phillips in Donau's car as the police cordon was tightened around the warehouse. Jim occasionally subvocalized into the tiny throat mike and then glanced at his companion who only shook her head.

Derek Mont Pelier was standing by the car, talking to Tanya. He was trying to understand why she and Elisabeth had both insisted that they had to be here. It was more than just Wanda and Erin being brought here; he had the weirdest idea that Jim was trying to talk to Wanda and get answers back through Elisabeth. He straightened when he saw Donau trotting back to the car, Alex beside him.

"The building is empty," he told them as he reached into the driver's seat and grabbed the bag containing Wanda's discarded cardigan.

Alex is behaving as if Carson went down a garbage chute. We can't go down that way, so we will have to look for the other end. They are calling up boats to patrol the river."

"There's another row of factories beyond this one, before you get to the river," Derek was alert and concerned.

"It's an old building," Donau explained. "It could have had an outlet to the river, though they should all have been diverted to a collection point."

He saw Jim's concerned face and promised, "We'll find Carson and the marine private."

He wasted no more time, and when he had gone, Jim asked Elisabeth, "Anything?"

"I told you, Jim, she's blocked me out. But I know she is still alive."

In an even softer voice, he asked, "What is she doing?"

Tanya turned and leant in the window, "She is getting answers."

Jim glanced at Elisabeth, to ask why she hadn't said so, but he saw she had gone pale and was reaching into her bag. She drew out a note pad and pen and began to write. He tried to see the writing, but it was in some weird glyph shorthand.

He was distracted when Tanya gave an inarticulate cry, and

seemed to slump. Derek caught her as she fainted. He eased her to the ground, and looked at Jim, hoping for an explanation. He only saw the other man shrug.

Jim had more than an uncomfortable feeling that he did know what Wanda was doing, and exactly how she was 'getting answers' and who was being questioned. He guessed that Tanya had just learnt that her mother might still be alive. Wanda would probably know how little time she had, and was being expedient. He didn't want to know exactly what she was doing, but it was working, for Elisabeth had not slowed her writing pace.

Derek's phone rang, and when he spoke it was to say, "I'll be there."

Elisabeth stopped, and shoved pen and paper into her pocket. She stepped out of the car, looking pale and clammy. "I'm coming with you."

"I am too," Tanya insisted, pushing herself to her feet, and standing unsteadily.

"Whoa," Derek held up his hands. "Where do you think I am going?"

"An underground bunker on the edge of the river," Elisabeth totally astounded him.

Alex led Donau along the riverbank, forcing his way through low bushes that showed signs that someone else had gone that way. He ran up to the back door and looked back at his human.

After edging carefully along, Donau tried the door and found it locked. He saw the fresh oil on the lock and hinges.

"Good boy, Alex." He patted the dog and gave him a small treat. "Now, we need to find another door."

Alex understood, and followed a weaker scent trail and stopped pawing at a ring in the ground. After a few moments of fiddling, he pulled at the ring and found the locked door below it. He called for reinforcements and then to Derek Mont Pelier.

Erin continued to watch her cousin with horrified fascination. Whatever odd mood had taken Wanda over, was getting results. The bastard was spilling out his mind, like his brain was no longer functioning. He was a hair's breadth short of losing control of his bodily functions. Then she felt the touch of Elisabeth/Tanya on her mind.

"Let us in. The police are about to blow the doors."

"Um, they'd better not see this..."

She had the image of Wanda in her mind, and heard Elisabeth, "Snap her out of it. Damn quick."

Erin went and shook her cousin, and got no response. She gripped both her shoulders and used her empathy. Once they had been linked on a really deep level.

"Enough!" it was a feeling, more than a thought, but it had the desired effect. Wanda suddenly shook her head and straightened up.

"The police are about to blow the door. Give me the tools."

"I'm almost done," Wanda told her, passing the tool sash while still staring down at the terrified, mind broken man without any remorse. She told her grandfather, quite distinctly, "Your only way to keep living is to tell the man who frees you, everything you know about all of your relatives, and answer all of his questions. If you do, he will protect you from the retribution of your relatives, who will certainly kill you for being such a craven coward. They will despise you for being broken by a mere young female."

Two almost simultaneous explosions compacted the air within the bunker. Booted feet raced in, yelling things that Wanda ignored.

"You said you were not Tanya," the weak, hoarse voice almost pleaded.

"I'm not," Wanda told him flatly, aware of the armed policemen in a circle around her, and of Erin refusing to move from beside her, of Elisabeth and Tanya forcing their way through.

"But I am," Tanya spat at the man on the floor.

The eyes that were reddened from the terrors inflicted, stared at two faces, differing only in the degree of cleanness, both showing no pity. Two more faces walked into his limited view, and then he did wet himself.

Tanya glanced at the spreading wet patch as she stood over him. "You didn't just have one daughter. You had three. These are the children of Katya and Katrina Tatarovich."

Wanda finished with, "Or did you never wonder why the diamonds were split into three? You who claim there is a curse on them have learnt what it truly is, but you will never speak of us."

Strong hands were gripping her shoulders, lifting her up from the man on the floor. Wanda didn't struggle, for she sensed this was Derek Mont Pelier. Different hands held her by the arms as he knelt down to examine her victim. Elisabeth, Erin and Tanya were being shepherded away by Donau.

Derek's nose twitched at the acrid smell emanating from the once well-dressed man. His eyes studied the scorch marks on the silken shirt, but when he opened the shirt, there was no mark underneath. He saw a drop on blood on the man's neck, and the fine red line – barely a scratch.

When the voice pleaded, "Protect me," Derek noticed the dirt around his mouth.

He glanced up at Wanda, and saw the expressionless 'shuttered' look, and the face devoid of colour.

He wasn't quick enough to warn the WEGA man, but the officer didn't release his grip when Wanda suddenly dropped. He was alert for an attempt to escape, but Wanda was out cold. She stirred when Donau's dog, nosed his way into her and licked her face. She tried to sit up, but didn't get far, opting instead to throw an arm over Alex.

Derek took charge and pointed to Tatarovitch's gun, considering why the owner had put it down. He saw the hammer used to nail down the metal tape and used the claw end to lever it back up. He came up so easily that he wondered why the man had been unable to wrest himself free. One of the armed policemen passed his weapon to a colleague and helped to free the apparent victim.

He spoke an arrest formula to the man when he was being helped to his feet and directed two of the policemen to take him to the central holding cells until he could be questioned.

He saw a knife on the floor that had been hidden by the man's body. He saw no blood on it and was relieved.

Wanda had made no further move and now Derek squatted down next to her. "What did you do to him?" He was being official, couldn't afford to be less.

"Mind games," Wanda told him, her voice muffled by Alex's furry coat. "Nothing that he didn't deserve a thousand times over."

She began to shiver, and Derek touched her face. He stood up and looked around. "I need a blanket, she is going into shock."

Donau had returned. He didn't have a blanket, but he did have the cardigan that he had used to give Alex the scent. He gave it to Derek and he helped Wanda into it and then helped her to her feet. Alex was pressing close to her, almost as a supporting third leg.

"Take her to your headquarters, Otto," Derek directed. "I will talk to her there."

When Donau automatically reached for his handcuffs, Derek shook his head, "You won't need them."

Derek gave instructions for the bunker to be sealed and guarded until the forensic team examined it. He was more concerned than he let on about Wanda. He was glad there was no blatant physical evidence of the torture he felt sure she had inflicted. Mind games she had said, and that sent chills down his spine.

The other three women were still waiting by his car, and he was about to object but one of the three ran to Wanda and threw her arms around her.

"Oh thank you, thank you," Tanya spoke in her native Russian, too full of emotion to think in any other language. "I cannot believe it! My mother, still alive."

Wanda forced herself to speak. "I hope that is still true. Is Jim going to find her?"

Tanya nodded and hugged her again. Now Donau, urged Wanda into his car, only then noticing that the American had gone. When he took his head out of the back seat, he saw Erin standing by the passenger door.

"I was told that you would want to speak to me too."

"Yes, I will. Get in then."

She opened the door, but Alex dived past her and over into the back seat.

"Okay, I guess that is better than being jumped on," Erin commented, with wry amusement. She didn't say more as she clipped in the seatbelt and leant back into the seat. She began to concentrate on the image of a still pool, aware that Wanda's mind was still like a roiling cauldron.

Somehow, Jim had expected this reaction and he had told her, just before he left, to "Snap her out of it fast."

While Donau drove over rough ground back to the road, Erin lowered her mental barriers, merged her mind with her cousin's and took in all the dark emotions and began to work at them.

Wanda fought her at first, full of self-loathing. "Are you disgusted with me?"

"No more now than five years ago. It is no different. You did what needed to be done, and I helped by increasing his terror."

"It was still torture. It makes me no better than he is, no better than those others five years ago."

"Ten minutes," Erin stated in her mind. "That is a mere instant when you think of how he has inflicted mental and emotional torture on his daughter for at least five years. Those others you think about, enjoyed what they did. You are not like that. You would not feel this bad if you were. So stop punishing yourself. Your job here is not finished. We still have to find Theo and Aleksei, and get you out of prison. You have to stay hard or that queen bitch will tear you to pieces."

She felt the change and was relieved when Wanda thought at her. "Yes, you are right. If I act like this at the police station, Tatarovich won't stay petrified. He has to be the one to sell out his cousins."

Erin considered that, and thought, "You want the family to kill him. What about Theo?"

"I know where he is, and where Ivana is. I told Elisabeth and she told Jim."

"Good," Erin said with mental emphasis. "Are you feeling better now, or still guilty by contamination?"

"Well enough. Starving though, and thirsty. I hope someone will offer the escapee some sustenance."

"I will insist," Erin promised. "So the morning sickness has gone?"

"Mostly. The damn hormones are still at work though."

Donau apologised at the need to restrain her again, but it was procedure for prisoners in the police building.

"It's okay," Wanda told him. "At least Alex likes me, either way. Are you taking me to the cells?"

"No, my office. Mont Pelier wants to talk to you."

Wanda merely nodded, and let Erin suggest that something to eat and drink would be appreciated.

"There's a small hand basin you can use to clean up a bit too." Donau had noticed that both women were begrimed, although Erin had made an effort to tidy up her uniform. "And I will have something sent up."

Wanda was happy to agree to anything that kept her from the prison for longer. However, she had no illusions that it would be much of a reprieve, particularly if any of the senior police saw her there.

There would be some that believed she had been trying to escape. She did want to know the outcome of the day's events, and she might learn that here, but would hear nothing at the prison.

Donau directed her to sit at a spare desk, and even pulled a chair over for her to use. Erin fetched another, and sat beside her.

"Wait here. Christian and Bauer can keep you company until you are needed. I have to report to the Chief."

He whistled to Alex, but the dog simply flopped down next to Wanda and panted.

Chapter 19 - Disregarded

Erin had questions, but her German wasn't that fluent, and Wanda needed to translate so that Christian would understand. She turned to where he sat at his desk.

"She wants to know if you found the two men she tied up at the warehouse."

Christian nodded and brought up two files on the computer. He asked Wanda, "Do you recognise them from the prison?"

Wanda stood and wondered over. "No, but I don't guarantee that I have seen all of the guards there. All I can say is that they are not the two who brought me here."

The Austrian had a startled look, as if something had just occurred to him. He grabbed his phone and pushed buttons rapidly. Wanda went back to her seat as he identified himself to the person who answered. He asked for the names of the two duty prison guards who had escorted the prisoner, Carson, that morning. He jotted the names down, and then asked if they had returned. He gave his thanks and ended the call.

"The two officers have not returned to sign off, and no others were sent to relieve them," he told the two women, as he began to dial another number.

Wanda guessed he was calling Donau, and she had a feeling of unease when he reported the two men were missing, possibly in the building. She glanced at Erin, who only gave a slight shrug. She hadn't sensed anything odd until the men forced them outside. And then they had other things to think about.

Alex was sitting up, ears twitching as if he sensed there was work for him. Wanda called him to her, and when he was close, she put her hands on either side of his head and tried to project an image of a man being mugged and dragged away. Alex woofed, seeming to understand.

Moments later, Donau trotted in, called Alex and went off. Erin offered to help.

Wanda slumped over the table, elbows on it and resting her head in her hands.

"You want to help too?" Christian asked.

"Hmm. Except I am kind of tied up at the moment."

"Well, maybe you still can. We didn't find those two black clad men. Can you tell me anything about them?"

"Is this on the record or off it? Should I have my lawyer here?"

"How would you prefer it?"

Wanda considered things, then asked, "Hypothetically, do you still have that building surrounded?"

"It should be, the forensic team are looking it over."

"Well, still hypothetically, if I were those two climbing monkeys, I would be hiding on the roof of a building, inside the police perimeter and waiting for night to sneak out. However, I did not suggest that." Wanda considered mentioning that they were related to Tatarovich, but decided they hadn't been able to help that.

Once again, Christian acted on her suggestion. Then, while they waited for news, Wanda made a pretence of dozing until Bauer returned with the food.

"Where's Alex?" Bauer asked.

"Off with Otto, looking for the two guards that came from the prison this morning. They are missing," Christian told him. "The other American woman is helping to search."

Bauer placed a bag in front of Wanda, and advised, "Eat quickly, before Alex gets back."

"I need to clean up before I eat. I have no idea what muck I have on my hands."

Bauer indicated a small wash basin and tap in a corner of the room, that Wanda had not noticed. He did not comment when she stood and went over to it.

Erin arrived back half an hour later and announced, "Alex found them. They'll be okay."

When she sat back next to Wanda and began to eat the food brought for her, she whispered, "I saw the prosecutor. He's still very agitated."

"Let's hope he doesn't see me, because I have no idea how to get Hauser here." Then Wanda had a sudden thought. "Have you given

Donau those diamonds back?"

Erin checked her pocket. "No, I meant to as soon as we got here."

"Do it – as soon as he returns. And don't open the bag."

"Why?"

"Do you remember what happened when I touched one?"

"It knew you!"

"Yes, and I think it used me. I think it recognises you as well, because the same thing is happening to you. It is making you forget about them."

"I'll do it," Erin promised, reaching for the bag.

"I have a better idea," Wanda twisted to look over at Christian, caught his eye and invited, "Can you come here?"

The policeman was curious enough to obey. Wanda nodded to Erin.

"Tatatovich had something in his pocket." Erin placed the leather bag on the desk.

Christian took it and rolled the diamonds out into his hand. They were faceted to be almost like marbles, and in his hand, they didn't glow. At that moment, Donau and his superior walked in, and Wanda tried to make herself small and inconspicuous as the report was given.

Erin stood, to see the stones better, but she couldn't help moving her hand to touch one of them. Wanda realised that she was feeling the same insistent mental sensation, and without thinking, grabbed Erin's arm to stop her. "No! Block it!" she sent mentally.

Her movement was noticed. "Carson! Release the woman!" The voice was that of the police chief.

Wanda obeyed, muttering, "Damn you!" However, Erin had stepped back, and the sensation had eased.

"Tatarovitch had these?" the chief demanded of Erin. "How did he get them? We had them locked up here."

His gaze moved to Wanda, and he glared at her. "Well?"

"Get my lawyer here and I will make a guess, but I damn well didn't take them again."

Donau moved closer and examined each of the stones. "I don't think that these are the same stones that we saw before. Ask Mont

Pelier to come here if you want a second opinion. Should we check to see that the other stones are still in the evidence safe?"

"Mont Pelier is still interrogating that Russian, but I will mention these to him, so he can ask about them. I will have someone check about the others. Why is Carson here?"

Christian was about to mention that she had been helpful, when he saw Wanda glance his way. She didn't want anyone to know what she had suggested. He said nothing.

Donau announced, "I was hoping to ask her more questions."

"I don't want trouble with that lawyer of hers. Have her taken down to the holding cells."

She knew Donau should have sent her there when she arrived, and appreciated that he hadn't, but now, they had to obey their superior. She knew that, and didn't want to cause them trouble. So, she patted Alex, received a lick on her hand, thanked Bauer for the food and pretended to ignore Erin.

Wanda didn't feel the need to be difficult, and considered the holding cell as good a place as any to have a rest, though what she really wanted was a shower to get the rest of the muck off her. However, that was probably not going to happen until she got sent back to the prison – if then.

And she wasn't in a hurry to go back there, so she meekly accompanied the officers summoned to escort her down to the cells.

She made herself comfortable on the basic cot bed, by sitting and hugging her knees. There were a great many images, impressions and thoughts that she had picked up from Tatarovich's mind that she wanted to sort through and consider. The most important things, she had thought to her sister, like the place that Theo and Aleksei had fled to. That wasn't Hamburg like the charter flight plan had indicated, but a private airstrip just outside Austria's border. Tatarovich was acting for his cousin whilst he was out of Austria, but accepted that Theo considered Austria 'his' just as he himself controlled crime in France.

An idea occurred to her. Tatarovich had wanted to know how she had known of the diamonds at Alpha Prime. He claimed that they were his, or rather his under the name he used in France. So where had that second set come from? And why did he have them on him?

She set her mind to filter through every miscellaneous detail that she had read in Tatarovich's mind. What she had received most clearly were the things of current importance to him, and the thoughts provoked by her questions. She hadn't asked about the diamonds, but when she had looked at them...

Yes...the ones that he'd had with him, he'd had a long time. They had probably been Ivana's once.

He'd only claimed that they had been stolen. He'd had one of his sons break in and take them, and they had just been returned to him. So...those others...at Alpha Prime...he'd heard about them from Theo, and Interpol. He was trying to convince the police that those ones were his. The bastard.

So he had come to Vienna, on that pretext and by chance, Theo had his people after her for other reasons. He had her passport, and had been happy to pass the thief to his cousin to deal with. Except, she had escaped.

Wanda concentrated on the elusive memory of when Tatarovich had first seen her passport and recognised the family likeness. Shock, and then anger. The latter emotion was because he had failed to get Tanya into his control, added to the fact that his daughter's useless whelp had proved to be so skilled, and taken something he craved from the moment he'd learnt of them.

Later memories, of the intense visceral thrill he had enjoyed when she had been sentenced to twenty five years in prison, morphed into how he had set Ivana up, and her horror when she realised what he had done to her, and how he had enjoyed seeing her dragged off to a French prison. He hadn't cared, except to gloat. Yet there had been something there, a fleeting thought about Ivana and her whelp, in the same place, unable to recognise each other.

Wanda was jolted from her immediate desire, of finding how Tatarovich had managed to get her sentenced for so long, but she mentally told herself to return to that point, after she had considered her own plight.

Someone was threatening the prosecutor, and that had to be

either Theo or Tatarovich, but would her so-called grandfather admit that to Derek? Would her command hold that long?

Even with the knowledge that Tatarovich was in custody, her own situation felt no better. She was isolated from the events happening upstairs, back to being a criminal and murderer, discarded, unthanked and unworthy of credit or consideration. For a while, she had been able to almost forget that she was just starting a twenty five year sentence and even if the appeal succeeded, it was unlikely the sentence would be reduced by much.

Would any judge want to if they learnt what she had done to that creature upstairs? Or if they learnt that she was his granddaughter?

At least she had the consolation that he would be in prison for a long time too. Unless the Family freed him, or killed him if he were indeed telling all to Derek.

She liked that latter idea...it would only take a word in the right ear...but that was a dangerous path. They might come after her too.

The time passed slowly, and Wanda had given up trying to guess what was happening upstairs. She was allowing herself to rest, with her mind set to wake her at the slightest sound. What woke her was the metallic clanging of the opening and then closing. She opened her eyes to slits to watch what was happening. Those that were led into the cell opposite were clad in black, but they now had fair hair revealed and faces betraying a mixture of emotions. In both, she recognised a likeness to Tatarovich. She wondered if the selection of cell was deliberate. She was in the perfect position to study them and she did so, by staying quiet and still pretending she was dozing. The guards didn't even glance her way as they had delivered these new prisoners, nor when they had departed.

She continued to watch them covertly until the guards had left. Then she opened her eyes and watched them circle within the cell like two caged panthers, and listened to their acrimonious whispers in Russian. They didn't know that their father was upstairs being questioned.

"Don't rely on daddy to get you out of there," Wanda startled both men by speaking in Russian. She didn't move from her seated position, and they had to look carefully to see her. When they did they both came to the bars to face her.

"What did you do, bitch?" one of them demanded.

"Me? Nothing. He's the one being questioned upstairs. He tried to kill me, by having me dumped into the garbage chute, remember? I'm only here until they get someone from the prison to take me back there."

The second of the two men laughed, as if she deserved prison. He was slightly taller than his brother and had a fine downy layer of beard.

"Laugh if you want, Uncle, but think where you are. You two good little daddies' boys will be in prison yourselves, soon. You will be no better off than me. Maybe worse, because they will say you are accessories to all your father's dirty deeds. I reckon he will sell you two out, so he can wriggle himself free."

"He wouldn't!" the first one contested. That one had a moustache but no beard and was slightly slenderer that his brother.

Wanda shrugged. "I can tell you two have never been caught before, and that tells me that you are good at what you do. Who other than your father knows you well enough to predict where you would hide?"

Wanda figured that they hadn't thought of things that way, and now those uncomfortable thoughts were tormenting them. Did they know what their father had done to their half-sister?

"No," the bearded one finally decided. "He won't talk, because if he is up there, he will be hoping we will free him."

"Too bad," Wanda commented with casual indifference. "As soon as he knows you are caught then. After all, he can't think much of his offspring if he could callously set his daughter up."

The two men glanced at each other, confirming her thought that they knew about Ivana.

"We don't believe you," the taller one stated flatly.

"Your choice," Wanda agreed amiably. "When you change your mind, if I am still here, let me know."

"Why? So that you can gloat?"

"No, so that I can offer you a chance to get out of here. In return for some information."

"No deal!"

"Fine." Wanda closed her eyes as if she was no longer interested.

After five minutes, during which the two men held a whispered conversation between themselves, the shorter man hissed for her attention. Wanda opened her eyes but said nothing.

"What chance?"

In answer, Wanda fumbled at the patch of plastiskin on her inner thigh, which held the slimmest of the tools that Erin had given her, took out a lock pick and pushed the false skin back in place.

She walked, casually, to the bars of her cell and held it up. It was obvious that both men knew what it was. Their eyes were fixed on it until they all heard the sound of the outer doors to the holding area being opened. The taller man nudged the younger, and they both moved back from the bars. Wanda did the same, and re-hid the tool where it had been, and sat back on her narrow bed.

The two uniformed officers, different ones to her earlier escort, stopped at her cell and opened the door. "Carson. Up! You're wanted."

"What for," Wanda feigned a yawn. "I am not answering questions without my lawyer."

"We have our orders, Carson."

They dragged her up, clearly in no mood to humour her. She let them turn her around and put the hand restraints on. She gave the brothers a look to suggest that they had lost their chance, and allowed herself to be led upstairs.

She was taken upstairs to a small room, where one of the officers remained and the other went out. A few minutes later, and while Wanda amused herself by imagining how easy it would be to overcome the guard, Derek Mont Pelier walked in and gestured the other officer out.

Wanda sat back and stared at him. He ignored her tactic, he felt he knew it was a mental game, and he sat across the small table from her.

"Are we still friends?" he asked softly.

"Yeah."

"Your grandfather is talking up a storm."

Wanda leant forward and said in a low voice, "Don't... call him...

my grandfather!"

"Very well. Tatarovich…has been talking freely. However, he still hasn't told us some things that we want to know."

"My treatment might be wearing off," Wanda suggested. "What won't he tell you?"

"Where the prosecutor's family is being held."

"Okay…" Wanda thought on that. It wasn't anything she had thought of asking when she had the bastard at her mercy. "Do you think he is not telling, or doesn't know?"

Derek considered. "I'm not sure. He knows of the abductions, he had to have."

"Did he say where Theo and Aleksi are?"

"Only that they flew out of Austria and were intending to sneak back a few days later."

"Did he say where he has been staying?"

Derek nodded. "A house not that far from the warehouse. One of Theo's properties. Why?"

"You know I have a knack for knowing how the criminal mind works….?" Wanda saw Derek nodding his understanding, and went on, "I was asking that bastard questions, while we were alone. He wasn't actually answering all of them…but I got impressions of things." She paused, trying to read Derek's acceptance.

"Go on…"

"Well, one impression I got was that Tatarovich wasn't actually the one who arranged for my long sentence, but he was expecting it. It is my guess, that Theo organised it. After all, in Austria, he is the one with the private army."

"How does that help us if we can't find him?"

"Are his properties being searched?"

"The couple we know of are. I don't expect any useful results."

Wanda considered other odd pieces of information, then asked, "Can I ask what sort of things Tatarovich has been telling you? Anything about Theo and Aleksi?"

"Some. The chief has people out checking what he has said."

"What about that call to the Prosecutor? Do you know where it came from?"

"Eighth district. Nowhere near the warehouse."

Wanda was thinking that if the jury had been got at by Theo, and now the Prosecutor was being pressured, that he might be due for another call about letting Tatarovich go. She suggested that to Derek, and added, "My gut feeling is that Theo will have the hostages close by."

"Except, we still don't know where he is," Derek reminded her.

"I know that. However, I have the glimmerings of an idea."

"What?"

"Take these handcuffs off and let me in the room with Tatarovich."

"No."

Wanda didn't think he'd agree. "Okay...plan B. Not as sure of results, and you probably won't like it either..."

"Go on..."

"You've got the bastard's two sons in the cells downstairs," she told him.

"I was aware of that. Did you learn anything from them?"

"Impressions, nothing definite," Wanda shrugged. "What I do think, is that they don't think he will talk about the family, but I think I have them worried that he will sell them out to get himself free."

"Have you indeed?" Derek smiled faintly.

"Now, this is the iffy bit," Wanda said, eyeing Derek. "As much as I want to go somewhere to have a shower and get clean, can you have me taken back down there indefinitely?"

"I could..."

Wanda continued, "Then have those two up for questioning, in separate rooms or one at a time. If you can make it seem as if their father has sold them out...I reckon that they are both highly skilled cat-burglars, and one of them pretended to steal the diamonds that Tatarovich had on him today...and maybe imply that he has also been ratting on his cousin Theo, perhaps given you a rough location of where to find him...without actually saying where...and that you are searching that place..."

"Whoa...slow down. I can organise that, but what do you hope to achieve?"

"Um," Wanda paused, wondering if Derek would renounce her idea. "Well, with a little illegal help, that you don't have to know about, I am hoping that they will escape from here, and run to warn Theo. But don't have Tatarovich down here with them. I get the feeling they are afraid to go against him, and if he is there, he'll insist they free him too."

"Devious," Derek smiled grimly. "The chief will take some convincing. And do you prefer that he isn't held down there while you are there?"

"No, you can bring him down. He won't be able to get to me." Wanda tried to sound innocent, but she didn't deceive Derek.

"Devious and dangerous," he summarised. "What else?"

"When I go back down, I might let it slip that you think I am in league with Tatarovich, and helped him get at the prosecutor's family because I hate the guy for piling extra charges on me. I might get an impression of whether they know where the prosecutor's family is."

Wanda waited for Derek to think the idea through. There was still no absolute assurance that any of her ideas would help the kidnaped victims. It had a better chance of catching Theo, and then it would be up to the police to make him talk.

"I will bring the idea to the Chief," Derek finally agreed. "The part about finding Theo, at least. If he agrees, it will take some time to set up the surveillance."

"How will I know if they do agree?" Wanda asked.

"What about…I come down to return the first of the brothers, and ask if you are going to co-operate?"

Wanda grinned, "That will do."

When she was returned to the cell, she was being 'difficult' – trying to shake off the guard's grip and cursing under her breath. In the cell, once she was free of the handcuffs, she went back to sitting on the bed with her knees up, but only after kicking the bed several times. She seemed to be oblivious to the first of the brothers being hustled out.

The other brother, the shorter, slighter one, tried to talk to her. She ignored him for a full five minutes before pretending to explode from pent up anger, coming to the bars and hissing out, "Those imbecile Austrian police think I am involved with your bastard of a father! And that I knew that he was going to take the prosecutor's family, and I helped him arrange it! Why would I do that? How could I do that? Anyway, your effing father wanted to kill me."

She turned her back, on her uncle and stood stiffly, staring at the back of the cell.

"Why don't you get out?" he suggested.

She let her shoulders slump, and half turned to reply. "What's the point? How could I get past the guards? Anyway, I reckon I will be safer in prison."

The man opposite became thoughtful, but Wanda only sensed it by his silence.

"Father didn't take the man's family."

"Crap! He's the one that wanted me, they said. The Prosecutor was told to let me go."

"No. Father wanted you, but Theo ordered it."

"How could he? That coward fled. Two months ago."

"No, he's back."

"Oh Great!" Wanda muttered.

"Why don't you get away? You could if you wanted to. Father said, that Theo said you were slippery."

"Why do you care anyway? You and the whole damn family think they own me. Your father is pissed at me because I did things against them, when I didn't even know they existed, and I damn well don't want to be part of it."

The blond man bit his lip and seemed to be thinking. "Look, I shouldn't be telling you this, but you're really no safer in prison. Our sister, Ivana...your mother he said...he keeps having her moved from prison to prison with different names each time, and always where she doesn't know the language."

"If you know that, then where is she now?"

"I don't know."

"Useless twat!"

"I wish I did. Really. But father would never say where she was. He thought Nikoli would try to get her out."

"Who's Nikoli?"

"Our younger brother. Father doesn't like him, because he refused to learn the business. But he is a wizard with IT stuff, so father tolerates him. Leo and I, well, we're like you."

"So, what's your name?"

"Stephan. Look, I don't like what he's doing to you either."

"You stood there and let him do what he liked," Wanda accused. "You obviously haven't tried to help your sister either. You're as bad as he is."

Stephan turned and moved stiffly a few steps away. Then he turned back, as if deciding something. "I won't say I am proud of myself, but I don't dare go against him. You don't know what he's like..."

After delving through Tatarovich's mind, Wanda did know what he was like. Easing off her outward hostility, she tried to project sympathy, and she came to the bars of her cell, so that she could talk softly. This Stephan was not as hardened as his brother, and his change from hostility gave her hope that she could influence him.

"Do you want to be free of him?"

"I can't, he'd kill me."

"You simply don't have enough incentive...that's all. I've been where you are..."

Wanda kept her voice so low, that Stephan had to listen hard to hear her. He sensed that this slip of a woman, had the answer he needed...

When she saw the blank look come over Stephan's face, she knew he had succumbed to the hypnotic trance, and that he was only aware of her voice.

"When they question you, volunteer all you know about the Prosecutor's situation, about his family, and where they are, and how to contact Theo. Ask them not to let on that you told them. You must not tell anyone that you told them. When you get out, the first thing you need to do is contact Theo. To get his help. To warn him that you think your father talked, that they told you he had. Say that you need his help to get your Father away. Wake now!"

Wanda had heard the first door opening. Stephan was suddenly aware of it too. She allowed herself a fleeting read of Derek's mind, and sensed that the police had agreed to take the risk and let the brothers 'escape'. She quickly retrieved the picklock and said, "Catch."

Stephan was not ready for it, and the small piece of metal clattered to the floor as the nearest secure door opened. He quickly grabbed it, "Why? You said..."

Wanda spoke quickly, "I've nothing against you! Just your father. Use it later, when Leo is back. Toss it back to me on your way out."

"But?"

"You can owe me one," Wanda insisted, then quickly back stepped away from the bars of her cell.

Derek accompanied an irritated Leo, who was being hustled along by a solid looking Austrian police officer. Stephan was ordered to the back of his cell, as Leo was pushed in."

"Stephan, we want to talk to you now," Derek told the younger brother.

"Tell them nothing," Leo told his brother harshly.

Looking at Leo, Derek said mildly, "That attitude won't help you."

He gestured to Stephan and the officer with him applied the handcuffs. As the three men emerged from the cell, Derek looked at Wanda and asked, "Have you decided to cooperate yet?"

His voice was stern, but he was smiling so only she could see it.

"You wouldn't recognise cooperation if your face fell in it," Wanda told him rudely, but she timed a wink, for when only he was looking.

Wanda went back to her bunk and sat with her back to the wall, and her feet on the bed, and told herself to be patient and wait. She was ignoring Leo, as he was ignoring her.

Half an hour later, she heard the outer security door open again, and thought it must be Stephan coming back, although she hadn't expected him to return so soon. She was sure Derek wouldn't let Tatarovich down while she was still there.

It was neither. Two police officers stopped outside her cell, and told her to stand facing the back wall.

"What now?" she demanded.

"You are going back where you belong. The prison van is waiting."

A small part of her wanted to go back, if only so she could have a shower. A bigger part wanted Tatarovich down here, within reach. The biggest part of her was angry at being dragged away, and not being able to know the outcome of her plan. She tried to struggle free, but the men held her firmly.

Chapter 20 - Insane plans

Wanda was so keyed up when she arrived back at the prison, that she was less than congenial company. It didn't help that the guards commented on her state of cleanliness, and she dared not make any kind of retort back to them. Nor was she going to explain what she had been doing.

They tried to rile her by suggesting she would not be allowed to go into the dining area in such a filthy dress, and that she had better get clean first.

She wanted to be clean, but she couldn't get a shower yet. That left seeing what she could do in the bathroom. At first, she didn't realise that they were not taking her back to her cell, but then she realised that they were taking her to the laundry. That had possibilities.

Her estimate of the time suggested that it was still half an hour before the meal time, and the workers would still be working there. It wasn't her day for laundry duty so she set her mind to recall the roster, and who was on this shift.

Inwardly, she groaned. Two of the long term prisoners, friends of Bridgette Wolf, were the supervisors.

"Earn your keep, Carson," she was told, and given a shove into the steamy atmosphere.

At first, no one noticed her, and she grabbed a wet dress from a pile waiting to be put in the dryer. She used this to clean her arms and legs, and then found the nearest washing machine and dumped it in to be cleaned again.

One of the workers caught her at it and challenged her. "What are you doing here?"

The two supervisors heard and came over, a nasty smile appearing when they recognised her, and saw her state.

"Emmy, Gretch," one of the supervisors called for two of the others. "Hold Carson."

Wanda knew what was likely to come next, and she had no hope to avoid it. Two women grabbed her, and dragged her towards one of the huge wash tubs used for scrubbing the really dirty washing.

They forced her head down into the tub, so that the two supervisors could each dump a bucket of grey water over her head. She held her breath and tried to struggle free.

Some water got up her nose, but she was able to blow it out when they dragged her head up. In that first moment of release from the water, the four women held her and stripped the dress from her. Not content to leave it there, they also tore off her underwear, until she was completely naked, and began to use the harsh scrubbing brushes where she was still dirty.

They only stopped when the siren for the end of the work shift sounded, and the guards overseeing the laundry came in to take the women back to the mess room. One of these was male and he made rude comments, but his partner was female, and she simply took one of the damp dresses from the pile and told her to get dressed.

"What were you doing, Carson? Trying to get out of showering later?"

"No, Mam. My dress was filthy."

She was sure they guessed there was more to it than that, but since the guards seldom stayed in the laundry while the women worked, they asked the two supervisors for the facts.

Their version was, as in similar incidents in the past, "The bitch was messing up our work, she needed a lesson."

The guards accepted it, since apart from being naked, dripping wet, and having signs of being scrubbed, Wanda was unhurt.

"We'll be reporting this, Carson," was the final word, as the laundry crew were allowed to leave.

Wanda knew it would not end there. It was really a no win situation. Had she complained about the treatment, she's have got worse. But by keeping quiet and accepting the fault as hers, they would want to make her squirm more, until she did start to complain or fight back. Then the guards would report her again.

It began during the meal, when her tray was jolted, and some of her food fell off. Then there were the kicks and pinches from passing prisoners – all cronies of Bridgette. Later, as they were released for the evening indoor recreation, she was subtly tripped, causing her to crash into the book shelf and send that toppling.

That was when she decided enough was enough, and struggled to her feet and launched herself at her latest tormentor.

She had frustration to work out, and anger, so while she wasn't fighting as effectively as she could, it was more than enough to get the better of her tormentor. It was one of Bridgette's crowd of course, or she wouldn't have done it, and the woman was stupid enough to fight back, so that when the guards arrived, and began using their batons, both she and her tormentor felt the solid whacks.

Wanda stopped fighting after the third whack, and allowed herself to be dragged away. Her opponent came after her and received three more.

She spent the night in solitary, and enjoyed the solitude. Though it meant that she missed hearing the nightly news on the television, and hearing if her afternoon's exploits were known. If they were, she'd be in for even more unwanted attention.

Her private source of information, Elisabeth, had nothing to tell her until quite late. Then she was able to report that Erin had told Donau what she knew of what had occurred at the warehouse, but had glossed over the bunker events by saying that they overcame Tatarovitch and immobilised him and then tried to humiliate him into talking. Erin, she said, had claimed not to understand what Tatarovich was saying.

Wanda asked, if she had heard anything from Derek, but she had neither seen him nor heard from him since leaving the warehouse, and Jim was nowhere around either. It was frustrating.

As she lay awake listening to the silence, she finally remembered that Jim had gone off looking for Ivana. He wouldn't find her.

Now, she had more information that suggested that Tanya's mother might be in the Vienna Women's prison, here, where she was. Tatarovich had delighted in the thought that neither she, nor Ivana would recognise the other.

Her first thought had been that she had never seen Ivana, to know if she looked at all like her own mother. Then she considered, surely Ivana would recognise someone who was like a twin to her own daughter. Another memory – Elisabeth telling her that Tanya's father had said she looked very like Ivana.

So, someone who looked like her sister, but older. Would Tatarovich have plastic surgery done to her – to change her looks? It was possible – somehow Aleksi had been made to look like Allan Wexford. Maybe he didn't have to, for even five years in prison could change a person. The face could be thinner, with more lines. She considered how five years of captivity, drugs and alcohol had aged the real Allan Wexford – the hobo versus his doppelgänger Aleksi.

If Ivana was being moved around, under assumed names, would she recall her true name?

In a low voice, Wanda murmured, "If he has the power to have her moved around, he could have more people, like that guard, to bring in drugs...Ivana's mind could be addled. That would be enough to make it impossible for her to recognise anyone, and if she thought Tanya was dead...I hope Theo kills Tatarovich!"

It had been part of her plan, and an aspect that Derek hadn't picked up on. He didn't know, in his bones, how protective The Family was. She hoped that if one of their own proved dangerous to the rest, they'd excise the problem – like Tatarovich had tried to do to her.

When her mind started going in the same useless circles, Wanda knew she needed sleep. She recalled a mantra for relaxation that she had been taught, and thought of the man who had taught it to her – Ivana's great-uncle, Jenha Mosellan. Seeing him in her mind's eye, gave her an answer to her question. One thing that would not change was the bone structure of her face – like that of herself and her cousins. The genetic inheritance from the Mosellan bloodline.

Stephan Tatarovich waited until it was very late, hoping that his father would be brought down to the cells. He was slumped on one of the cot beds, while Leo was angrily pacing the ten pace square area. His brother's muttered curses were directed at their father who must indeed have told the police about many of the robberies he had sent them to do. It had to have been him; how else could the police have found out? Neither of them was prepared to take captivity without a fight, or admit that they would be sent to prison.

"What if the relatives find out that he has been telling things about them?" Stephan asked Leo. "We have to get him out, before they decide he's a liability."

"As far as I am concerned, if we can get out of here, he can rot!" Leo snarled. "We need to warn cousin Theo, or they will be after us too. I'm even wishing I'd done a deal with the bitch when she was still here."

"Leo, I can get us out, but do you think we can take on the guards here and the police?"

"What? How?"

Stephan showed him the tool Wanda had tossed to him. "Ivana's brat gave it to me."

"What did you promise her?"

"Nothing. She said we'd owe her one."

"Let's go then."

The police building wasn't deserted, but at that late hour, few people were around. The guards at the holding cells were settling down for a quiet nightshift. The stealthy opening of the security door from the inside, was totally unexpected, and one guard had no warning and the other no time to act. The first fell unconscious from a blow from Stephan's fist, the second, was felled by Leo, who leapt across the table, before he could hit the emergency alarm. They wasted no time trotting up the stairs to the ground floor, and running for the outside door. They were relying on their fleetness of foot to elude pursuers. Even so, they were seen, and the eerie alarm began when they were less than five metres from the building. The brothers raced for the nearest shadow and kept running.

Three hours later, after avoiding the frequent police patrols, the brothers drew near the house where they had been staying. They watched from cover, and Leo cursed under his breath when they spotted the police watchers.

"They're just waiting for us to come waltzing in. Father must have told them. We can't go there to get our stuff and we have no money either."

"We can call Cousin Theo, or Aleksi," Stephan proposed. "Surely they can help us get father out of the police cells."

"Are you mad? If we admit that we left him there, Theo will have a piece of us."

"Well, the Austrians hadn't brought him down there yet...and if we tell them that father was talking freely, and we had to warn them."

"They'll kill him, and probably us."

"We can tell them we didn't say anything, and why would we tell the police about this place. All our stuff is here."

Leo snarled, "Let's get away from here and find some money."

They found a closed up shop, and entered by picking the lock with the tool Stephan had. The till had very little cash in it, and they took it all. Then, while they were there, they put through a call to Theo.

Stephan watched the street from through a crack in some venetian blinds. He listened to his brother's half of the conversation, but couldn't tell who he was speaking to. He just had the impression that the person at the other end was entirely unsympathetic to their plight.

Finally, Leo slammed the phone receiver back down in its cradle, and strode to the door.

"He's sending a car for us."

"Will they help us get father?"

"Theo said he'd handle it. I think he has an agent in the building. He just said he'd take us somewhere we could stay until the heat died down."

Even though they kept a constant watch on the street, the brothers were not aware that they had been seen and followed from the house to the shop. The car that stopped outside, was followed once the brothers had scuttled to it. The house where the car took them, was discreetly surrounded, and the watchers were alert for any indication that either Theo or Aleksi was there. The special tactics team were ready to move in if it became positive that either of those two were there.

In fact, Leo, Stephan and their driver waited in an empty house.

At the police building, Tatarovich was finally taken down to the holding cells. He had no idea that his sons had been there and escaped. He had every expectation that they would come and release him.

If asked, he would have said he had told the police nothing, since he was unaware of the hypnotic commands that had been laid on him. He believed he had thoroughly denigrated his daughter's brat.

The holding cell guards, warned to expect an attack, did not disobey the command to free Tatarovich. One raider held a high powered hand gun to the back of one guard's head. The other raider kept his aimed at the second guard. Both men were restrained using their own handcuffs, while the prisoner and the raiders fled. They were released within minutes, while several groups of WEGA men skilfully followed the fleeing men.

While it was expected that they would join up with the earlier escapees, it was soon proved otherwise. This group went to an office building in the second district. The building was surrounded and all known exits were covered.

Half an hour later, when the order to move in was given, they searched the building and found it empty. The order was given for the house in sixth district to be raided. A dark haired man had been seen going in, but that place too, was empty.

Consultation with the utility authorities, revealed that each place had access to the underground tunnels.

In the morning, Wanda was allowed to re-join the other inmates at breakfast, and all the while she was eating, she was glancing at the other faces she could see, trying to find one with a familiar look. During her work period, again in the laundry, she looked anew at her fellow workers, but dismissed all of them. She turned her attention to trying to reach her sister's mind, except that she couldn't fully concentrate on that because the women who were cronies of Bridgette were trying to get her in more trouble, and she needed to disoblige them.

She continued to look around at everyone during the exercise period, but with so many women in the prison, she couldn't be sure she was seeing them all. Some were in the section for psych prisoners.

Finally, near the end of the exercise period, she felt a response from her sister.

"What's been happening?" Wanda sent with her mind, as she continued her purposeful fast walk around the perimeter of the yard, scanning every face she saw.

"We don't know," Elisabeth sent. "Jim is still away. Derek hasn't been around and there has been nothing on the news. We're just waiting."

"Same here," Wanda sent. "Is Erin around?"

"Yes, why?"

"Has she had any luck hacking into prison records or court records for Ivana?"

"Limited success. Not all the prisons have computer records going back."

"Tell her to keep at it. Tatarovich has been able to keep her being moved from prison to prison – different names and crimes probably. They may each have been short term sentences. His mind believed that neither Ivana nor I would recognise each other."

Wanda outlined the ideas she had considered during her sleepless hours in solitary, and finally suggested that Erin look at the psych prisoners too.

"We'll get busy on those new ideas," Elisabeth promised, sounding glad to have something to do.

"While you are at it," Wanda sent, trying to sound casual. "See if you can get a list of all the prisoners here. I might as well check out this place for something to do. I want to know how many women are here in the different sections, and if you find pictures, look at them – particularly the facial bone structure. Tell me any you think I should check out further."

Elisabeth wasn't fooled. "Do you really think she might be there? Right under our noses?"

"I don't know, but I intend to be sure one way or another."

Wanda sensed that her sister had turned her mind to her suggestions, and she decided to change her tactics. If Ivana was here, she would not be one of the dominant personalities – she was more likely to be one of the 'mice'. So when her path drew near one of these timid loners, she slowed and went to speak to them. They were afraid of her too, for the word about how she had faced down Brigitte had spread. However, she spoke kindly to them, promised to stand up for them, in exchange for telling her who they were and why they were in the prison.

When the siren went for the end of the exercise period, she had only spoken to six of the 'mice', but none of them resembled her idea of Ivana Krinsky nee Tatarovich.

As the prisoners shuffled back into the building, Brigitte's cronies, including her cell mate, eased their way into positions around her, jostling her as they uttered warnings to stay away from the 'mice'. They subsided when Wanda uttered feasible threats back at them – feasible because they had seen how well she had fought the day before. However, the stalemate would only last until Brigitte was released from her extra week of timeout.

During the evening meal, Wanda seemed to be paying no attention to anyone, but even while she was recalling myriads of details that she had noticed during the exercise period, she was aware of her cell mate and two others, moving in on one of the 'mice' she had spoken to. The woman had picked a table right in the corner, by herself, and had kept her attention on eating quickly.

The woman's eyes were wide with fear, but from what Wanda could see, the three women had simply sat near her and were eating.

Since walking around while everyone else was eating was an invitation to loss of privileges, Wanda did not get up until the guard indicated that eating time was over. Then, she quickly returned her tray and plates to the tub near the kitchen, and moved with casual ease past groups of chatting women.

The mouse being cornered by her cell mate, had said her name was Helene. Wanda moved behind those standing over her, caught the words, "...I swear, that was all. She just asked who I was and what I'd done."

Helene was swaying from side to side, and seemed extremely edgy. That suggested things to Wanda that were confirmed when she saw her cell mate pass something small to her. Helene made a rapid motion of hand to mouth, and visibly swallowed.

"You could have asked me what I was doing," Wanda said mildly when her cellmate and the two other women turned away from Helene.

The three women took in her stance – her feet slightly apart, her weight balanced on the balls of her feet, arms free, and the stood immobile, while Helene slipped out from behind them like a squirt of water.

"I didn't expect you to tell us," Wanda's cellmate, Gertrude, admitted tamely.

"Just because you and all of Brigitte's other sheep go around doing things you won't admit to, doesn't mean I'm the same. And if I want to go around here meeting everybody, that's my business. It amuses me."

"You never asked me about me," Gertude challenged, with more animation.

Wanda snorted. "I didn't have to. I was told the very first day that I deigned to be around, and you confirmed it the first night we had to suffer each other's presence. So don't think you can make me stop or I might find other amusements that you sheep won't find funny."

While Gertrude decided not to say any more, since she had to share a cell with this indomitable prisoner, but one of the other two weren't so intimidated.

"You don't want to get involved with Helene, Carson. She's crazy."

"Is that why you slipped her a trank, then?" Wanda kept her voice low this time. "I suppose that slimy looking guard brought them in?"

The three women all looked surprised. They'd have no idea how she could have observed the transaction.

"You're guessing," Gertrude accused.

"I note that none of you are denying it," Wanda countered. "So, if she's crazy, why isn't she in the psych section?"

Gertude began to smirk, since she knew things that her cell mate didn't. "She was, but they reckoned she was okay to join us. They were full over there and needed a bed for a worse case."

"Austrian women must be weak minded cows if the psych section is full." Wanda's taunt got the bite she wanted.

"They only have twelve beds in there!" Gertrude continued to smirk. "I bet you don't even know where that section is."

"It hasn't yet amused me to find out," Wanda told them, but it wasn't quite the truth. By observing from the window of the time out cell, she had a fair idea. However, she wasn't going to hint at her interest.

Before any of them decided to say more the guards came to hustle them out of the mess room.

Wanda glanced around the gathering area, but did not see Helene, or any of the other mice she wanted to talk to. It seemed that they preferred their cells unless they had to be elsewhere. She decided to head back to her own cell, but via the lower level cells.

She didn't get very far, towards the first floor cells, for a guard stopped her.

"You don't belong here, Carson."

"I was looking for Helene," Wanda tried, peaceably.

"This isn't a social institution. Get back to your area."

She decided to obey, and hope she wasn't reported for trouble making, again. She had only five more days before Brigitte was back from time out.

Her own cell was empty when she got there. Gertrude tended not to return until lock up time. So that meant that she had half an hour to herself.

Without her cell mate's disruptive presence, Wanda could think over the day's observations, and to consider ways to get into and out of the psych section, unseen and unmissed.

Her first problem was to get out of the cell section. The best scenario was to find somewhere to hide in the exercise yard, so they wouldn't force her inside. Then she would have to hope no one would miss her. She could convince Gertrude not to speak, by implying her absence was for official reasons. The fool of a woman had made a fuss about her not being around once, and had been in trouble herself for making a false report. She's not be keen to make a fool of herself again.

Anyway, if she managed to stay outside, she'd have to get to the psych building fairly promptly.

The whole idea was extremely foolhardy, but Wanda didn't see it that way. She felt that the inevitable punishment would be worth it if she found Ivana and helped her out of her father's influence.

Still, she had no wish to be caught visiting the psych section. She'd be missed eventually, but she hoped to be back in the exercise yard at worst, and at best elsewhere in the main prison, when that happened. So in the time before lock up – she concentrated on recalling every detail that she had seen of the prison exterior, and of the guard positions and rounds.

By the time Gertrude returned, a minute ahead of lock up, Wanda had pinpointed the one place where she could climb up to the roof unseen. It was an unlikely place, because from ground level, when the prisoners were exercising, it was in plain view. However, when the yard was empty and guards didn't need to be there it was in a blind spot. Her task tomorrow would be to find a hiding place outside.

Wanda was lying awake, and her cellmate was snoring gently, when she felt her sister's mind reaching for hers.

"Lisbeth?" she thought back. "Any news? I hear nothing in here."

"They have Aleksi, but he's not talking. And they recaptured Stephan and Leo – Tatarovich's sons," Elisabeth began. Wanda had the feeling that was the good news, and her sister hadn't got to the bad part. She was right.

"Theo sent his private army to the police building. They got Tatarovich out. He and Theo escaped. Well, they were followed to a house, and surrounded, but when the police moved in, there was no one there. It was discovered then that the house had an old exit to the cellars. They are all interconnected and eventually lead to the catacombs. Derek and Donau spent the day searching down there, hoping to find the Prosecutor's family."

Wanda hadn't given the missing woman and children any thought since returning to prison. There was nothing she could do anyway.

"Any luck with the records here?" Wanda asked instead.

"Three possibles out of three hundred and eighteen prisoners. Two are in the psych section, one in the main part."

"Who are they? And can you think the faces at me?"

"First, Helene Reidel. She was in psych and got moved out."

"I've met her, and you can rule her out," Wanda sent.

"Erika Fischer," Elisabeth looked intently at the printed photo she had obtained. After a minute, she went on. "The other is Monika Federova."

Wanda had the two faces memorised. "How long has each of them been here?"

"Fischer? Um, she's been there three years. She was convicted of slashing a teenager with a knife."

Elisabeth shuddered, and Wanda sensed it.

"Federova is meant to be schitzo, and has been there for nearly a year. She murdered her husband."

"What do you, Erin and Tanya think?"

"Tanya doesn't recognise either of them. But, if what you learnt is right, she wasn't expected to. Could you?"

"Not from where I am. I'd have to get into the psych section."

"Can you?"

Wanda sighed to herself. "Not officially. And I don't want to be committed."

"But you have an idea?" Elisabeth sensed.

"Yeah, I've been thinking about how to get in there…and my idea is insane."

"So you think she's there?"

"I think I want to be sure if she is or not. I feel I have to try. Trouble is, I will only have one chance, and I don't have much in the way of tools."

"What about what Erin gave you? Do you still have it?"

"I gave one tool to Stephan, but I have the other two. I will have to make do."

"What will they do if you are seen?" Elisabeth betrayed her concern.

"If they see me, and I don't stop and drop…maybe shoot me," Wanda considered, and then went on quickly, "However, I don't intend to be seen. What I will do is talk to Helene again, see what she knows about those two women. I'll get her to tell me the routine in there, before I try anything."

"I think the idea is too dangerous," Elisabeth admitted. "When you mentioned it, I started having a very bad feeling."

Wanda didn't want to admit to the same sensation, so hid the thought from her sister.

"Are you going to go over the roof?" Elisabeth asked.

"Am I that predictable?" Wanda sent an image of herself looking shame faced. "But yes. I think I can get in and back here, without them thinking any worse than I stayed outside in the yard."

"Be very careful," Elisabeth insisted,

"Always," Wanda promised.

Chapter 21 - Abduction

Wanda heard the prison alarm system begin, and over the eerie sound, the eruption of booted feet into the yard she had left. She wasn't immediately worried, since she had already reached the roof of the psych wing, and if she stayed flat, she could only be seen by helicopter.

Getting that far had required patience, attention to detail, and careful timing. But the actual actions needed had been easy. She had hidden in a shallow space at the edge of the exercise yard, where two of the old brick buildings formed part of the yard wall. Her constant mantra of, "Don't let anyone see me," had seemed to work, for the guards hustled all the other women inside, and none of them even looked her way. As soon as the yard was silent, she climbed the wall, in this blind spot, using the cracks between the bricks and rough patches to get a grip. She stopped on the roof, hidden by a low parapet, until the change of guards, when the tower guards were less attentive. Then she scrambled up over the roof ridge of the east wing, and down into the angle between the roof and parapet there, while she checked her way to the south wing where the psych prisoners were kept.

The buildings were connected, but the roof was not a clear way. She had spotted what she thought was a skylight, and was commando crawling towards it when the siren began.

She guessed that she had been missed after the evening meal, for it was still half an hour before dark, and lockdown was an hour away.

She continued to move forward, for the sense of urgency that she had been feeling all day had escalated with the siren. All her senses were on alert even though her mind was busy considering what she had learnt from Helene. The routine in the psych wing was different to that of the main prison. If she didn't get to talk to her two targets within the next hour, they would be tranked to sleep and she would have to hide until morning. And that, would escalate the risks she was already taking.

Many times before, she had done equally dangerous things, but never for quite so personal a reason.

Her estimate of the time, let her guess that the psych prisoners would be getting ready for bed. She needed to keep moving, and not think of the search going on behind her. From the sounds and shouts, as well as the barking of dogs, she knew the search of the yard had found nothing. Her intuition suggested they would search the prison and the workshops and when they still didn't find her, they would widen the search.

The unmistakable sound of a helicopter approaching, made her hurry. She had reached the roof hatch and was having trouble opening it as it felt like it had been sealed shut. Yet her flat tool had slipped into a gap and she was moving it around the frame, slowly prying the window glass out of it.

The hatch was only just wide enough for her to slide into once the glass was out of the frame. She risked it being noticed, judging the need to be out of sight as more important. She slid in feet first, lowering her body so that her feet dangled and she hung by her hands. The helicopter flew over, as she dropped to the floor of the dark space below.

She guessed that the drop had been about five feet, but she had landed and let her knees bend, and then converted some of her momentum by springing back up onto her feet. She stood then, to listen, before beginning to explore the room.

Apart from the light coming in through the skylight, the room was dark. The only window faced away from the evening sun. Yet her eyes adjusted to the dimness, and she began to feel her way to the wall and around the room. She found the door, and debated turning on the light, and finally decided to turn it on and off – just long enough for a memorising look around.

The room was twice as large as her cell, and contained maintenance equipment. She spotted two torches on a shelf by the door, and grabbed one after dousing the light. Her next target was a pair of coveralls that were hanging on a rack next to a locked cupboard. They were too big for her, but she donned them any way and almost laughed when she saw the id tag pinned to them.

Something had fallen when shed dragged the coveralls from the peg, and when she felt around for whatever it was, found a cap. With a practiced movement, she gathered her hair, twisted it into a bun, and tucked it under the cap.

Then she checked the pockets, finding a small notebook and a stubby pencil, some twine, a pocket knife, and some electrical tape. Before she moved out, she used the torch to have another look around and to rifle through a toolbox that was sitting on the floor in plain view. She took two screwdrivers and a small wrench.

Then she went to examine the lock. She knew at once that the lock on the outer side of the door needed an electronic keycard, or had a number key pad to punch in a code. Getting out wasn't a problem, but returning would be. She had a solution for that though, she tore off a length of tape, and taped over the tongue of the lock so that it wouldn't extend fully. She would be able to push it open for her return.

A further idea occurred to her, when she gave a last glance around. There were two step ladders leaning against one wall. She took the lightest of these and set it up under the skylight, just in case she was in a hurry when she was leaving.

After the briefest review of her plan, Wanda walked out of the room as if she had every right to be where she was. As she moved, she instinctively checked for the locations of the security cameras, and timed the red indicator. Three seconds on every quarter minute – the same pattern as for the main prison. From then on, her movements were half stealth, half overt.

In the stairway, she timed her passage during the interval between the red flashes. She was out on the second floor without it detecting her. Helene had told her that Monika and Erika had rooms on that level. The third floor where she had entered had the 'gathering lounge' and an exercise room. The first floor had the interview rooms, visitor's room, dining room and clinic.

If her estimate of the time was correct, the inmates would be getting their nightly shower about now. So she walked openly along the passage, but kept her head looking down, glancing rapidly at each door she passed. There were six doors on each side of the passage, each with a slider for the occupant's name, and a viewing window with a patient style clipboard hanging below.

Wanda found Erica Fischer's room, and risked a peek at the personal data. A glance at the age, was enough to rule her out. Fischer was too young to be Ivana.

Monika Federova's room was at the end, near the staircase leading further down. The door was slightly ajar, and she paused there, pretending to check her pockets for something, but actually listening for sounds from within and glancing at the patient data.

She waited for the security camera active light to go off before slipping into the room. In there, the cameras were aimed at the bed and the toilet, which was in a corner screened by a curtain. They would not see her entering, or slipping into the small wardrobe. She was glad that there were no drawers in there, and there was room for her. The space held only a coat and some outdoor shoes. It seemed that Federova didn't have many clothes, apart from the prison issue dresses, and what she did have fit into the three drawers next to her bed.

Wanda pulled the door shut, as far as she could, for there was nothing to grip on the inside, and she kept as far to the hinge side as she could, and listened for noises. She murmured her mantra of "don't let anyone come here and see me".

Noises were muffled in the wardrobe, but she could still faintly hear the sirens from the main facility. Nearer, she was beginning to hear a trolley rattling along the passage, and voices.

She began to review her options for the next stage of the plan. If she was sure that this Monika was Ivana, and the age on the chart outside gave it a reasonable chance, she was going to have to contact Jim or Derek somehow. She could send the information via her sister, if she was awake or not otherwise occupied. It would be too great a risk to find a telephone, and even if she succeeded in getting back to the prison side, she was going to have to face a 'please explain' from the Warden.

She couldn't magic a patient out of here by herself, and the patient was probably going to be drugged to sleep anyway. Yet, as she thought that, she had a sudden sense of urgency. She considered the feeling – it wasn't her danger sense kicking in; yes, her position was dangerous, but not immediately so. She hadn't even confirmed if Monika was the person she was seeking, and she was going to have to wait a bit longer to find out.

While she waited, she felt the tentative touch of her sister's mind. A kind of, 'are you alright' and 'are you busy' message.

"I'm fine for now," Wanda sent the assurance, intending to be misleading, but her sister wasn't fooled.

"What are you doing? The news is saying there has been an escape."

"Yeah, well, it might look that way..."

"Wanda? Where are you?"

She gave her sister an outline, and added, "Stay available – if Monika is Ivana – I need you to pass the word to Jim."

"He isn't back yet. Should I tell Derek what you are doing?"

"Um..." Wanda was sure he wouldn't approve. "Lisbeth, let's see if it is her first. I am pretty sure I can sneak back into the main prison and find somewhere to hide. I'm going to be for it, either way, but I won't have escaped. I just have to wait here until Monika comes back and I can have a word with her. I will tell you what I learn. If you tell Derek now, he'll probably call here. I don't want them to know I snuck in here."

"Okay, I'll wait," Elisabeth didn't sound sure.

Wanda's attention changed to listening to voices in the room. They were muffled by the wardrobe door, but still sounded as if the warders were treating Monika as if she were a simple minded child. Telling her to put her clothes in the drawer, go to the toilet and take her meds.

A second voice, softer than the other, spoke for a moment, but Wanda could not hear the words. However, the warder replied with, "We don't have time for that nonsense tonight. If you disagree, talk to your doctor next time he comes. Take your meds, Federova."

Finally, after the shuffling, flushing and creaking noises ended, and the outer door was snapped shut and locked, the outer room was quiet. Wanda counted to six hundred and carefully opened the wardrobe door. She edged out, and moved to where she could see the red sensor light, but still be out of its range. She timed the periods when it was active, and then used one pause to dash to the bed, scan the woman's face and dash back. There was a light still glowing in the ceiling, only a very dim one, but it would be enough for the camera to see the woman on the bed. It was enough for her to get a mental picture of the facial features of Monika Federova.

It might be her, Wanda decided, but she needed to be sure. The woman's apparent age seemed right, the facial structure too, though the hair colour was black, not light brown.

In another pause period of the camera sensor, she went back to the bed and gently shook the woman. She didn't wake, so she risked gently opening one eyelid and flicking her torch to see the woman's eye colour. It was blue – like her own eyes and those of her sister and cousins.

Wanda still wasn't sure – she would need to wait until she woke, and talk to her. It meant staying in hiding, and increasing her risk of punishment. Even though she wanted to be sure, she debated the wisdom of staying in the wardrobe – she had enough for her to get others to look into this prisoner. If she were found here, the wrong people might learn of her interest in Monika Federova...she really should leave. Yet, even as she thought that, the urge to stay where she was became overwhelming. Obeying the stronger urge, or intuition, Wanda slipped back into the wardrobe and curled up to doze.

During a period of wakefulness, later in the night, Wanda sensed the Erin/Elizabeth/Tanya link.

"What? What is so urgent?"

"Wanda, my mother has a long scar along the inside of her right forearm." That was mostly Tanya.

With a surge of expectation, Wanda sent, "I will check." She stood up to let her muscles unstiffen. She had just edged out when she heard the room door being unlocked, and had to dash back into the wardrobe. She didn't close it completely, and listened through the crack, deciding with relief that it was only the warder doing a routine bed check.

Wanda let the breath she was holding out slowly and breathed deeply a few times to settle herself. When she edged out once more, she waited for the red light to come on and grew alarmed when it did not. Had the physical bed check been because the system was down? That meant the system could start again, any time.

Deciding to take the risk, Wanda dashed to the bed, fumbled under the covers for the woman's arm, and risked using her torch to check for a scar. A faint line of white showed up.

She dashed back to the wall, out of the camera view, and thought elatedly, "She has a scar! It is Ivana!"

Now that she had the proof, it was time for her to head back across the roof to the main prison.

She moved to the door, and touched the handle, expecting it to be locked, but it was instinct to try it first. The handle moved all the way. Only then, did she realise that she hadn't heard the door being relocked when the bed check was done.

Through the crack in the ward door, Wanda heard someone pushing something with trolley wheels. Her danger sense flared to full, and she ran back to the wardrobe to hide. The combination of the alarm being off, the door being open and someone with a trolley at this weird hour alarmed her. They might not be coming to that room, but...

She stood rigidly still, hardly daring to breathe, with only a narrow slit to look through. The rattling trolley came closer, the outer door banged, and a voice hissed a curse. The curse was Russian!

That settled in her mind the reason for the odd events. The person with the trolley had a lit torch on it, and she saw the flash of light as the trolley was pushed towards the bed.

They were going to abduct the sleeping woman, and Wanda considered what to do. She could take on one of the men, there were two she had caught as shadows passing the gap, possibly both, but then what? She couldn't get Ivana/Monika away herself. What if she overcame both, tied them up and then left to get back to the main prison? Probably no good, someone else had to be in on the scheme – they could free the men and they'd continue their task. If, instead of leaving, she went to rouse the guards in this section, they'd not listen to her. They'd have her slammed into solitary so fast, her head would spin. And it might be one of the duty guards in on things.

Even though she was grinding her teeth with frustration, she stayed where she was, trying to see all she could through the slit. If she got back to the main prison, she could get a message out.

Wanda was completely unprepared for the door in front of her to be jerked open, and her moment of shock was enough for the man there to bring the orifice of a hand gun up to touch her nose.

The wielder spoke in an urgent hiss. "Boris! Igor!"

Wanda wasted no time berating herself for not sensing this man, the look out – she was already calculating ways to escape and the chances of success. Her attempt to get a response from her sister failed. Elisabeth was likely asleep.

"Out! Hands above you."

With a gun touching your face, obedience was the most prudent action. The man with the torch, flashed it in her direction, it wasn't so bright that it dazzled her, and it gave her a glimpse of the men, who were dressed like she was in coveralls of some dark colour.

"That's Carson!" one exclaimed, and his voice seemed exultant. Wanda tried to read his mind to see why he was pleased. She sensed more than 'heard' that someone wanted her. Well, these were most likely some of Father Theo's 'army', so it meant that either Theo or Tatarovich was behind this. She'd bet on it being the latter. If he thought she was onto Ivana's whereabouts, he'd want her moved. The trolley meant they were not simply going to kill Monika – or why bring it? Her own position wasn't so predictable.

Wanda flicked a glance around the room, imprinting everything into her memory. Then she watched the eyes of the man in front of her, there was just enough light to see them as a faint gleam.

The shape of the eyes changed as the mouth smiled. "We'll tie her up and bring her with us. Igor, grab another trolley."

For an instant, the man's eyes looked away, although the gun hand was steady. Wanda ducked and dived for the partly open door. Right then, she didn't care if others saw her, if it meant these men were seen and challenged.

Something hissed past her ear. A moment later, a second 'phutt' seemed to coincide with a stinging pain in her side. She staggered but put her hand on the pain and pressed as she regained her balance. She got two more steps before she was shoved in the back, and she fell nose first to the floor. A weight sat on her back, making it hard for her to breathe. Her arms were forced behind her, and she felt something like taped being wrapped around her wrists to keep them together.

When the man eased up, she tried to struggle, but a fist hit her hard in the back of the head, causing blackness to threaten her. Her body would no longer obey her, but she could still hear and her feet were being taped now.

"Why don't we just leave her here for the guards to find her?"

"Fool, she's seen us! And a tied up escapee would look suspicious, when we are meant to make this look like an escape. Hurry with that other trolley – this is already taking too long."

While Wanda lay breathless, unable to move, the men lifted Ivana/Monika from her bed and folded her into the trolley. She was vaguely aware that they were shoving dirty bed linen in on top of her.

The second trolley arrived all too quickly, but the man must have carried it, for the first she knew of it was when it was set back on the floor with a minor clatter. She hadn't time to recover enough, when she was lifted in feet first and pushed down by the shoulders. All she could do was try to resist being folded in as Ivana had been. The men were out of patience, for a fist came at her from the side. Wanda sensed it coming but couldn't move out of the way – in the fraction of an instant before losing consciousness, she sensed her sister's mind.

Chapter 22 - Waiting game

Derek Mont Pelier returned to the hotel room where Elisabeth, Tanya and Erin were alternately pacing and flopping into chairs. When he arrived, three pairs of eyes fixed on him, and the women became statues, as they waited to hear what he had to say.

"Nothing!" he summarised. "A laundry truck left a short while before I alerted them. It was allowed to leave because that wing wasn't in lock down."

Elisabeth felt like she was going to cry. Derek had not said a cross word about withholding information; he hadn't needed to. She wished now that she had confided in him, and told him earlier what Wanda had been doing, but she hadn't wanted to get her sister into more trouble.

Derek went on, "The police are looking for the truck, and the helicopter will refuel and join the search. It won't get far."

He glanced at the three women, their tense postures hadn't eased. They were all still staring at him, and he finally exploded, "Why the hell did she do such an asinine thing?"

Tanya answered, her face white, "She found my mother." She met the angry gaze of the tall Interpol agent, and seemed to be daring him to call that reason stupid.

Derek had not expected that answer. "What?" He calmed himself and went on, "What is this about?"

"I thought my mother was dead. But Tatarovich said he had rescued her – he told Wanda, thinking she was me. He was punishing her."

"Why did she think your mother was in that prison?"

Elisabeth answered. "He implied that neither would recognise the other."

Erin added, "He thought wrong."

Derek shook his head in amazement, and admiration. It was another instance of reasoned method behind Wanda Martin's apparent madness.

"This business is getting more and more complicated. I hope we find them both alive."

"If they were going to kill them, why take them out of the prison?" Tanya asked. Derek's comment had sent a lance of fear through her.

"Exactly," Elisabeth insisted. "And I told you, Wanda is too stubborn to give up and too damn ornery to die. And if I find out anything more, I'll tell you. I promise. But she isn't dead now, but I just don't know where she is."

"And the three of you are sure Tatarovich is behind this?"

"He has to be! Him or Theo. The men who took her and Ivana, recognised Wanda. I think they are probably Theo's people."

"Well, the Austrian police have a full scale hunt for both of them. We must hope they find them and the other missing people. Why don't you all try to rest?"

Tanya and Erin, who were standing, both moved to chairs and sat, but Derek decided it was a lost cause trying to stop them worrying. He decided to help himself to a drink from the small supply in the room.

Erin spoke from the chair where she had retreated, causing him to pause as he began to sip.

"It has occurred to us that these people tend to repeat successful methods."

Derek glanced at her, but continued to take a mouthful of the less than top quality brandy. He considered all he had learnt of 'The Family', and most of it had been from Wanda, and accepted the idea.

"So what method might they be repeating this time? Theo disappeared into the cellars...and this abduction was set in motion after that. Are you suggesting they will take Wanda and your mother into the cellars?"

Elisabeth spoke up, "The cellars go everywhere, so rats can vanish there, but they also suggest places to hide stuff."

"I assure you, that idea has been thought of. But we searched those cellars – with Donau's dog. Units are still searching."

With an impatient twist, Elisabeth turned to look at him. "There are countless miles of the things."

"So, do you have an idea?"

"Yes! Maybe look at the idea from side on. Theo kept Allan Wexford, the real one, prisoner right near where he was living. And by the sound of it, he has control of a fair bit of property. I would say that those rats have gone to ground in one of the places, and it will be near the cellars, and they will take their prisoners somewhere nearby."

Derek was impressed, he hadn't yet thought things out that way. "Yes, that is a very perceptive theory. I will see that the Austrian police look into that. Anything else?"

"Not at the moment." Elisabeth looked away and slumped further into her chair.

Derek finished his drink and left the room. He wanted to be where the action was, and so he went back to the police building, aware that Donau would have been alerted and would most probably be there, trying to rest after the long search in the underground tunnels.

He hadn't told the Austrian that two people had been taken from the psych wing, just that he'd had word that an attempt would be made to remove one of the psych prisoners. At the time, before that astounding revelation, the name Monika Federova had meant nothing. That Carson was with her, had been senseless. It would have done more harm than good, if he had mentioned Carson in the warning. The police might have considered her being there another piece of proof that she was actually working for the Russians, not against them.

They still might, but that would depend on what was found, when that laundry van was found. Though surely, they would not believe that Carson, an American who had only been in the prison for a short time, could have known that the psych wing had a laundry service. The main prison didn't. They would have to think that she was not involved.

No, he wanted them to think that – but he couldn't assume so. It would be better to warn Donau. He at least, seemed to have an open mind, and respect for Carson in her other guise of Wanda Martin.

At the police building, he met Donau coming down the stairs, Alex keeping pace with him.

"Come on! They've found the laundry van that left the prison.

Abandoned, and partly obscured in trees."

Without a word, Derek changed direction, and kept pace with the Austrian. "I have some other information. Carson was with Federova when she was taken."

Donau almost stumbled on the lowest step. "What? We've been hunting everywhere for her, and you tell me she was in the psych wing. How do you know that?"

"Nevermind. I know it sounds unbelievable, but let's see what they find with the truck. We already know that Tatarovich doesn't like Carson. It seems that Federova is another of his victims."

"We'll see," was all the agreement Donau would give.

"She did help you catch him."

"He still got away."

"Carson didn't help him get free."

Donau growled. He was tired and frustrated.

Five police cars surrounded the truck pull in area where the laundry van had been abandoned. The site was cordoned off, but Donau and his companion were allowed through. Alex stayed close until Donau gave him a command and he moved to sniff at the pile of laundry that had been strewn on the ground, and at the two overturned wheeled laundry hampers.

The forensic team had already arrived, but were waiting for Donau to finish examining the site.

"We have only had a cursory look, but there is blood on some of the linen sheets – a fair bit," one of the technicians reported. "I am told that there were two bullet holes in Federova's cell wall."

"Yes," Donau agreed. He knew that, but decided to ask, "Two hampers? I thought only one of the psych patients was missing."

His attention was caught when he heard Alex whine softly. The thin high pitched sound was the dog's equivalent of worry. He left the technician and went to see what Alex had found. He was staring at the blood-stained sheet.

He glanced at Mont Pelier, saying tacitly, "You were right."

To the technician, he said, "Run a blood type on the blood. Compare it to Federova, and if it doesn't match, compare it to Carson. Two hampers suggest two people escaped or were abducted, and it is too far to believe that Carson's disappearance and Federova's are not connected."

To his dog, he said softly, "Search."

Alex was off like a shot, following a scent only he could detect, but he stopped when he got to the road, and sniffed in all directions. The story was obvious; the two women had been taken off in another car. Donau pointed out tyre tracks and let the technicians begin their work. He went back to his car where the Interpol agent had retreated out of the way.

"You seem to know too much about what is going on here," Donau accused. "How did you know Carson was in the psych section, and how the hell did she get there?"

"I didn't know, but once I knew the missing inmate, it became logical."

"You are going to have to explain this to me. I can believe Carson capable of getting there. Her skill at Alpha Prime is evidence enough. But why?"

Derek murmured softly, "I have the notion that Carson believes that Federova is another victim of Tatarovich."

"Are you trying to say he set Carson up? Was she under duress when she went to Alpha Prime?"

"Not then, but later. I believe her when she says she did not kill anyone, or assist anyone to kill."

Donau clamped his lips, deciding not to contest that point. "Victim? How?"

"Set up – put in prison. False charges."

"Are you also implying Carson was set up? I can't see it. Rudy Wagner is an experienced detective. Anyway, Federova has been in and out of prison all her life. She is in for killing her husband and daughter."

"One of those young women that you might have seen at the riverside warehouse may be Federova's daughter."

Donau frowned, "I think I should question those women, and find out what their connection is to all this."

Derek shook his head. "There are a few highly confidential matters involved. You are aware of Wanda Martin's affiliation with the US Government?" Donau nodded, slowly, waiting for the other man to continue. "There are things that she cannot talk of, even if questioned by you. She is related to those young women, and they are doing everything they can to help us find Tatarovich and Theo. It's personal – so you can believe they will leave nothing unchecked. One of them has been locating records of property owned or controlled by either of those men, here in Vienna."

"So you believe the missing women could be at one of those places?"

"Or near to one. Another of those women reminded me that Theo kept the real Allan Wexford prisoner right where he was living – for five years. She also reminded me that since those two escaped from us into the cellars, they probably came out through some property owned by one of them, and may have places to stash victims and other stuff down in the tunnels."

Donau groaned. "You've seen enough to know that those tunnels go everywhere under the city. Heavens knows where they go. Do you really want to spend another day getting lost in them?"

"Truthfully, no. However I don't like the idea of – sometime in the future – that someone will stumble over five skeletons."

"Five?"

"Prosecutor Neubauer's wife and children are still missing. I am hoping that Carson and Federova will be put in with them, and that Carson will find a way to get them out."

"The blood was Carson's," Donau revealed his guess. Then he said, "Let's hope then. Do you really trust Carson that much?"

"I do. And I am not saying she hasn't done some criminal things here. However, think of the fact that your dog likes her, and if nothing else that she has a good heart."

"Hmm. I will see if I can find where the nearest known entrance is to the cellars from here," Donau decided. "Coming?"

Wanda roused, aware only of a pounding in her head, as if she were in the hollow of a large drum. Awareness of a lack of sound in her ears, followed, and she identified a headache. At first her concentration was on relaxing the muscles in her head, and slowly the pain abated to a point when she could begin to think. Where was she? What had happened?

Memory returned slowly, and when it did, she stiffened reflexively – was she still in danger? The question was forgotten as the intense pain erupted in her side, near her hip. She emitted a stifled moan, and forced herself to relax again, as she did a mental inventory of her condition.

She'd been in a worse state before, and survived, therefore she could again. She was bound, arms behind her, and at the ankles. What had they used – yes, surgical tape – could she tear it? No – with so many layers, it might as well be steel but maybe she could wear it away – but how?

She heard something scurrying away in the darkness – too big for a rat, but what? Her special senses seemed sluggish, but there was no danger – for her danger sense had never failed her.

"Mmmm," she tried to speak but her mouth would not open.

No one answered her, and as she strained to listen, all she seemed to hear was the sound of water dripping nearby.

She would have to help herself then. In her mind was the intense desire to see at least a little in the dense dark. The area smelt of damp, dust, rot and a little of human waste. She moved slightly, so that her hands touched the surface under her. It felt like wood – dry, dusty, splintery, old, but with thin gaps between narrow slats. Some kind of basic flooring to keep the area flat.

Wanda considered how she could move – to find what the walls were made of. Pushing up was beyond her – she was weak, and her arms had no strength. All she could do was push herself further onto her side, to fall on her front where her nose was greeted with a stronger smell of decay. She had to control a bout of nausea, and then steel herself to roll further, onto her injured side and then to her back.

The pain made her nearly black out, but she tried to breathe deeply, and held on to consciousness by a narrow thread. She had to stop, control her breathing, and relax.

The scuffle of movement came again, and she tried to speak, "Hmmm."

"Who...who are you?"

The voice was high pitched, like a frightened child.

"Hmmmmmm."

"Can't you talk?"

"Hmm, hmm." It was the nearest Wanda could get to "Uh, uh."

Then she began to feel tentative fingers touching her, and trying to find her face.

"It feels like papery tape," the voice said.

"Hmm, hm, hmmm!" Wanda wanted the child to hurry and get it off.

"Lochi?" another voice broke the silence. A woman's voice, fearful and abrupt.

"Here, Mama."

"What are you doing? Come back here."

"Mama, the lady is awake."

"I told you to stay away from them."

The hands left her face and small scuffling sounds told Wanda that the child had moved away, somewhere to her left.

Wanda managed another roll, and felt herself touch a wall. She was half way between on her side and on her back, so her hands could feel the dusty rock wall. It felt like natural rock, rough sealed with cement. Now though, the wall seemed to be faintly glowing, and she focused on a rock protrusion and considered how to sit up so that she could try to abrade the tape around her mouth. Some of the weak feeling persisted, but now, with the rough wall beside her, she might be able to push herself up. As soon as her body began to bend, her injured side protested, but she kept going until she was sitting. Only then, did she stop to let the pain settle down again, and her head which had begun to pound again in sympathy.

Once she felt able, she began to rub the tape on her face against the protruding rock. It took time, and she could feel the scrapes on her cheek. After what seemed a long time, she freed her mouth enough to speak.

"Lady, I have no intention of hurting you or your kid," Wanda stated, leading up to asking for help.

"I don't believe you. I know who you are. You're a murderer, and that other woman probably is too."

Wanda held back her instinctive denial. "I won't expect you to believe I am not, but you will have to admit that I didn't walk in here under my own free will. And if you were able to recognise me, I assume there was light when we arrived?"

"Yes," the woman admitted.

"Well, then you know I am tied up. Can you at least believe that the people who put me here – us here – don't like me? Think that I might be able to get out if I were free? Is the other woman tied up?"

There was silence. Wanda decided the idea of getting free had done it.

"Don't you want to get out of here? I can do that – if I were free."

She heard shuffling noises, and felt hands touching her again.

"Where are you tied?"

"Hands and ankles. They used surgical tape."

The woman went to her ankles first for Wanda had her hands behind her.

"Thanks," Wanda said, when her ankles were free. She felt the woman inching along the floor to get to her hands. She inadvertently kneed Wanda where she was injured, causing her to twitch in pain.

"What's wrong?"

"I'm sore there, don't worry about it. Do you know where the light switch is?"

"Not in here. Somewhere outside the door."

"Okay. Can you help me up?"

Wanda needed that help, but once she was on her feet and the initial giddiness had passed, she pushed away from the wall.

"Was it just you and Lochi that was in here?"

"No. Lilli is asleep."

"Am I likely to step on her?"

"No, she is against the far wall. What can you do?"

"Get us out – I hope. What is your name?"

"Angelika Neubauer. I know you are Carson, but who is your friend?"

"Monika. She should stay asleep for a while longer – they drugged her. I don't know what she will be like when she wakes."

Wanda moved away from Angelika, in the direction opposite from where the woman had come from. Her guess that this was the wife of the Prosecutor had been confirmed. Heavens knew what her husband had been telling her about "Carson the murderer", but right now she was more interested in outsmarting 'The Family' than holding grudges against the man who had sent her to prison for twenty five years.

Following the wall, which at first was the cement coated stone, she came to a section where there was more of the rotten wood forming a wall. It was like the false floor of this dug out cellar. She guessed it was a divider to an adjacent area, and kept following it around. She came to a change in the wood. This was smoother, and when she knocked on it, the sound was a dull thud. She let her hands explore what she thought was the door, and finally felt a metal plate with a hole in it. In an instant, her mind had flicked through dozens of old locks. This one was very old, it would be little trouble to force open.

Wanda checked the pockets of the coveralls she still wore. The few tools she had stolen were gone – not surprising – but the men had not searched her further. In the process, she felt where the fabric had stuck to her, and which was now crusty dry. Her wound had bled a lot, but she couldn't worry about that now. She was functional, that was all that mattered.

As she unzipped the coveralls, and felt down to where the plastiskin was still stuck to her leg, relieved to feel it. She unstuck it, and brought it out, removed the tools by feel and rolled up the plastiskin and stuck it in a pocket.

She knelt down, so her head was almost level with the lock. She felt for the hole again, and then used one of the slender metal pieces to investigate the lock. The little clicking noises seemed loud in the cell, but Wanda worked as quickly as she could, while she sensed it was safe.

Angelika ghosted up behind her. "What are you doing?"

"Picking the lock."

"In the dark?"

"Won't be the first time. But I do need to concentrate."

Wanda took a deep breath, and thought clearly to any powers that might be listening. "I need to get this lock open. We need to get out."

She resumed her attempt, and it almost seemed that she could see the inside of the lock in her mind. But there was something blocking the hole. The key was in the other side of the lock. She sat back and considered. She didn't have a tool to turn it from this side...

Moving carefully, she twisted to feel for a gap at the base of the door. There was, but she could only put her fingers under it, and an inch of her wrist.

"What's the matter?" Angelika asked.

Wanda explained and added, "I can push it out, but I can't get my hand under far enough to reach it. And I don't have paper or something to push under to catch it. I could still work on the lock, but the key would be much easier." She had an idea, and wondered if the woman would allow it. "How old is Lochi?"

"Five. Why?"

"I was wondering how far under the door he could reach."

"Lochi, come here to Mama." Angelika kept talking so he could find her. She explained to him what they wanted him to try.

Wanda added, "Lie on your back, your arm will go under more easily."

Wanda felt a little body wriggling past her legs. "I can get it right under," Lochi said, excitedly.

"Ok, get out again, and let me work for a bit."

When they heard the key fall beyond the door, Wanda let Lochi feel around, and talked him through moving his arm.

"I feel it!"

"Try and move it towards the door. Sweep it this way," Wanda told him. When she heard it slide on the inner wood flooring, she felt down and found it, then helped Lochi wriggle free.

"You're a right clever boy, Lochi. What say we see if the key will unlock the door from this side?"

It did, but Wanda held both mother and child back. "Wait. I will try to find the switch, and check the area."

Wanda opened the door, outwards, a tiny slit, and listened first, but allowed her other senses to tell her what they would. She was sure their trick with the key had not alerted anyone, and she still sensed no other presences. She opened the door wider, and felt around the frame on the outer side for a light switch, and found none. Then she tried to follow the wall, but her feet hit something that rattled. It seemed their prison was a room at the back of junk storage cellar.

She moved slowly after that, feeling with her feet for a clear way through. It wasn't straight, but her mind mapped the route, even though she could see nothing.

She reached another door, and this time her exploring fingers found an old style switch – not a wall switch, but a dangling cord, right beside the door. Before yanking it, she let herself sense the aura around her. She didn't feel there was danger, just the need to be cautious. A dim light came on, revealing piles of ancient, dusty, broken household junk.

To herself, she thought, "I doubt that Theo would keep guards here, but how often would they check?"

To Angelika, she asked, "Do they bring food to you?"

The woman was standing in the doorway of their prison, holding Lochi back.

"I haven't seen anybody while I was here – except when they brought you and the other in – they had us turn our backs from them. We've had no food, or water. We tried drinking the stuff that runs down the wall, but it is gritty and tastes awful."

That didn't help, Wanda decided. They could come back at any time – or never. She tried to send a message to her sister, but again, she felt no reply. Studying the other woman though, she guessed from the dark shadows under her eyes, that she was dehydrated, and from that decided that she and her kids had gone missing even before the Prosecutor had taken the call that had agitated him. Before she had been used as bait.

Wanda examined the lock on the outer door. It was the same vintage as the other one, but this time the key was not in the other side. She set to work with the makeshift tools, and within a couple of minutes, the lock clicked open. She turned the door handle, and pulled. The door rubbed the frame, and make a squeaky sound. She stopped and listened, to see if anyone had heard the noise. Feeling that it was safe, she slowly inched her head out and saw only a dimly lit passage going left and right.

At that moment, a high pitched wail began and Angelika hurried back into the inner room. Wanda closed the door again and went after her. She could see Monika now, a huddled form near the right hand wall, and paused to check her breathing and pulse.

To Angelika she said, "I want to go and find a way out. I think you should wait here. We can't go until Monika wakes up, and it will be easier for me to find the way out and come back rather than have all of us going in and out of dead ends."

Wanda had the idea that the woman wasn't listening.

"We have to get out of here! Lilli...she has a really high fever. She only just fell asleep before you woke up."

The slightly higher pitch to Angelika's voice, betrayed her incipient panic.

"Let me look at her," Wanda insisted, and she gently pushed Angelika aside, and knelt down to where the tiny girl was whimpering on a hard bed that was no more than her mother's jacket.

Wanda estimated that the girl was only about two years old, and she did indeed have a fever. She drew on her paramedic training as she examined the girl, looking for rashes, or other outer signs of the cause, and at the same time considering options.

Angelika was standing rigidly as Wanda examined her daughter. Lochi was clinging to her skirt.

"We need to get her cooled down, and try to get some fluid into her," Wanda said decisively. "I will go and see if there is anything in that junk out there that we can use. If you have a handkerchief, try wetting it in that trickle, and washing her with it – perhaps blow on the dampness."

Wanda stood and stepped aside, as Angelika began to follow the suggestions. Lochi detached himself from his mother and followed her out.

"Stay back, Lochi. I will look, but I need you to be ready to help."

By stepping carefully on and around various pieces of rubbish, Wanda found a metal wash tub, but had to move a lot of other stuff to get it free. She took it to Lochi, and continued looking for something to use to direct water into the tub. The best she could find was an old roller blind. Two broken wooden chairs, might be able to support the blind. Nothing else gave her any further ideas. Lochi, from his position in the walkway, had seen two cups, and pointed them to her. She was able to extricate them with very little difficulty.

Wanda carried her findings into the inner room and began to assemble her makeshift water catcher. The chairs helped to support the blind, but not close enough to the wall. Wanda asked Lochi to help hold the blind close to the wall, so the water flowed down the blind, into the tub. She took the two cups, and directed some of the flow into them, and when nearly full, set them on one of the chairs.

"Angelika, I have filled two cups, let the dust settle a bit, then dip your finger in and try wetting Lilli's lips with it. If she tries to suck your finger, keep dipping it and letting her suck. If she rouses enough to sip the water, let her."

"The water is filthy," Angelika protested.

"Right now, it is all we have, and Lilli needs the fluid. If the tub fills, you might consider unwrapping her and splashing the water over her."

Once the other woman was busy with her daughter, Wanda checked Monika again. She was still deeply asleep.

"I'm going to see if I can find a way out. I won't go far."

"What if those men come and find you gone, and blame me?" The words were calm enough but Wanda sensed the terror she was hiding, so that her son would not be scared. It wasn't working.

"Tell them you were glad to see me go. You were frightened of me, once I had freed myself. Okay?"

Angelika nodded. "You are not what I expected...not like what my husband said."

"Yeah, well he doesn't really know me, and was told misleading things. Anyway – I will be quick."

Wanda went back to the outermost door, and repeated her earlier precautions before emerging into the tunnel like passage. In this section, there were opening on one side only. The other side was native stone. She reached out and touched it, placing her hand flat.

"Please, keep the people inside there safe." She pictured the two women and the two children, and thought of the evil that threatened them. And this time, as had sometimes happened in the past, she seemed to feel some power moving – but it might have been a breeze.

She moved to the left, the way that the breeze seemed to be coming from, and kept her ears alert for any sound. Gradually, as she zigzagged along passages and cross-passages, the sound of trickling water became louder. She followed the sound, until stopped by a grating that blocked the way into the water drain. To one side, water was pouring out of a pipe. She couldn't go out that way, but it gave her a direction to follow that might lead to the street. The breeze that came from the flowing water, smelt of fresh wet air.

Now, as she retraced her steps, she paid more attention to the doors she had been passing. She picked the locks on several at random. In one section, she saw steps going up into a house. In another, in a different passage, the doors hid more storage rooms. The houses were a definite possibility.

She was returning to the cellar where the others were, and was hearing a voice echoing around the stone walls. A nagging sense of urgency made her begin to trot back. She had no trouble returning, and the sound grew louder and louder. The yells were coming from within the chamber she had left – Monika had woken.

Wanda entered and relocked the door behind her. She strode into the inner room, where Monika was in a heap on the ground yelling in some mixed dialect.

"Quiet!" Wanda hissed, infusing the words with her 'command' tone.

Silence, fell, broken only by the sound of water running into the tub. Lochi was still manfully holding it, in place, even though his eyes were wide with fright. Angelika held Lilli close to her chest.

Crouching down next to Monika, Wanda now spoke quietly. "I am sorry if I scared you, Monika, but I need you to be quiet."

"Where am I? Why are you doing this to me? I've been good. I have."

"I'm sure you have Monika, and as you can see, you are not in prison anymore."

"Who are you?'

"My name is Carson," Wanda said, aware that Angelika was listening. "I am a friend of Tanya. Do you remember Tanya?"

Monika looked up, and echoed the name. "How can you be? My Tanya is dead."

"No, she is alive, and so is Stefan." Wanda mentioned her husband, to see how much she remembered.

"You're wrong. Papa said I killed them. He showed me pictures. He told me I was sick and had to be locked up."

"Your Papa is a lying bastard."

"No, he loves me. He's trying to help me," Monika's protests were muted now.

Her statement had the ring of truth to it, or at least a truth Monika believed. Wanda kept her cursing inside her mind. She did not have the time to try sorting Monika out now. Yet, at the same time, she was relieved. She was sure Monika was really Ivana Krinsky, and on some matters, Tatarovich had not scrambled her mind.

However, she needed to do something to keep Monika calm. Speaking very quietly, Wanda put her into a hypnotic trance. "You are no longer sick, Monika. You have paid for any wrongs you did. You have been released. Your father does not need to find you more treatment."

Monika was nodding slightly with each sentence and Wanda continued. "There will be some formalities to complete, and the current treatment to taper off…" The authorities would need proof of her wrongful incarceration. "But now we need to get out of here. Can you help my friend Angelika with her children? Will you trust me?"

"Yes," was the whispered agreement, and Wanda tapped Monika's shoulder to wake her.

Wanda stood up, and said quickly. "I just need to check the other way. Be ready to leave when I come back."

Her thought was that there had to be an exit to the street nearby. If she couldn't find it, there were the houses, but she shivered at the thought. What if she chose the wrong one and Tatarovich was there?"

She let some inner instinct guide her, and the air was getting colder. She was shivering. The coveralls over her prison issue dress, was little protection. When she began to walk up a steep slope, she felt the entrance had to be close by. Then she stepped into water, and the thin jiffy shoe on her right foot became instantly saturated. She didn't need to see to know there was a tiny river of water in this part of the tunnel, and she took it to mean that she was near the exit. Hurrying, in spite of the dark, she came to a solid wood door. It was locked, but she still had the tools to open it.

As soon as she opened it, a gust of wind pushed it against her. She kept her feet, and held it as she looked out. A gust of wind driven rain soaked her. Rain hadn't been in her plans. She wanted to bring the others up, hide somewhere close, and call the police. In this weather, she needed to find shelter for them. Staying in the entrance here was too risky if Theo's men came looking for them.

She stepped out, and looked around. She was in a dim corner of some kind of yard. Light came from streetlights along a road, and dim security lights. Two buildings backed onto this yard, and a quick dash to the nearest and a look at the lock, told her they were too modern for her to open with the tools she had. She scanned the yard, but there was nowhere to shelter or hide so she trotted towards the street, where the occasional cars went past with their wheels swishing in the wet road and throwing up spray. Wanda hoped the rain would at least keep people off the street.

Wanda stood close to the wall of one of the buildings and scanned the far side of the street. The lights reflected off wet walls and glass. Enough signs were visible to suggest these were shops. Several had an awning of some kind, but they were touching each other, and there was nowhere to hide. She saw several people trotting along the street, head down, hurrying to get out of the rain. Wanda decided to imitate them, and ran for approximately fifty metres along the road, glancing both ways, looking for a niche to hide the others. Just as she was about to turn around, she saw a gate between a hardware store and a flower shop. After a quick glance along the street, both ways, she forced the lock and went inside. The area was sheltered from the worst of the weather, by being small and surrounded by tall buildings. It had piles of stuff, places to hide...it would do.

Her danger sense began to niggle her, as she approached the gate again to go out. She was cautious, peeping out around the wood first. Two figures, with umbrellas trying to twist out of their hands, went past. As soon as they were two shops away, she slipped out and began to run back towards the laneway to the cellars. She heard footfalls behind her, and looked over her shoulder, a man sized shape was lumbering after her, so she increased her pace. Aware of that danger, she didn't heed her danger sense, and so was unprepared for the figure that stepped beside her and grabbed. She almost tripped and fell, but her balance was instinctive.

A voice was saying, "What were you doing coming out of Bauman's yard?"

Wanda didn't answer or wait to hear more, she twisted and had a glimpse of the brown uniform the man wore, as he fell to the ground. She was already racing off, ignoring the shout to stop, and hoping the guards didn't decide to pull out their guns. Behind her, she heard a car engine rev, a wheel screeching turn and realised the guards were coming after her by car.

Debating whether the guard had seen enough of her face to recognise her, Wanda kept running. When she should have turned between the buildings, she slowed, but decided that she had no way of knowing the allegiance of the men. Her inner sense was telling her to run, not to trust them. If they had been police, she would have risked it…maybe…but these guards might be Theo's people looking for her. She ran around the corner of the next side street. The car was almost on her, but the light turned red and it had to wait. It gave her time to find another wooden gate. This time she didn't try to pick the lock. It was quicker to heave herself up and over the top. She didn't stop through – the men would check anyplace that she might have gone, and this yard seemed like a dead end.

She paused to look around, and grinned as she saw the pull down ladder of the fire escape. She scaled it in seconds and pulled the lower ladder up. Then, she lay on the landing, close to the wall and kept still. Nearby, a car door slammed. Wanda watched the gate, a head appeared over it, and torch flashed around. She heard a man giving orders – to check the other side of the street. Then her worst fear was confirmed. She heard her name mentioned. They had recognised her as Carson – and the police were coming. She had to move.

Her first impression of the yard had been of a dead end, but from her position on the landing, she had a different view. The yard below had a carport along one fence, providing shelter for four cars. At the end was a space for hanging washing. A high fence hid the adjoining property, more units or flats, but from this high, she had a glimpse of back yards. She could climb the fence and elude the followers that way. If she hurried, she would beat the police, if they decided to cordon off the area.

If the police were not working under the theory that she was an escaped murderer, she might have given herself up and made them listen to her. Maybe. If they had to catch her, she would rather be caught helping the abductees.

As she began to make her way over back fences, and the police sirens drew closer, she began to feel an urgency to get back to the others. That need overrode any other thought she had. She dared not return to where she had come out – that would be swarming with police. Maybe they will find the open door to the cellars…but they would not know why it was open, or they might think only she had been hiding there.

But there had been houses with entrances to the cellars and she had a mental map of where they were, and how far away they were. She had a chance to get to one of them if she moved fast.

The sirens did not come near – the street, when she emerged was quiet. The houses she wanted were across the road, and they were all built so they touched each other. She could not slip between them to the back, so she would have to go through one. She studied the nearest five houses – two had lights on in the upstairs rooms. The other three were dark. She checked the street and ran across the road to the nearest one with no lights. She couldn't even make herself approach the door – something repelled her. There was no time to wonder why, just to run to the furthest of the three.

The sensation did not occur there, and she quickly forced the lock and dived inside, being as quiet as she could and holding the door firmly as she relocked it. Wanda stood still then, listening to see if anyone had been alerted by her entry. The only sound she heard was the ponderous ticking of a clock, and she waited no longer. The only light she had to see was coming in through a semicircular window over the front door, it showed her a passage heading to the back of the house and she went there, moving carefully, lest her wet jiffy shoes squeaked on the polished wood floor.

She was probably leaving a trail of water but she could not worry about that. She would be long gone when the people awoke in the morning.

The passage ended in a laundry, and the door to the cellar was there. Solid, and with a lock that had not been opened in a very long time. It took her five minutes to open it, and by that time she was feeling a sense of dread close to panic. She pulled the door open and it protested as the wood door and frame parted. The noise was loud, even with the sound of rain on the windows. She didn't wait to be found, and slipped through, finding herself on a set of narrow steps going down. She turned and pulled the door shut.

Now she felt the urgency to return to the small group she had promised herself she would protect. Once again, her instinctive sense of direction led her to where she had to go. Sensing danger, she hurried, but did not forget caution. When she reached the cell, the outer door was closed, and relocked. She listened at the door, but all she heard was her own laboured breathing, but something felt wrong.

In her mind, she asked the powers that be, "Is it safe to go in?"

She felt an overwhelming sense of, "Hurry."

For the second time, she picked the lock of the outer door, and when it opened, and there was no light within, she went in, shut the door and switched on the light. She was already hearing someone frantically trying to shove the door against something that rattled. A child was crying, Lochi she guessed.

"Damn," Wanda swore. She began to toss aside the junk that had been thrown against the inner door to block it, since she had removed the key. "Angelika, I'm coming."

Some of the junk was heavy, and she could not lift it, and tried to shove it. The exertion made her side explode in pain, and she thought the wound might have opened again. It didn't stop her. Her senses were telling her she needed to hurry.

Part of her mind was listening for someone to come along the passage, but she knew she would only hear them when they opened the door. If Theo's men had been here, then they would know she was missing. They hadn't wanted to take her at first, until they recognised her. Surely they had gone to report to Theo. That meant Tatarovitch probably knew she was with Monika. He would want her found, so that she wouldn't talk to anyone.

"Monika?' Wanda called out.

Angelika's voice answered. "They came and took her and wanted to know where you were. They were hurting Lochi so I had to tell them."

"You did the right thing," Wanda called back, still moving junk as fast as she could. Now though her mind was thinking, "Will he expect me to come back?"

The answer came immediately. Tatarovitch would know she would. As soon as he learnt where she had been, he would think she knew who Monika was. He'd be expecting her to bring back help.

The rest of Vienna might think she was a callous uncaring killer, but he knew she wasn't. He had ensured she was convicted of a crime that would be heinous to her mind.

The question was, how much time did she have? They had taken Monika, would report her absence...

Her danger sense flared to full, and she ran to the door and doused the light. She pressed against the wall as the key turned in the lock and the door opened. She reached sideways and felt for an old lamp that she had seen there, but didn't grab it yet.

She was prepared for the light to go on, and counted on a moment's surprise when the man saw the junk had been moved. The man who stepped in, spun around, saw her, but by then it was too late. Wanda's foot hit him hard in the face and he went down, falling into some of the junk. His companion had that much warning, and pulled a gun, but Wanda grabbed the lamp and threw it at him. As he moved to avoid it, she kicked him in the groin. He bellowed with rage, holding himself and trying to fire the gun, but Wanda dived towards him, both arms stretched out and hands clasped. The attack was like a pile driver hitting him in the chest, driving the breath in his lungs.

"It's not your night, you bastard," Wanda told him as she delivered a follow up blow that sent him into unconsciousness. She swiftly gathered up the gun the second man dropped, and shoved it in her pocket. Then she searched both men, tossing the first man's gun into the rubbish, and taking a knife from each of them. These went into another pocket of her coveralls.

Angelika's efforts to open the door were getting more frantic – she had stopped when the light had gone off, guessing the reason, but now it sounded like she was kicking the door.

"I'm coming," Wanda told her, loud enough to be heard. "I'm moving stuff as fast as I can."

Finally, she had enough room to open the inner door part way. Lochi came out first, and then Angelika, carrying Lilli.

She was crying, and holding the little girl like a favourite doll. "Lilli...I think she isn't breathing!"

Wanda moved back, giving the woman room to come out, and then she said urgently, "Let me see her!"

Angelika resisted the request, but Wanda gently took the child's limp body and felt for breathing and a pulse.

"How long has she been like this?"

"I…"

Long enough, Wanda thought as she placed the child on the flooring and commenced CPR. She kept checking for a pulse, and as minutes passed, her mind grew angry.

"No, dammit! You are not meant to die!"

To whatever power might hear her, she pleaded, "Help Lilli to live! I wanted her safe. She's an innocent child – one of those louts in the other room deserve death, not this child."

Lilli coughed, and a trickle of dirty water bubbled up in her mouth. Wanda turned her on her side and more water dribbled out. She then checked the breathing and pulse – thready, but there.

The girl wasn't out of danger, but now there was hope – but she needed help, soon.

"Lisbeth!" Wanda screamed mentally.

Chapter 25 - Darkness

Elisabeth Willard awoke from a deep sleep with Wanda's call in her mind.

"Wanda? What?"

Elisabeth felt the message drum into her mind. Wanda was with the Prosecutors family, the little girl needed help urgently, she was going to get them out – they were close to where the police were already looking for herself.

"On it!" she thought back as she threw the bedcovers off and reached for her phone to call Derek Mont Pelier.

He had stopped trying to learn how she knew things like this. He just accepted it.

"I will arrange the ambulance, and get Donau and his dog out there too. It might be no help in this rain, but we will see. Is she going to give herself up?"

Elisabeth asked her sister a question in her mind, received the answer and answered Derek. "No, once she gets the Neubauers out to the street, she is going to look for Monika. While she was finding the way out, some men came and took her. Derek, I want to go with you. Please."

"Let the police handle this."

"Wanda isn't going to let them stop her," Elisabeth warned. "I think she's hoping to find Tatarovich."

"I understand. This is personal," Derek agreed gently. He understood the bonds of family. "Trust me to help her."

"I have such a horrible feeling..." Elisabeth admitted.

Donau picked Derek up on his way to the centre of the second district, to where a cordon had been created around the place where Carson had been seen. A door to door search was being made. His ID let him through, and he arrived at the command post as some of his colleagues were helping Angelika Neubauer and her children into an ambulance. He saw Rudy Wagner standing under an umbrella giving orders and dived out into the still teeming rain, to go and talk to him. Derek emerged and trotted after him, thinking Alex had the right idea of staying in the car.

"Rudy!"

"Otto, who called you? I've got this covered."

Derek inserted, "Carson was seen around here?"

"Yes, sir. Neubauer's wife said Carson helped free them, but I reckon she knew where they were and is trying to make us favour her."

"Or she and Federova were taken by the same people who took the Prosecutor's family," Derek suggested. "Have you seen any sign of Federova?"

"While it is a long shot to say that Carson escaped on her own, it's an even longer shot to suggest that people got into two separate sections of the prison and abducted two people from inside."

Donau filled his colleague in on the findings relating to the laundry trucks, and how one of the laundry trolleys had bloodstains on the dirty sheets.

Wagner shrugged. "Carson was rescued once before, wasn't she… probably was again. She's part of this."

"Why did they take Federova?" Derek asked bluntly. Wagner shrugged again.

"We are searching the tunnels. If Federova is in there, we will find her, and Carson too."

"If Carson is accessory to the abduction, like you suggest, why would she free them?" Derek asked.

"I personally don't believe she is in league with the abductors, and we need to find her before they kill her."

"Oh, we'll find her," Wagner assured him. "There are teams going into the tunnels and cellars from outside the cordon, and moving this way, There are other teams watching the drains and anywhere that she might come up to the street. "We are about to move in from here."

"I'll get Alex," Donau decided, and he trotted back to his car.

Wagner said to Derek, "I don't want Carson or Federova staying loose. The city is nervous, having two double murderers on the loose."

Alex went in first, stopping just inside to shake water from his coat. He sniffed the walls and began to trot. In a very short time, he led Wagner, Donau and three WEGA officers to the lighted room where two men were just rousing, and muttering rude curses in Russian. They were no match for the police in their present state, and were quickly handcuffed and led outside.

Derek waited in the tunnel and simply observed the interior of the cellar.

Donau followed Alex to the inner door, and had to move junk to open the door wide enough to get in. He saw the water collecting attempt, and the tub that was well over half full. He saw Alex nuzzling something white and went over. He picked up the discarded surgical tape, as Alex gave a little growl that meant he smelt blood. Carson, he believed had been injured, and had probably been tied up. They would not have needed to do that to Monika who would have been in a drugged sleep.

He directed Alex, "Seek! Find your friend."

His dog looked at him, not understanding which scent to follow. Donau let him sniff the tape, and he gave a woof and trotted off.

When Donau went off after his dog, Wagner and Derek followed. They encountered the returning WEGA men.

"I was told to tell you that according to Frau Neubauer, Monika Federova was here, but was taken out while Carson was away. Carson took her and the children to the street entrance and said it was safe to go out, but she was going to find Federova and come out later. Carson knew her, Frau Neubauer said."

Wagner gave a sour laugh. "I reckon she's taken off, probably with Federova. I reckon we'll be lucky to find either of them. Did she say who took out the Russian thugs?"

"No, but she saw them unconscious when Carson got that inner door open again."

Alex gave an impatient woof, and Donau stopped listening to the WEGA man's report and went after him. He sensed Mont Pelier following him, and then heard Wagner's heavier breathing and the boots of the WEGA men.

They all followed Alex through a maze like route and came

upon two more unconscious men. The dog kept going, but Wagner paused to direct the WEGA men to secure these men as well, and keep following.

Alex was sniffing at doors, but he suddenly reversed and went back to the first of the group. He barked. Donau tried the door, it wasn't locked. He and Wagner entered cautiously, with their weapons drawn.

They found Monika Federova curled up in a ball, in the laundry of the house. She was whimpering, as the man of the house kept a gun aimed at her. Donau stepped forward, pushed the gun down and produced his ID.

"What happened here?"

"I came down for a drink, found a trail of water from my front door to here, and found her. My wife went to call the police."

Donau sent Alex searching, but he went to the front door and returned.

Two WEGA officers were helping Monika up, and handcuffing her. Derek tried to speak to her but she stayed mute. He watched her led outside, keeping his thoughts to himself.

"Carson came through here?" Wagner demanded. "Did she go out the front?"

"Was a lot more water at the front," the house owner offered.

"She probably eluded the security patrol by coming in here, and then went out the door here to go back to the others," Donau gave his opinion.

Wagner didn't quite sneer as he said, "And she took out those two toughs on the way? She must have had help."

Derek had a different view. "It's simply a matter of leverage. Someone who has been trained would find it easy. Those two men in the passage, were heading away from that cellar. I would say that Carson came at them from behind and succeeded in getting Federova from them."

"Carson is short and slight. I still can't see it," Wagner insisted. "If she got the woman away from them, why leave her in the house to be found, why didn't they both go off."

"If it was not their choice to leave the prison, perhaps it is her intention to ..."

"Give herself up?" Wagner interrupted. "I don't see her anywhere? She's not coming back."

Donau looked around for Alex, then called him. They heard him woof, somewhere ahead of them, but out of sight around a corner. He took off at a run, making use of the little torch he carried. He came to a grating that was hanging half open. Alex was looking down into the water channel. Donau tried to see what had his dog's attention, but his torch didn't penetrate the darkness. He could hear the sound of water running into an echoing space, and icy damp air came up at him.

"Get a torch!" he directed, and one of the WEGA men went back to the house where the other escapee had been found.

Wanda had seen Angelika and her children go out into the rain, sensed the police, and retreated. She ran back to look for Monika/ Ivana, knowing that she had very little time before the police surged in there in force. Once they did, she was history. They wouldn't listen to her. She was, as far as the police were concerned, an escapee, an escaped murderer. They'd shoot if she didn't give herself up...

She mentally added up the time between leaving to look for the way out, and getting back, moving stuff to get Angelika out, helping Lilli, getting them out...Monika might be long gone. But her instincts, or some subtle power, was telling her otherwise. With all the police activity, Theo and Tatarovich, might still be close by, lying low. But if the police were doing a house to house search, they would not want to be seen.

"They repeat successful tactics," Wanda muttered aloud. "So they pick hideouts with rat holes. Like those houses with back doors leading to the cellars." She recalled the house that had subtly repelled her when she was coming back. She must be near that now...would Monika have been taken there?

Wanda moved cautiously forward, returning to where she had re-entered the cellars. Then she heard a voice, sharp, authoritative, and very close. She flattened herself into a shallow depression and listened, hoping the speakers did not come her way. The answering voices were low, and seemed to be moving away – but they had

Russian accents, and one was a woman, protesting.

The accent was familiar, Monika's, and it was cut off abruptly. Wanda risked edging to the junction of the next passage and taking a look.

Her mind was translating the commands, as she watched several figures walking away from her, while a torch flashed around the tunnel ahead of them.

"Take her to the boat, go as far as you can and then leave her for the police to find. That way they will concentrate their efforts somewhere else."

The speaker went back into the house, for a door shut firmly, the sound echoing in the tunnel.

"Bastards," Wanda hissed in the direction of the house. "You can wait..."

If she helped Monika, the police wouldn't move away.

The same leashed anger that she had felt in the cellar, came over her again, mingled with memories of hunting other vile creatures in dark passages. She moved with very little noise, gaining on the unsuspecting men. Already she was planning her attack, picturing the steps she needed to take to use her small size to advantage. Surprise was the biggest advantage, followed by the contempt of the bigger heavier men. The first fell face first to the ground after she had leapt and kicked. The torch went flying and was now pointed further into the tunnel. The second man, who was shoving Monika along, threw her aside and drew a knife, twisting and snarling.

Wanda wore a feral grin, lost in the darkness, but with the light behind the man, she had a further advantage. She was weaving from side to side, and he was waving the knife in front of him, at full arm's stretch. He was moving forward, but Wanda was just as slowly backing away. The first man was crawling towards the torch, he would flash it towards his mate...

Wanda kicked out, connected with the man's arm, and heard the knife clatter to the stone ground. The man recovered quickly, rushing to where he guessed her to be, but his grasping hands clasped air. In the instant of beginning to kick the area in front of him, he felt his leg lifted. He fell against the wall and pushed back, but something hit him at the knees, and he felt himself somersault over the woman, and he blacked out when his head hit the wall. He came too, tried to get up, then felt something sharp, dangerously close to his private parts. Something that was jammed in between two of the cobbled stones.

The light had disappeared. When he called to his partner, he only heard a whisper of a groan. The women, he guessed, were long gone. Father Theo would not be pleased.

Monika sat hugging her knees and hiding her head. Wanda urged her to her feet, wanting to get her to safety before the men woke up, or Theo needed to scuttle back into the tunnels. She wanted to be free to follow them.

"Come on," Wanda used a touch of 'command' in her voice and this time Monika obeyed. She edged around the unconscious men, eyeing them like sleeping snakes.

She followed until Wanda stopped outside the house she had walked through.

"Monika, listen...I want you to go in there. There are steps leading up into a house. Go through the house, and out into the street. I want you to give yourself up, okay? Don't fight them, okay? You are better off with them than with your father."

"No..."

"Yes!"

"What are you...? Are you coming too?"

"No, I have one more thing to do first. You have nothing to worry about – you didn't escape someone took you out of the prison. You woke up in a cellar, and then they came for you again. I got you away."

"I will be in trouble..."

"Not as much as I will be," Wanda admitted. "Look, I will make you a deal. If you give yourself up, I will prove to you that Tanya is not dead. She is here in Vienna, with her cousins...your nieces."

"What! But I..."

"You didn't kill her. Your father lied to you...now go in!" Wanda opened the door and gave Monika a shove. "Go!"

She shut the door and moved quickly to the one further on where the man had come from. Her hand reached out to touch the lock, but her danger sense flared to full strength. Someone was just beyond it, and she sensed fear. A key turned in the lock and she ran past the door and pulled herself into the shallow alcove of a sealed over door, and tried to flatten herself against the concrete.

The door opening was silent – the hinges well oiled. Yet now Wanda could hear someone pounding on a door, probably the front door.

"Come on Pieter," Theo spoke quietly. "The boat is this way. We will be gone before they get in."

Tatarovich made a reply, in a quieter voice.

Theo answered, "Forget the bitch. If she is smart, she will be a long way from here, running as fast as she can. If not, she'll be caught and sentenced to extra time. We can deal with her later."

Wanda thought to herself, "Neither of you were smart to interfere with me!"

She spared no thought for the foolishness of going after these two alone. Her mind was focussed on her hunt, and the prey was within her reach.

"Don't let them hear me coming," Wanda mentally prayed to whatever power sometimes helped her. She felt a breeze waft past her, coming from ahead of the two men, and she slipped out after them as they began to walk towards the storm drain. Theo, the taller of the two, had a torch, but he used it rarely. It seemed that he knew this part of the tunnels well.

Wanda stared at his silhouette and prepared to attack. She sprinted to gain speed and then leapt, her feet landing in the middle of Theo's back, knocking him down hard. She twisted and landed back on her own feet and heard Tatarovich's savage snarl of pure rage.

She didn't need him to tell her that he was out for her blood.

"You won't kill me, old man," she taunted, swaying from side to side, ready for him to react. He was not so comfortable in the darkness, and he was dressed in a suit. He pulled a gun from his pocket, and fired once, but instead of the bullet flying straight down the tunnel, and hitting the infuriating bitch, it hit the rock of the wall and ricocheted from wall to wall. While he was further blinded by the flash from the gun, he felt his arm twisted, and the gun fell. He heard it skitter away as if it had been kicked. He cursed in Russian, vile gutter oaths.

Wanda had gone past him, but a movement of the air made Tatarovich twist around, and grab. She felt him catch the coveralls, and try to pull her off balance and throw her against the wall. The rage in her mind, anger at the evil this man had done to her, and to her aunt, turned her into a fury – fighting instinctively, aware of his every move, even though it was dark. She kicked his lower body and punched his face, eliciting more curses. He tried to poke and scratch at her eyes, but her head kept dodging him. He used his grip on her clothes to throw her to the ground, and when he thought he would land on her, he found she had rolled free. He hit out, catching her by luck on her injured side.

Wanda bit of a cry of pain, and fought off the feeling of intense weakness. She had to finish this...

Sense came back to her suddenly as if lightning had jolted her mind. Her head felt like it was on fire and she felt hands around her throat, squeezing her airway shut. Wanda's mind cleared enough for her to recognise her peril. She must have passed out for a short while, enough for Tatarovich to get her.

A breeze ruffled her hair, and it smelt of damp and mildew. Her head was hanging over a drop down to the river, where the water was rising and running fast. Her attacker wanted her to die, was intending to toss her body in the river. As the inner darkness began to close over her, when she only had seconds before her body shut down, she arched her back and pushed with her feet, and she grabbed the clothing of the man on her. He was unprepared to somersault into the air, and his hands released her as he tried to save himself from the fall into the river. He grabbed at his victim again, but felt himself twisting in the air as he seemed to fall in slow motion.

The landing was hard. Wanda felt the body under her 'splat' into the edge of the water, but she was too busy trying to gulp air into her lungs. Her head seemed to be splitting, and she pushed up and tried to feel her head. Her hand came away, sticky with blood: she could smell its metallic tang.

Her mind grew fuzzy again, and she could not understand the words she seemed to be hearing.

"Hold on!'

"Don't pass out!"

"Stay awake!"

She couldn't seem to do anything, she had no strength left. She let her body collapse, and felt the cool water soothing her hurts. Her feet touched something hard, but her head and shoulders were floating. The water pulled at her, jostled her, and she settled onto her back, content to drift into darkness, where there was no pain.

Donau grabbed the torch from the officer, gratified that it was a particularly bright one. He immediately shone it down towards the water, and saw a figure starting to drift with the rising water. He couldn't tell if it was Carson, for he knew she had probably stolen some coveralls. He shone the torch straight down the wall and saw the maintenance ladder. He didn't think as he began to climb down. Wagner moved to stare down. "Are you mad! The water is rising fast."

Alex shoved against Wagner, and barked down at his master. Donau yelled up, "Stay." However, a short time later he gave another command, and Alex launched himself from the top of the ladder, used Donau's arched back as a stepping stone and then landed on the narrow area that was not yet under water. The ledge that ran both sides of the normally three metre deep channel.

Alex ran along the ledge, in the direction of the water flow, as Donau went to the figure he had seen. He recognised Tatarovich. The man was dead, and it was obvious that he had fallen. He called up and requested the body be removed before the water took it away.

Then he shone the torch around, looking for Alex. When he couldn't see him, he called out, and heard barking. His dog sounded frantic.

Donau was aware that someone else had descended and was looking at the dead man, but his concern was for his dog, and whatever it was that had him barking. He began to run, the torch showing him the ledge, and it touched Alex just as his dog dived into the water and began to swim – the current catching him and sweeping him along faster.

"Alex!" he called, but the dog either didn't hear or was to intent on what he was doing,

It was hard to see anything in the water, since the current was strong and the surface rippling and eddying. He thought he saw something in the water, but it disappeared under one of the arches,

He tried to go further, but the path ended at the arch. He would have to swim to get around it.

"Alex, get back here!"

The dog kept paddling, and was swept out of sight under the arch. Donau kicked off his shoes, and was about to dive in when he was grabbed from behind.

"No!" Derek Mont Pelier said firmly. "It is too dangerous to dive in here. You do not know what is under the water or flowing with it."

"But Alex..."

"You cannot help him. There is still room for him to swim under, but you could not. There is a chance that he will find a place above water, further down. What was he doing?"

"Someone was in the water," Donau said. "I just caught a fleeting glimpse of a dark shape."

"There was blood in the passage – at two different places. The first spot had blond hairs stuck to a rough patch of rock. If Tatarovich was with Theo, I think Theo got away, unless he is the one in the water."

"No, Alex would not have gone after Theo," Donau's voice seemed strained. "But I think he would have if it were Carson in the water. She was the one I told him to find."

"Where does this drain flow to?" Derek asked sharply.

"The culvert near Technistrasse. It eventually flows into the river, but there is a net across the entrance to catch rubbish. Though with all the rain, it is likely to rise so high that the water flows over the barrier."

"Come on then!" Derek urged, grabbing Donau's arm gently and urging him back. "We can't stay here. The water is rising and this ledge is already awash."

Donau realised that he was right, for by the time they returned to the ladder, they were splashing through water that was several inches deep. One of the WEGA men was still standing on the ledge, he urged Donau and Derek to get up, and then followed them.

"The body has gone to the morgue," Wagner told them. "You finished in here?"

"Yes," Derek answered before Donau could. "We need to watch

the outlets from this drain. Alex went in after someone in the water. It might have been Carson."

Wagner let Donau go off, and took control of the search. He wasn't so sure there had been a body in the water. Carson could have thrown something in to make them think it. She might have pushed the dead man down there too – expecting him to float away and not be found.

Donau returned to the cellar door of the house where Monika Federova had been found. He returned the torch, with thanks, and requested permission to walk through to the street. He got grudging permission.

"Why not? My wife has put towels down, since it is like the main street through there."

The voices started up again, or perhaps they hadn't stopped. The babble made it hard for her to drift.

Why did she have to wake up? She felt warm, comfortable. Then her head bumped on something, reigniting the piercing pain, and her mind woke up. She was in the water! For a moment, she thrashed in panic, but her arm felt something soft, and a slight whine reached her physical ears.

Her body was being turned around, her feet were being dragged under something rough and solid, but her coveralls had been snagged on something and being pulled another way. The whine came again.

"Alex! Silly dog! You shouldn't have come after me."

The whine came with a little more volume – all he could manage with his mouth full of her clothes. He was trying to swim against the current, and tug her towards the edge. She had no energy. There was too little room to use her arms to swim: she couldn't even push herself away from the archway, her arms simply collapsed. All she could do was try kicking with her feet, but even that wasn't much.

It must have helped a little, for she was aware when Alex reached a ledge that was level with the water, and dragged her onto it. She wanted to collapse there, but now her memory was returning, and she knew the water was rising. She and Alex had to get out.

Nearby, she heard water flowing as a solid waterfall, from

somewhere above, splashing into that in the channel. It made her look up. Above was a grating, and faint light came through it. It was a street drain – could they get out that way?

She forced herself to crawl to the edge of the torrent, to feel on the wall. Finding the rungs of the ladder gave her hope, but she had no strength to pull herself up. All she could do was hook one arm around the uprights, and the other around Alex. A deep instinct told her that they needed to share heat to survive.

She must have passed out, for she woke again with Alex yelping. His legs were flailing against her, the water was up to his chin, and the current was trying to drag him away from her. He had a grip on her clothes, once again. Now she moved her freezing cold fingers under his collar and tried to grip it. She let the water float her up, and grabbed the next rung up. She scraped her arm, but the cold water deadened the stinging. She did not dare let the ladder go.

When her head touched the grating, she had to stop. She had neither the strength nor a free hand to try to lift it. All she could do, was ease her arm out a bit – to give Alex room to squeeze between her and the ladder, and hope they would both be safe.

Donau raced to his car, and left the area as soon as he could. The streets were fairly empty, the result of hours of heavy rain, and the onset of full night. He drove as if possessed to where the drain emptied out into the river, stopping the car with the headlights made the turbid water glow. He took a brighter torch from his car, and played the beam over the water, but it was murky, full of dirt and rubbish being flushed from the drains, roiling with the current and the immense amount of water being forced out of the entrance. This culvert was normally almost dry, but now it was three or four metres deep. He took off along the walkway that paralleled it, heading for the netting that trapped rubbish. It was straining to hold what had already been flushed out. He shone his torch on it – examining it inch by inch.

Derek stood with him, to support him with his presence, since he had little else to offer except hope. At least the rain had finally stopped, as the storm moved past the city. Above, the sky was beginning to clear. He glanced at his watch, activating the light. It was well past midnight. Then his phone rang, startling him.

He didn't recognise the number, and simply gave his name as he answered it.

"Derek?" Elisabeth Willard's voice was recognisable, even though it sounded strained. "Where are you?"

"What's up, Elisabeth?" He was in no mood to formal with the Senator's daughter.

"I...this will sound odd...but...could Wanda be in the water?"

He was startled, but Elisabeth had been right about Wanda before.

"Yes. We think Alex is with her. What can you tell me?"

Through the earpiece, he heard a sigh or was it her breath catching?

"I think...they are stuck. Between arches, if that makes sense? On a ladder, near a street drain...but Wanda's mind is vague. I don't think she is doing too well. It's like she is moving away..."

"Otto and I are looking," Derek tried to infuse his voice with confidence. "I will pass this on."

"Tell me how it goes," Elisabeth asked, her anxiety apparent from the tremor in her voice. "Please."

"You will be the first to know," Derek promised, and he was striding over to Donau as he ended the call.

"Otto!"

"What?"

"We need to check the street drains, between the cellars and here. They might be stuck in a high area between arches."

Donau turned and looked at the entrance – there was no longer a gap between the top of the water and the keystone of the opening. "Yes. Yes." He ran back to his car, forcing Derek to run to keep with him.

He drove back towards the city centre, along the road but this time at a slower speed. He paused occasionally and called Alex's name.

Down in the drain, Alex twitched his ears and wriggled. He began to bark, but the woman who had kept him above the water, didn't move. He wriggled more and tried to lick her face. There was no reaction. He whined. Still she did not react. Alex barked, listened and barked again.

"Quiet!" Derek hissed, grabbing Donau's arm. "Listen!"

Very faintly, they both heard a dog bark twice, pause, bark twice again. Donau was out of his car and running down the nearly deserted street, towards the sound and calling his dog's name.

Derek moved into the driver's seat and followed in the car. He pulled up next to where Donau was crouched staring into a street drain. He had his arm through the grid, just touching his dog, and aware of the still figure of Carson.

"They are both down there, clinging to a ladder. Carson is holding Alex there, but I can't feel a pulse."

Derek took out his phone and dialled the number of the Chief of Police. He had no qualms about waking him, and leaving it to him to activate the emergency services they needed. Then he dialled Elisabeth, and the phone was answered immediately. "Yes?"

"We've found her, but it isn't looking good." He knew she would want the news straight. He heard no further response from her for a long moment. "Hurry, Derek," was all she added before ringing off.

At the hotel, Tanya and Erin listened to Elisabeth's part of the conversation. After she put down the phone, she told her cousins, "She's not dead! But I can't get through to her. Derek said it isn't looking good."

Erin felt the fear Elisabeth was trying to hide, and decided, "We need to go down to the garden, together, and think at her. Like we did before."

"Yes. Come on. Hurry."

Tanya thought to grab their coats.

No one was around to think it odd that three barefoot women were sitting in a circle on the drenched grass. Even if there had been, none of the cousins worried about getting wet, and what they were trying now, they had done before, with success.

They were all grandchildren of Anneliese Mosellan, and they, along with Wanda Martin, had a mental connection to each other, and at times they could use a power they only knew of as the 'aura of the earth'. In the past, they had managed to summon it to help, to hide, to heal. It was still an instinctive skill, and it worked best when they were in direct contact with the Earth. Now, they wanted to use the connection to send energy to the one of them that needed it.

It had worked before, and that time, Wanda had been a great deal further away. This time they were close and they did not dare to believe anything other than that it would work.

They joined hands, to make it easier to merge their talents. Tanya, like Wanda had some projective telepathy, Erin was predominantly an empath, Elisabeth had some of both, but she also had the strongest link to Wanda, since they were sisters.

These talents were a classified secret, for no one liked the idea of someone deciding to use them for a vile purpose. They didn't know the limits of what was possible, but they did know they could help each other.

In their own individual ways, they had a sense of Wanda's mind. Now, they tried to find it – a faint presence amongst the predominantly sleeping city. Elisabeth had felt it - a fleeting touch that drifted in and out of her awareness. Now she knew that Wanda was in water, probably suffering from hypothermia, and needing energy to warm her. Now, she caught the vague sense of her sister and held it. Tanya and Erin added their own energies to surrounding that spark of life, and together they thought of warmth flowing to that spark.

"Is the baby okay?" Elisabeth thought at her cousins.

Erin, the most sensitive to that, considered. "Yes, for now. I think Wanda has concentrated her essence there too. But her system is working very slowly."

"David mentioned that," Elisabeth told the others. "She did something once, to slow her automatic functions, so she wouldn't bleed to death. I think Derek might have heard about it. I will call him in a bit."

In a distant way, they sensed when Wanda was lifted from the water, and into the street and waited.

"I don't feel any change," Tanya voiced after five minutes had passed.

Elisabeth broke the circle of hands and pulled out her phone and called Derek.

"She's not dead!" she said as soon as Derek answered.

In the quiet garden, all three heard Derek tell her, "They can't find a pulse of heart beat and she doesn't seem to be breathing. They have been doing CPR."

"Don't let them give up! Try again! Give her a thump to get her attention. I think she has done something weird – slowed her circulation. She isn't dead yet!"

The paramedics had given up, were about to cover her over, when Derek knelt down to make his own assessment. After what Elisabeth had said, he recalled something his doctor sister had told him in confidence. He put his hand on Wanda's neck and kept it there.

"I felt something. Twice now – about two minutes apart. Keep the CPR going and get blankets here."

The paramedics began again, and Derek stayed close. His eyes flicked to Donau, crouched down next to Alex who was now swathed in blankets. The sound of an ambulance siren grew in volume.

A doctor came with the ambulance, and when he checked the woman's vital signs, they were up to one beat every half a minute. It was a very strange case, and no one believed that the woman would be normal, if she survived.

Still, as the ambulance rushed towards the hospital, they continued to give forced respiration.

Warmth was beginning to seep through the cold extremities towards the core of warmth within. Wanda's mind stirred sluggishly, aware but not yet thinking.

Pins and needled of returning circulation hardly registered. The voices of doctors and nurses seemed like unintelligible babble to her ears. The voices in her mind were clearer, more insistent.

"Come back. You are safe."

"No," Wanda thought at them. Not yet. She had to protect the precious life within.

Chapter 27 - Time to step back

Of no use at the hospital, Derek returned to the hotel. He went up to the room being shared by Elisabeth and her cousins, and got no response to his quiet knock. He doubted that they would have gone to sleep – not until they knew about Wanda. He turned to go to his own room to change into dry clothes, but had only gone a few steps when the lift dinged. He looked that way and saw the three women emerging from it. He walked to meet them, and observed that they all looked to have been sitting on the wet ground. However, they all seemed serene.

"Let me organise some warm drinks for you all," he suggested, deciding not to comment on their state.

"You are a polished diplomat, Agent Mont Pelier," Elisabeth said with a faint smile. "My father would have demanded to know what the heck we'd been doing sitting out on the wet grass."

"Mine would have said a lot more than that," Derek admitted. "I will, instead, assume you had an excellent reason, and I would intuit that they were successful."

Elisabeth nodded, but didn't explain. "How is she?"

"In excellent hands, and showing signs of recovery." Derek opened the door of the room for the women. "They did x-rays. She has a severe concussion. Also, she had a bullet in her side, and a multitude of scrapes and bruises."

"You look like you have been getting wet and dirty too," Erin remarked, seeing that his suit was looking less than impeccable.

"My part was merely observing," he said in reply. He closed the door and went to where the small kettle sat on a side bench. Amongst the tea and coffee supplied, he found a container with chocolate powder and decided to make use of it. As he waited for the kettle to boil, he had the feeling the women were waiting politely for him to reveal what happened.

"It has been an eventful night," he remarked when he had the drinks ready. He handed one to each of the women and took up his own cup. "I am sure that most of this will be on the morning news, but Monika Federova is safely back in custody.”

Derek was watching Tanya and saw various emotions play across her face.

“Wanda is sure she is my mother,” Tanya told him. “I want to see her.”

“We all do,” Erin said softly, looking at Tanya. “But Tatarovitch has screwed with her head. She will need help.”

How these women had known what Wanda had thought, when they had no contact with her this past night, Derek decided not to question. Instead, he went on, “The police have Alexsei, Leo and Stephan in custody.”

“We know that,” Elisabeth said impatiently. “What about Theo and Tatarovich?”

“According to Monika, Carson went after them. We believe Theo was injured by her, but he got away.” Derek watched for reactions, and was disappointed.

After a while, Elisabeth sighed. “If it were anyone else but Wanda, I’d say I wish she had finished the job. There was more?”

“Yes. Tatarovich is quite dead.” He saw the women shudder, as if they had shared the vision in his mind of the man splattered on the ground.

Elisabeth’s voice was toneless when she asked, “Did Wanda kill him?”

“There will need to be an investigation,” he prefaced his remarks, “But I believe he was trying to kill her. There are bruises on her neck, consistent with someone trying to strangle her. It seems that they both fell into the drainage channel as the water was rising. Tatarovich fell onto the edge of the water; Wanda must have landed in the water. When we climbed down, Donau’s dog jumped in and began to swim towards something.”

“Remind me to buy a treat for that mutt,” Erin said with feeling.

Derek wondered how they felt about their ‘grandfather’ being dead.

“Was there more?” Tanya asked.

“Yes. Angelika Neubauer and her children are safe. Wanda found them and helped them out. The little girl is very ill, but should recover. Apparently she had stopped breathing, but Wanda knew what to do.”

“Of course she did!” Elisabeth said flatly. “Not that they will give her any credit for that! So now we just have to get her out of that stinking jail, and absolve her of those put up charges."

"I do not think that rushing at this point would be advisable," Derek said quietly. He sipped his drink before explaining further. "Yes, the prosecutor is probably grateful to her now, but we do not want a backlash from those who think that his change of attitude to her is an emotional reaction."

"Put that in simple language," Tanya grumbled.

"No, he's right," Erin agreed. "It is a complicated situation. We want the counter evidence to be water tight, like Jim said. Wanda is tough enough to survive in that prison. While she is there she might even help some of the others to survive better."

"Like my mother?" Tanya asked.

Elisabeth then blurted, "I am going to ask that lawyer of Wanda's to take her case on too. I will even pay his fee myself. We haven't looked at her case yet, but I bet it is a frame up like Wanda's."

"Might I suggest you wait until you have all had some sleep before thinking on that?" Derek suggested. That they were immediately thinking of helping yet another person, impressed him.

"Yeah!" Erin yawned. "I think we might be able to sleep now."

Wanda was spared questions for almost three days, until her body temperature was back to normal and the doctors were confident that she had recovered from the frigid immersion. Then, the doctors were able to remove the bullet that had dug a groove into her hip, and she needed time to recover from the surgery. During the third day, they ran tests of all kinds, to be sure she was 'normal'.

The oddity of her greatly slowed pulse and heartbeat when she had been rescued had been shared amongst the hospital staff, and many were talking of her as being in 'cold sleep'. If she had not been under minute by minute guard, due to her escapee status, the news media would have fought their way in to interview her.

The doctors had first go at asking her questions, about that strange state she had been in. Wanda acted amazed, and shrugged off any knowledge of it. However, she knew what she must have done, again, and she was under oath not to reveal it as it was classified by the US Government.

Her lawyer arrived next, an hour before the expected police onslaught. His greeting was not, "How are you?" but "What the hell kind of stunt were you trying to pull?" He stared down at her.

Wanda grimaced when he had to remind her that, "Escaping is serious business. They will be within their rights to extend your sentence."

She knew exactly how much trouble she could be in. "I was not intending to leave the prison precinct, Mr Hauser, and I have that guarantee that they won't add any extra charges, relating to things I did here in Vienna."

"Which…" Hauser paused to be sure his client was paying attention, "is only as good as the reason you come up with for being a damn fool."

"The Neubauers are safe," Wanda said, trying to distract him.

"Is that your reason? You knew exactly where they were? You went straight there? Obviously, you are in league with the abductors. Try again!"

"I hope you don't believe that," Wanda told him, what defiance she had mustered was completely gone. She looked down at her hands and said, "I went into the psych section to see if Monika Federova was my aunt. I intended to go back."

Hauser was silent. It seemed like a completely random reason. Wanda glanced up just as he opened his mouth to speak.

"I couldn't get anyone else to find out – because they would have moved her again if they knew that someone was asking questions," Wanda said quickly.

"What has that to do with anything?" Hauser asked, confused.

"Ask Derek Mont Pelier. He will give you the details," Wanda suggested. "Do you remember him asking me about a Yuri Tatarovich?"

Hauser nodded.

"He is, or was, part of the same Russian crime group as Theo and Alexsi. I think, Theo's father and Yuri were brothers. Pieter Tatarovich, the one who visited me in that jail, is Theo's cousin."

"I gather he is related to you. Is this how you know all this?" Hauser's tone was implying all sorts of dire things.

"No. I mean, yes they are related to me, as much as I hate to have to admit it, but no, that's not how I knew. I didn't think Pieter Tatarovich was still alive until he came and saw me."

"I can understand your aversion," Hauser's expression betrayed that he knew more about the Russian family than he let on. "It makes it seem more likely that you are a criminal, working with those who took the Neubauer family."

Wanda shrank back on the bed. It would be no use trying to insist that the women in "The Family" were pampered and spoilt rich brats, and only the men were involved in crime. He'd want to know how she knew, and she didn't want to betray how much she knew about those bastards.

"Why don't you tell me everything that is relevant that you did, or that happened to you, since you conceived this insane idea – up to when they found you in that gutter drain."

"Well, I stayed out in the exercise yard, and when the guards weren't looking, climbed to the roof and crawled over to the psych wing," Wanda began, giving the briefest summary of that feat.

"And no one saw you?" Hauser shook his head.

"Anyway, I got into that wing via a skylight, into a maintenance room. Pinched some coveralls and an ID that was with them and walked down to the floor where the people sleep. I knew some of the layout from a women who used to be in there."

"I think security is going to be tightened after this," Hauser warned her.

"You see, I did them a favour..."

"Keep talking. The police will be here all too soon to ask the same questions."

"Well, my timing was off. I got to Monika's room, and hid in her cupboard. Some of Theo's thugs came in pushing laundry trolleys – the cameras were off, the door had been left open after the last bed check. I thought I was safe in the cupboard, but I wasn't. They took me too."

"How did you even know that such a woman was there?" Hauser asked with irritation.

"It's classified. Just pretend that I still have that ear receiver."

Hauser took a deep breath, and kept his voice calm. "Very well. Go on."

"I am now sure that Monika Federova is actually Ivana Krinsky, nee Tatarovich, and that bastard that came to see me has set her up like I was and for the past five years has been screwing with her mind. As soon as she saw me, she should have thought I was her daughter. Tanya and I look like twins!" Wanda didn't try to hide her feelings. "I had to do it! For Tanya!"

Hauser stared at her, and his client's blue eyes stared back.

"How exactly do you fit into the family?"

Wanda considered what she needed to say. Some of it was classified but...

"My mother, Tanya's mother and Erin's mother were triplets. The children of Pietr Tataorvich. Erin is the marine private who was helping with the IT stuff on the cartel records."

"I see," Hauser said, as he gave in to the need to sit down. This client had a knack for creating major complications. "Tell me what happened after you were taken."

Wanda obliged, giving him the events with her usual degree of detail. She admitted to overcoming two lots of Theo's thugs, and attacking Theo and Tatarovitch – so that they could be caught by the police.

"What happened? You let Tatarovitch get the better of you?"

"He got lucky. He kicked me where his cousin's thugs shot me."

"You attacked him, when you'd been shot?"

"I wasn't feeling too bad. He wouldn't have known..."

"He called your bluff, you mean. And he almost ended your life."

"Yeah, well, he didn't. He was trying, but I woke up. I realised that I was in a bad spot and reacted."

"What did you do?"

"Honestly, I'm not really sure. Something I was trained to do – it was instinctive."

"And that is everything?" Hauser demanded.

"Everything I am sure of," Wanda agreed. "Did they find Theo and Tatarovich?"

"Theo? No. Though the police feel sure he was injured. There was blood and some blond hairs on the stones." Hauser studied his client before continuing, wondering if she had deliberately killed and was hiding the fact. "Tatarovich, is dead. He fell down to the drainage channel, landing on the stones at the edge of the water. You were lucky."

He saw her body shudder, and believed that she had not deliberately killed him.

"I wasn't sure that I really knew that," Wanda admitted. "I was almost blacking out. I couldn't breathe. I think I landed on him, but I must have blacked out then. I don't recall anything else until I was here."

"I wish I could give you some advice, and be sure you would act on it," Hauser said, shaking his head. "So I will merely ask. Haven't you done enough? You came here to find two people, and you did that. Why didn't you leave it at that?"

It was an excellent question, and what she thought was the true answer was too weird to mention.

So she gave the next best one. "Why? Because I don't like leaving jobs unfinished. And sometimes, what needs to be done, can't be done following restrictive and arbitrary rules. I will not hide the fact that I am glad Tatarovich is dead, but he did not have to come to me to gloat. He should have left me alone."

Even though Hauser agreed, he didn't say so. Instead, he advised, "I think you should step back and let the police do what they are paid to do."

"Maybe," Wanda shrugged. "I've given them most of the answers they need. I hope they appreciate it. If they don't they can drop their stupid charges and deport me."

Hauser sighed. It wouldn't be that simple. He would have to produce new evidence to prove that she didn't do most of the things she was sentenced for.

"You are a most troublesome client," Hauser sighed. "However, when you are questioned, I do not want you to be so obliging. The police have Alexsei, and they have his suit which has blood on it, from Wessler and Lunn. So far, he isn't talking. Have you any ideas?"

She was about to say no, but then a possibility occurred to her. "While I was residing in the holding cells, I spoke to Stephan Tatarovich. I gave him a tool to get out..."

"You what?"

"Derek knew it. It was so we could locate where Theo was..."

"Fine. Please don't mention that to the police. What about Stephan?"

"I told him he and his brother owed me one."

"So..."

"Maybe you could offer him a deal. Maybe he spoke to Alexsei and heard what he did?"

"And if he knows that you killed his father?" Hauser suggested a flaw.

"I don't know about Leo, but I had the impression that they were both scared to go against their father. Stephan, I think might be relieved that he is dead."

"I will see what I can do there," Hauser promised. "Will you behave while we plan your appeal?"

"I can help..."

"I know you want to, but please, let others help you now."

Hauser saw Wanda drop her head, and he thought he saw tears beginning to form in her eyes.

"Alright," was the stifled answer. "I was just trying to keep my mind off twenty five years' incarceration for things I didn't do."

"You aren't completely innocent," Hauser said softly. "And now it is time for meekness, not confrontation."

His last words were a warning, for the police questioners had arrived. Wanda glanced at the door, disappointed that Donau was not one of the group, but relieved that Wagner wasn't. These men were strangers, and she hoped they were unbiased. If they didn't have preconceived ideas, maybe they would listen to her and their evaluation would be accepted.

Chapter 28 - Nothing to look forward to

Wanda requested that the curtains around her bed be closed, once the police and her lawyer had gone. The regular guards were happy to sit near the door, for they could see how pale she was, and had heard the nurse saying she had done too much and should rest.

She wanted to rest, and sleep, rather than endlessly second guess how the interview had gone. The policemen had been watching her like a hawk watches prey, and she had worked hard to make her body language agree with what she said. That had taken concentration and energy that she didn't have to spare. Trouble was, they were experts at not betraying their reactions too.

Hauser had seemed pleased with how things went, though, and had promised to visit her when she had recovered more.

Sleep didn't come easily. She had refused a sedative, since they would affect her in strange ways, so she had resorted to repeating a mantra for relaxation that she had been taught some years ago. She thought of the man who had taught it to her, and felt he would have been proud of her. With that in her mind, she managed to sleep for a time.

When the nurse came into check her pulse and temperature, she roused, but pretended to be sleepy. Once she was alone, her mind dwelt on her future. She didn't regret acting to help her aunt. Nor, did she regret her part in Tatarovich's death. He had been an evil man. She did wonder what it was about those diamonds that had sensed her and drawn her into her current trouble. Surely they were not alive? Or had it been the power that she called the aura of Earth, making her its agent?

Was she really sorry it had?

No. It really wasn't that different to the times she had been part of Jim's team, doing things to make an important difference to people or countries.

Trouble was, she had done all she could. For now at least. That damn "Family" was still around, and the other members were just as bad.

Before her mind could begin to think of ways to close down "The Family", she told herself firmly, not to start. Another part of her mind argued that while she had problems and mysteries to solve, and the adrenaline fuel of danger was pumping through her, she had forgotten that she was a convicted felon, forgotten the twenty-five years she had to endure.

She tried to picture the appeal, and while it was pleasant to dream that all charges were dropped and she was exonerated, honesty forced her to admit that the best Hauser could do would be to have some of them dropped. She wouldn't walk free, even when he had done his best.

When she tried to resign herself, she couldn't. Oh she would survive in that prison, one day at a time, as she had when she was a teenager. But there was nothing there to challenge her mind, to keep her active enough to remain healthy.

This night in the hospital might be her last night of comparative freedom. They wouldn't keep her here much longer. They would take her back to the prison, and she would be stuck in solitary for weeks. Stuck in a box cell, where she couldn't even look out the window and imagine freedom.

"Time out" was for minor infractions of the rules. Escaping was a major transgression.

Chapter 29 - To protect not punish

Jim Phillips arrived back in Vienna with Max and Grant, and quickly caught up with the events of the last week. He heard the official view, via Derek Mont Pelier, and Wanda's view, when Hauser came to talk to him with an idea he had conceived.

Since he knew Wanda better than anyone else currently in Vienna, with perhaps the exception of her cousins, he made his own evaluation. He understood exactly why Wanda had acted as she had. Her instincts had been right on target. If anyone had started asking about Ivana, she would have been spirited away – as indeed her father had tried.

He had spent the past week following a lead to Ivana's whereabouts. He had started at a French prison, only to discover that Ivana had been taken from there for 'treatment' in Italy. No Ivana Tatarovich or Krinsky had been treated in Italy. The lead had petered out.

When Elisabeth had called him and mentioned Wanda wanting to check out the Austrian prison, he had known he needed to return at once to Vienna. On the plane flight, he had considered Wanda's actions in Vienna. As far as he knew, all had gone according to Wanda's plan until her inexplicable stealing of those diamonds. Then either bad luck or bad judgment had dogged her. He didn't believe it was the latter. It was more like some power had decided to use her as its agent of vengeance.

Still the mystery of the diamonds could wait. If they had indeed once belonged to Anneliese Mosellan, then the answer was related to the strange blood she had passed on to her daughters and their children. Anyone else would scoff at that idea, but he knew things few other people did.

Only good had come out of her 'crimes' – but a rigid justice system didn't look beyond the fact of the crime. He knew for a certainty that Hauser wouldn't be able to achieve true justice for Wanda Martin. He was a talented and dedicated lawyer, but for all that, he had no 'pull', only passion.

When the plane landed in Vienna, he went briefly to the hotel where he had stayed before, and spoke only to Derek and Hauser. He suggested that Max and Grant stay and keep an ear out, but he booked the first available flight that would get him to Washington.

Grant drove him back in a hired car, but quizzed him on the way.

"What can you do, Jim? She knew the rules. If we are caught, the Secretary disavows any knowledge, and he doesn't like her."

Jim had thought this through already. "True enough, if this was one of our usual missions, but this wasn't. It was meant to be a simple come and find a missing person, and she did that. No one could have expected this to blow up in her face. And in every way, she followed her training. As an investigator for the State Department, she ferrets out threats to America's national security. When she sensed something was wrong, she followed it and found that a Russian criminal had wormed his way into a sensitive government position. There is plenty of evidence that he planned to defraud the government through trade deals negotiated by his cover alias of Allan Wexford. I'm sure you can think of other ways he could have screwed the US."

Grant nodded, as he continued to drive. "And if they knew she was an agent, naturally they wanted to neutralise her credibility."

"Exactly. Derek says Aleksei isn't talking, but he had to have been the one who set Wanda up. I will need to give evidence to the investigative team, and Heinrich has been promised consideration if he tells all that he saw. If push comes to shove, Derek is not averse to us giving Aleksei some persuasion. There is enough evidence to cast doubt on the murder charges. But all that is not enough. Private citizen or not, Wanda has done the US a major service, and she deserves their reward, not a tacit acceptance of a lengthy jail sentence."

"You won't get an argument from me," Grant said quickly. "Is there anything else Max and I can do while you go home?"

"Yes. There is. Start the process to get Ivana Krinsky an American refugee visa. Also, see what else you can find out about her original sentence, in Russia. If Tatarovich was able to spirit her out of the prison, he had to have help in high places. Quite a few places – since he has had her moved around. He could have easily arranged false charges."

"Will Ivana be safe in the prison?"

"The warden has placed special guards on her, and ordered a psychological review. She will be well enough for now."

"And Wanda will behave?" Grant asked, only partly in jest.

"I have a few ideas there," Jim managed a smile. "After I go and tweak a few favours, I will talk to David."

Chapter 30 - The end of the nightmare

The aircraft was a military one. It had come from the American Base in Germany, and was enroute to the States, when it was diverted to pick up a group in Vienna.

Wanda didn't care if it wasn't the height of comfort. She was going home.

She didn't care that she was handcuffed as she was led to it. It was one that didn't fit into the docking lounges, so she had been able to avoid the media, by leaving through the ground floor maintenance and service passages. It meant crossing the tarmac and using the mobile stairs.

If any of the reporters were looking out through the viewing windows, they might still be looking for her in the violent orange prison garb she had been wearing when she arrived at the airport.

That had been intentional misdirection, for Jim had arranged for some US military style fatigues to be ready for her to change into.

When she had left the court at the end of her appeal, the sensational outcome had the newspaper and TV journalists clamouring for an interview. She had been hustled away, but Hauser had given a carefully worded statement, that revealed little more than the court spectators had learnt, had praised the fairness and persistence of Austrian legal system, the open mindedness of the chief Prosecutor, a who had been the first to insist that a new trial be arranged, when new and compelling evidence had come to light.

So since she had been exonerated of the double murder, and the true killer was now awaiting trial, and her jewel theft charge had been downgraded to breaking and entering, her sentence had been greatly reduced.

That had seemed to be the end of it until word had leaked to the press that she was to be deported back to the States to serve her sentence. A minor furore had erupted, and reporters once again tried to interview her as she was driven from the prison. However, the number of reporters that persisted to the airport was only a fraction of the original number, as the police announced the result of the task force investigation, and the shocks arising from that press conference overshadowed her departure. Her existence was insignificant when the residents of Vienna, and many other parts of Austria were reeling from the revelation of two major crime enterprises and the arrest of many prominent businessmen.

Wanda was only aware of some of this, as she allowed her police escort to lead her to the plane.

"You know, I hope you and I can meet again sometime?" she told him.

"You don't hate me then?"

"No, you were doing your job, and at least you were willing to listen."

"So, who will you be next time?"

Beside them, a German shepherd woofed.

Wanda chuckled. "Alex will know. He was right about me, all along."

"So it seems," Donau said, with a wry chuckle. "Tell me if you will, who is the real you. Martin or Carson?"

"Martin," Wanda said immediately. "But Carson is still me. Or rather, who I used to be."

"And what about Monika Federova?"

"It has been kept quiet, but her real name is Ivana Krinsky, and she will be coming to the States as soon as a visa and passport have been arranged."

Wanda didn't enlighten him that Ivana was already on the plane. He didn't need to know.

They reached the foot of the mobile steps, and Donau released her arm and invited, "After you."

He held Alex back with him until she had reached the cabin, where she waited for him to remove the handcuffs. He was only just quick enough, for a two year old bullet raced at Wanda. She turned so her healing side was out of the way, and instinctively scooped up her son, and held him in a bear hug as he plastered wet sloppy kisses on her face.

David walked forward and gave Donau a nod and a grin. For as soon as the little boy had spotted Alex, he was wriggling from Wanda's grip to get down and pat him.

When Donau had make the introductions between the boy and his dog, Wanda explained, "Davy is my son, Inspector."

Donau's smile was full of warmth as he watched Alex trying to lick Davy's face.

Davy returned to Wanda after saying goodbye to Alex. He immediately demanded, "Up!" and clung to her like a limpet, saying clearly, "Daddy says I am going to have a brother."

"I told him it was going to be a sister for you," Wanda corrected, and then she turned to Donau. "Thank you for being my escort."

Davy didn't modify his volume when he objected. "I want a brother."

Donau grinned, waved and retreated.

"Davy, you will have a sister. Get used to it. Now go find Auntie Elisabeth or Auntie Erin. I want to hug Daddy."

The aircraft door was being sealed, as David enfolded his wife in a heartfelt hug that ended too soon. "The plane is on a priority schedule. We have immediate clearance to take off."

Wanda followed him to a seat, passing a group of four air force personnel who were trying hard to appear to be noticing and hearing nothing. She saw Tanya talking quietly to Ivana further back.

David was still talking, "Jim said he will catch up with you back home. He is finalising some loose ends here. Anyway, let's get seated."

"Where's Davy?"

"Don't fret. Elisabeth has him. She wanted us to have time together."

Wanda glanced back and saw another familiar face.

"Derek is coming with us?" Wanda asked in surprise, then thought maybe it wasn't so surprising, and dropped that mystery in favour of another.

She dropped into her seat and fastened the seatbelts. Her hand went instinctively to find David's as the plane began to taxi. She closed her eyes, as the realisation that she was free to go home, finally became real. When the plane gathered speed and began to lift, Wanda felt the weight of the past three months dropping away.

When they were finally at cruising height, Wanda asked, "How did Jim manage to get me deported?"

David squeezed her hand. "I think he pulled a few strings, cashed in some favours, blackmailed a few people, and pointed out how you had unmasked a Russian spy who had wormed his way into an important government position. Unfortunately, the Senator is taking some flak, but nothing he can't handle."

The Senator would be her father, Charles Willard. "He can always claim that he sent me in to find things out."

"I don't know if he said that or not," David admitted. "Though he did tell me that he had advocated for you to be assisted, because of what you had uncovered. Oh, and he warned that the VP is, well, finding it very distasteful to have to agree."

"Stan Russell is an old sourpuss anyway." Wanda dismissed the man as unimportant and asked instead, "Do I still have a job with the State Department?"

"Oh, yes," David said with an evil chuckle. "Our friend Derek, only had to imply that he would snap you up to work with Interpol. Russell very quickly decided that the US still needed your investigative skills."

"Derek wasn't joking. He has suggested that several times."

"I know," David admitted. "He spoke to me about the idea. I said we would get back to him. He told me there was no rush. I should let you wind down first."

"So, why did he decide to hitch hike? Was it to enter the US incognito?"

"No, he said he'd like to visit his sister. The one that's married to their representative with the United Nations. But, well, do you really have to ask?"

"No..." Wanda doubted that anyone, except maybe Ivana, would miss the besotted looks Derek and her sister were giving each other. "I wonder what the Senator will say."

David smothered a laugh. "I'm wondering what Vera will do without her live in baby sitter. Aren't you glad you left home before she married your father?"

"I'd have eloped."

"I'd have been in that," David agreed, intending to keep the conversation away from Wanda's time in jail. He sensed that she was not ready to share that yet, and would need time to get that period of her life behind her. They would have time to work that out when they were home. What she needed now, was to feel like she was coming home after a successful mission.

Not surprising, Wanda seemed to have sensed the thought. "Remind me...never...to get myself put into solitary again. It is a foul and degrading experience. Total mind sapping boredom. I feel as if I have been punished for every single crime I have ever done."

"It's over, hon. Put it behind you."

"I will, but it reminded me too forcibly of that other time when we were away and I was..."

"That's over too." David leant closer and put a finger on her lips. "You did a great deal of good in Austria. You should be proud of it."

Wanda sighed. "We didn't get Theo and the damn "Family" is still around."

"Oh, so that is what is bugging you?" David teased. "You are not the genius of your family, but an inevitable by-product."

After slapping his hand playfully, Wanda countered with, "If you must think that...I consider my skill with locks is a mere hobby, and my skulking ability as an inheritance from the Mosellans."

The seatbelt signs had gone off, and David noticed Erin approaching with Davy.

"This little man says he is hungry, and I think he ought to eat and sleep," Erin suggested. "However I have an idea about something."

Wanda sensed that the ideas wasn't just about Davy. "What?"

"Ivana has been pretty lethargic since the doctors weaned her off the drugs," Erin began. "I have been trying to start helping her, but she is sort of closed off. Tanya can't even get through. I think if we all worked at it, we can get through to her."

Erin glanced at Davy, and added, "If we can start working from a more distant memory..."

Wanda understood. They would see if Davy's antics amused her, and could be a wedge to open up Ivana's memory of Tanya as a child. Then, if Davy fell asleep with her, it would reinforce the memories.

David stood up, and announced, "I think I will get Davy's food ready. Why don't you bring him back to the little lounge area?"

He must have guessed the idea, for what he called the 'lounge' was simply the forward most cargo area, where there was a rudimentary kitchenette. It was also right behind Ivana's seat.

Davy squirmed free of Erin, and began to run around the empty cargo area. His squeals caused Ivana to pay attention to him, and a faint indulgent smile played on her lips. Wanda slipped into the seat beside her while Tanya pretended to chase him, and Davy was hyped up and running around like a swatted blowfly.

"Don't you wish you can harness some of that energy?" Wanda commented.

Ivana glanced at her, and then down at her hands where she had them in her lap. She didn't answer. Wanda placed one of her hands on Ivana's. The touch gave her a much stronger sense of the older woman's fragile mental state.

"Pieter Tatarovich is dead, Ivana. Your father, my grandfather, cannot hurt either of us again."

"How can you be related to me? Your name is Carson. I have never met anyone called that."

David scooped up Davy, and shooshed him, so Tanya and Erin could move closer to Ivana. Elisabeth stood up and excused herself from Derek and came to join them.

"Mama, you are safe now," Tanya went to Ivana's other side. Ivana still showed no sign of recognition. She kept her eyes down. Tanya repeated her words, but sent them mentally.

Ivana looked up, her eyes wide with terror.

Erin sent waves of reassurance, while Tanya persisted. "We want to help you, Mama."

"Who are you all?" Ivana asked, truly believing that she did not know them.

Tayna's eyes began to fill with tears, and Erin spared some energy to soothe her sense of rejection.

Wanda began speaking very quietly to Ivana in Russian, all the while patting her hand, and within a minute or two, Ivana was relaxed and in a hypnotic trance.

"What is your name," Wanda asked.

The unemotional response was, "Monika."

When Wanda gestured, David passed Davy to her and she sat him on Ivana's lap, and asked Davy to be very good and sit quietly. The little boy sensed the importance of the request and obeyed, wide eyed. He snuggled into Ivana when she instinctively cuddled him.

"Can you remember when you held your little girl?" Wanda asked. Ivana smiled.

"What is your name now?"

"Ivana Krinsky."

Tanya looked at Wanda and soundless words passed between them. Then, with Tanya feeding memories of her childhood, Wanda spoke to Ivana, getting her to remember them too, and to begin to talk about them.

Derek moved to stand beside David. "How are they doing?"

David glanced at the taller man and shrugged. "I think they can help her. Wanda and Erin have had some special training."

"In psychiatry?"

"Not exactly," David temporised. "The details are classified...sorry. But they are her family, and that is what they want her to realise for now."

"Is there anything you can tell me?" Derek asked.

David glanced towards the cockpit to where the four servicemen were busily exchanging stories. "Not really. Not now."

Derek changed the subject. "So what will be happening to Wanda when you reach America? I know the official story."

One of the servicemen came past enroute to the toilet cubicle. David waited until he returned to his seat before answering. "We will be going to a State Department base, that isn't too far from our place. They will want to check the women over. Officially, Wanda will be being detained there. Unofficially, she will be going home. That is, give or take a few discussion sessions with VP Russell."

"Is that likely to be a problem?" Derek asked with concern.

"No more than normal," David shrugged. "What will you be doing besides visiting your sister? I can introduce you to Senator Willard if you want."

"I think I can manage that," Derek said with a faint grin. "I also wish to speak with the FBI and other agencies about 'The Family'."

"Makes sense," David agreed. "I do have a question though."

"Then ask, David."

"What is happening about those damned diamonds that

Tatarovich said he owned?”

"Ah those," Derek acknowledged. "I have taken into Interpol possession, two pouches of those oddly tinted diamonds. There is a rumour that there should be a third pouchful to complete the set."

"That is what Wanda thinks."

"I have asked some of my colleagues, who are experts in precious gems, to look for more of those diamonds, and to try to check the ownership of those we have."

"Can you tell me anything more?"

David shook his head, and looked away.

"I saw the odd effect they had on Wanda. I am convinced that they rightly belong to the descendants of Tatarovich's wife – the mother of Ivana and her dead sisters."

"That was my feeling too," David admitted. "Though as far as we could discover, the bastard never married Ivana's mother."

"Is that what concerns you?" Derek asked, sensing David was unusually quiet.

"No. I don't want Wanda and the others anywhere near the things."

"Perhaps you might explain?"

"Please don't think I am crazy, but Erin told me about when they had Tatarovich cornered. From what she said, and I agree, something about the damn things 'possessed' Wanda. And I can't explain what I mean. Let me just say that I would like to send them back where they came from."

Derek shook his head. "I would really like to know what it is that you are hinting at."

He watched the colour drain from David's face, and the younger man's body go rigid.

"No you don't."

Derek drew his own conclusions and decided to change the subject.

Epilogue

"Are you sure that is suitable work for a pregnant woman?" Derek Mont Pelier asked casually.

Wanda glanced up from the post hole she was digging, eyed the speaker in his light coloured designer suit and once polished shoes, and said, "I'm pregnant, not crippled."

She turned her attention back to her task and then added, "Are you sure you should be walking through horse paddocks in those clothes?"

Derek chuckled. "Touché". He watched her for a while then said, "David said I would find you here, though this wasn't what I expected."

"We live on a farm, even if it is really only a hobby farm. The work still needs to be done."

She wasn't telling him what he wanted to know, so he probed, "And it is your turn to dig holes?" There was a hint of humour in his voice.

"Yeah! So, what can I do for you? Teach you how to mend fences?"

"I might just watch," Derek said quickly. "This suit isn't designed for it."

Wanda chuckled.

"I really just came out to see how you were. Elisabeth told me that you had been released from that State Department Facility."

"They wanted to debrief us. Find out all we knew about Alexsei and the rest. So after their endless questions, they really only wanted to check me over – inside, outside and upstairs. Nothing I hadn't expected, and all's fine."

"That pleases me," Derek told her as he watched her pick up a post and slip it into the hole.

"How long have you been home?" he asked next.

"A few days," Wanda answered, as she packed dirt down around the post.

"So how long will you be digging post holes?"

Wanda rested her shovel against the post and gave her attention to her visitor. She placed her hands on her hips in an almost stern manner. "Who sent you down here?"

"I volunteered...for the reason I said. And I am not the only visitor. There is a regular welcome home party happening at the house."

Wanda relaxed her stance and reached for the shovel again. "I know, but I am not feeling particularly sociable right now. This mindless hard labour is letting me work certain things out of my system. And, it is more productive than kicking myself, and when I am sick of it, I might just realise that I cannot do everything myself."

"I see," Derek understood how she felt. "You have some very staunch friends."

"I know, and I am glad that you seem to be one, and I am not ungrateful for all you have done. I should have thanked you earlier, so please accept my heartfelt thanks now."

"Then you must also accept my thanks. You helped me a great deal too."

"It is nice of you to say so...it helps make ...well everything... worthwhile."

"It isn't just me you helped. There is Nicole Wexford, and Rachel, and the real Allan Wexford. Not to mention your aunt."

"And I pissed off my grandfather, and a pack of cousins that I wish I didn't have," Wanda looked at Derek to see his reaction. "And I made Nicole's life complicated. Did Elisabeth tell you that she is divorcing the Allan Wexford she married, so that she can marry the one she thought she'd married in the first place?"

"Ah, yes, she did mention that," Derek admitted. "She didn't know the latest about your Aunt though."

"She's going to be okay. My friends at Rockwater – the state department base near here – have found her an excellent psychologist, who speaks Russian too. She's gone to Washington with Tanya to be reunited with her husband who is beyond overjoyed. He, like Tanya, had thought Ivana was dead."

"So, you are not down here just to avoid your friend the Senator, then?"

Wanda stopped tamping down dirt, to admit, "I didn't know he was coming. I only knew about Elisabeth, Nicole and Rachel. Who else is there?"

"Well, the Senator brought Allan Wexford...he wants to thank you in person."

"Did he bring Vera?"

"No, he apologised for her. She wasn't feeling up to the trip."

"Probably wasn't feeling up to being nice to me," Wanda suggested. She glanced at the four posts she had replaced, and then stared in the direction of the house. Then she decided, "Maybe you could tell David that I still need to work off a bit off cussedness. Especially if the Senator is there. If I don't..."

"Is he such an ogre?"

Wanda laughed. That definition depended on whether you knew how to irritate him.

"No, he's nice. You will get along fine with him. It's just that he and I often rub sparks off each other. Well, it used to be all the time, and that's probably more my fault than his. Right now though, I don't want to."

"I think you under rate him," Derek proposed.

"Not really. It's better now, since his eldest daughter is officially dead. I can be a bit obnoxious at times. He can pretend I am just some ex-con that his daughter befriended. Better for you too."

"Me? How?"

"How?" Wanda echoed him. "Think of your royal reputation. Even though your father is grateful for what I helped to do, having his son interested in the sister of a criminal may be a bit much for him."

"I am sure he doesn't think you..."

"Derek, he knows what I am, but won't mention it. That is not the problem or my point. I just wanted you to know that if you and my sister decide to take liking each other to the next level, there is nothing for your family or any interfering anybodies, to complain about. Elisabeth is my opposite and only good things can be said about her."

"Are you match making?" Derek asked, amused when Wanda grinned at him.

"Not really. I am just pleased that she has finally met a nice guy." Wanda's grin became more like a smirk. "I haven't said a word about your family to her. She can have the fun of finding out. Just like you can have the fun of finding out about the rest of her family."

Derek laughed aloud. "Am I that obvious?"

She nodded, emphasising each movement. "But I also know you had a more old fashioned upbringing and guessed the rest. Vera might be a problem though – if you look like spiriting Elisabeth away – but don't let her stop you."

"Fair enough," Derek turned his head back towards the house. "I'll head back then, and see you when you come up."

"No, blast it. I'll come with you. I have probably done enough for today, and I can't expect David to handle Davy and all those guests."

"I am sure he can," Derek contradicted. "It will be good for him, and he did manage to survive without you."

"He shouldn't have had to," Wanda said disgustedly.

Derek nodded to himself, having guessed right. "Dig another hole then."

Wanda stared back at him. "Yeah...one more."

Darkness had fallen and their guests were preparing for bed. Davy and Rachel had been asleep for several hours. Wanda took a dripping plate from David who was up to his elbows in soapy water.

"We should change roles. You can be the house person, and I will be the outside worker."

"Not on your life, wife!" David said flicking water at her. "We're a partnership, we share all jobs."

"What about fence holes?" Wanda suggested.

"I will be generous – you can do them all if you want," David said hurriedly. "Particularly as it makes you less twitchy." He took his left hand from the water, shook it and used it to hook Wanda around the waist. "I am just so glad, that you are back here with me where you belong."

"Yeah, I'm glad for me too. And I have to admit that it was fun to have everyone here tonight. This place is meant for a lot of people."

"Does that mean you don't intend to stop at two kids?"

Wanda shrugged. "However many come – but...I am not planning to outdo the Senator."

"It might be fun trying," David chuckled.

"True," Wanda agreed. "And if Derek and Lisbeth hook up, between us we might out do him."

"Seems like the Senator and Derek hit it off," David commented.

"And Nicole and Allan are all over each other."

"Another love-struck couple," Wanda grinned. "I can tell Rachel likes this Allan better than the other."

"She's a smart kid. At least she won't be being raised as a member of 'The Family'."

Wanda couldn't repress a shudder. "That is one of my nightmares. That one or more of those unmentionable creeps decide to come back at me...us."

"Not if they are wise, they won't," David promised. "Changing the subject, do you think you can help Rachel with her nightmares?"

"Do you mean, can I undo the work of all those highly paid shrinks? They should have left her alone. Elisabeth was right, making a big thing of it all was what did the damage, not me clunking that nurse on the head."

"Rachel certainly likes you," David said.

"She's one up on Maddie," Wanda chuckled. "Actually having met me. But I suggested to Lisbeth that she bring her and Nicole. I can help them both."

"What about Vera? That imposter pretended to be her brother," David reminded her.

"Her? Well she was never that close to her brother, though from what Lisbeth told me, I think that she is finding that her true brother has mellowed. She can work things out for herself."

Seems like you have everything worked out," David commented neutrally, pulling the last dish from the water.

"We have worked it out," Wanda said giving David a playful poke in the ribs. "I am grounding myself until this next baby is born, and you are going to sit on me if I don't act like a normal mother to be."

The End

Other Novels by Margaret Gregory

WANDA: FROM BAD TO WORSE

If she was going to die young, like her mother, Gwen Willard was determined to die rich and she had very few years to do it. Her first step was to leave home. She met Hooch, who taught her some exciting and illegal skills. She was the Draco's lucky mascot until she came to the attention of the police. Then her uncanny knack for predicting trouble, warned her to flee to the city and change her name.

Life wasn't easy. She was 15, had little money and no regular job, but her new skills came in handy. Then she crossed the path of an evil and unscrupulous man and she didn't want him to have his way.

WANDA: CHOOSING CRIME

Wanda was free. She was never going back to jail. But she was homeless, almost penniless and Harrison Franklin had a long and vengeful memory.

Jim Phillips had a long memory too, and Wanda had saved his life. Could he save her from Franklin?

WANDA: RISKING LIFE TO LIVE

The euphoria of successful heists were what kept Wanda Dean alive. At 23, she was crime boss Harrison Franklin's top agent – well paid for absolute obedience. That's all that mattered. Until she met Mike Johnston and her boss ordered him killed. For that, the Franklins were going to pay. In Risking Life to Live, justice conflicts with loyalty and the penalty for betrayal is death.

WANDA: A NEW LIFE - HIDDEN SECRETS

Even before beginning as a covert agent for the US Government, Wanda is abducted by a foreign operative. After being rescued, there are signs that she had been subjected to hypnosis. With an important government gathering imminent, her handler must ensure she is not a security risk.

Can Wanda's psychic extra senses help her recognize and resist the implanted commands and clear her for secret work?

WANDA: A NEW LIFE - FIRST MISSION

On her first covert mission for the US Government, Wanda calls on the skills that made her a skilled thief to convince a revolutionary general that she's an ideal recruit. When her team mates' covers are blown, it is up to her to ensure that two missing scientists and confidential Government documents are not smuggled out of the US.

WANDA: FULL CIRCLE

Three generations after the alien Kumatan left Earth, their own world is suffering from alien invaders. In desperate hope, one returns to Earth seeking help - little knowing they had left one of their own behind.

Wanda, a child of the third generation, answers the call.

ERIN: THE FORCING OF WISDOM

For years, Erin has used the intricacies of cyberspace to banish unwanted emotions. Others call what she does hacking, and her manipulations criminal, but now her skill was exceptional - in, out, traceless. She was wrong. Someone betrayed her.

Travis has dangerous plans. He needs an electronics expert – one he can coerce through fear. Erin was perfect.

With the inescapable threat of prison looming, Erin accepts his offer of sanctuary. When she realises his intentions, she is in too deep. But the terrifying of innocents is unforgivable. She cannot walk away. She is an empath and shares their distress. She has to help them, even if it means prison, and insanity...

ERIN: THE CALL

(including ELISABETH AND TANYA: BLOOD CALLS TO BLOOD.

Elisabeth's sister, Wanda, had been missing for half a year. Multiple authorities had found no trace of her, or her two colleagues. Yet she knew her sister was still alive and had answered a call for help from an alien who had once lived on Earth.

Elisabeth, along with her newly found cousin Tanya, have started to sense things from her missing sister. Enough to know that she is in dire trouble, but not enough to help her.

While looking for traces of the aliens, Elisabeth makes some unexpected discoveries about her family. Yet even with the help of a second newly discovered cousin, she fears she is not strong enough to help her sister and the others to return.

ERIN: THE CALL

Convicted cyber-criminal, Erin Mason, is startled into awareness in an unfamiliar place, with no memory of escaping and only vague memories of getting there. Voices in her head were urging her to go west, and they were getting more urgent.

After a chance meeting with covert agent, Jim Phillips, when she helped save his mission, he realised that she might be the key to another, more personal quest – to find three missing state department agents.

All he must do is keep Erin safe, and hide her from an intense police search, until he can introduce her to cousins she was unaware of.

However her uncontrolled psychic gifts conflict with a logical mind that prefers the ordered intricacies of computers and electronics. She only wants to shut out the voices and the madness she sees looming.

Can Phillips convince her to help him, before the forces of the law find her?

THE SERPENT'S SHADOW

Three books in one.

Janna consorts with terrorists to protect her friend Prince Ali from assassins.

Former cyber-criminal, Erin, becomes part of the merchandise of stolen tech secrets.

Jim Phillip's team is sent to neutralise the leader of the terrorist Cobra Sect.

KORVU: THE BEGINNING

The prequel to The Wild One

Jai Ansuni was the first female Atapi sorcerer for thousands of years, but she dare not reveal it. However, when tribal sorcerer, Stacion Ansuni escalates the enmity between Atapi and Kumatan to an ominous level. Jai and her womb mate, Con, try to mitigate his atrocities but can two young Atapi, not even a score of years old, win against the powerful sorcerer?

THE WILD ONE

Sixteen year old Jai Cassidy thought she was finally free of her family until she is discovered by her other relatives...the ones that aren't human. Jai uses her natural perversity and cunning to escape their control, but catapults herself into the middle of a deadly feud between two alien races.

ATAPI SORCERESS

The sequel to The Wild One

Jai Cassidy is beginning her mission of reversing the decline of the non-humanoid Atapi. As a sorceress and an Atapi-Human hybrid, she is vehemently disliked by the male Atapi sorcerers and the humanoid rulers of Korvu. Her task is complicated by the treachery of a group of alien engineers, who are inciting insurrection and harsh reprisals.

THE TYMOREAN TRUST BOOK 1 - POWER RISING

The Tymorean Trust - When peace rules Tymorea - Peace reigns in the universe.

Chosen to be the Advocates of the mystical and incorporeal Guardians of Peace, twins Tymos and Kryslie must first learn to control and use the power rising in them - or it will destroy them.

On Tymorea, only the ruling Triumvirate Governors are powerful enough to guide the strong-willed alien-bred twins until they have mastered their power.

THE TYMOREAN TRUST BOOK 2 - GREAT ONES

The peace of the Guardian Planet, Tymorea, is in deadly peril. War there will create ripples of unrest and destruction throughout the settled universe.

Tymos and Kryslie, still adolescents, have barely mastered their power and Llaimos is still less than a year old, but they are the three chosen to be Advocates of the mystical Guardians of Peace, to safeguard the Tymorean Trust.

THE TYMOREAN TRUST BOOK 3 - RETURN TO EARTH

Even before the war on Tymorea, the Elders foresaw that Great Ones Tymos and Kryslie would have an imperative mission on Earth.

But as the Tymoreans prepare to build an Earthbase to support them, they discover that specifications for two vital protective shields are missing.

Now, nearly a century later, Tymos and Kryslie must find his work and build the generator before the base is found.

THE TYMOREAN TRUST BOOK 4 - EARTH MISSION

Just before their graduation from the prestigious WSRA Washington University, Tymos and Kryslie Ward deliberately disappear.

The Great Ones have foreseen the capture and death of the new Tymorean missionaries and discovered that the leader of the Eastern Imperium plans to undermine the United World Nations.

Tymos and Kryslie must protect their kin and prevent a potentially devastating world war.

THE TYMOREAN TRUST BOOK 5 – ALIEN CONTACT

Tymos and Kryslie Ward, hide their Tymorean intelligence and abilities while working as low ranked technicians at the WSRA's lunar base. When an alien ship arrives at Lunar One, pursued by a powerful enemy who will stop at nothing to get what he wants, only the two Tymorean Great Ones have the knowledge and abilities to overcome him, but to do so they must risk their sanity, and their souls.

THE TYMOREAN TRUST BOOK 6 – INVASION

Great Ones Tymos and Kryslie go to rescue the crew of Earth's first deep space mission – and discover that Ciriot space pirates have discovered Earth's location. When the Ciriot invade in force, the Great Ones reveal themselves so that Earth can gain vital help. However, Kryslie becomes the victim of Ciriot, who want to control her mind and make her betray the people of Earth.

TRICKS

Tom and Jo Dwyer had a reputation for playing tricks – and getting detention. They didn't seem to care about that, so long as they made their class laugh. That was until someone began to turn their tricks against them, and it was no longer funny.